End Games in Bordeaux

ALLAN MASSIE

QUARTET BOOKS

First published in 2015 by
Quartet Books Limited
A member of the Namara Group
27 Goodge Street, London W1T 2LD

A catalogue record for this book
is available from the British Library

ISBN 978 0 7043 7376 1

Typeset by Antony Gray
Printed and bound in Great Britain by
T J International Ltd, Padstow, Cornwall

END GAMES IN BORDEAUX

For Claudia and Matt with love

END GAMES IN BORDEAUX

I

It was strange to be idle. Sometimes Lannes thought that he was like his peasant grandfather from Les Landes, who, even when settled in his chair by the fire after supper, would keep his hands occupied, mending a piece of harness, whittling the head of a walking-stick, stitching the nets with which he trapped migrating birds, or cleaning his gun. Even the business of keeping his pipe going seemed a sort of work, occupation anyway. He had been a silent, suspicious man, reluctant to display the affection he nevertheless felt for him as a boy.

Now, since his suspension, Lannes found himself wondering to what extent his own life had been his work, how it had defined him, given him the sense of his being. True, he had often told himself that family was more important than work, more important than anything else in his life. Nevertheless without work he was diminished. And home which had been a place where more was left unsaid than spoken since the boys, Dominique and Alain, went their separate and frightening ways was now more silent than ever, with Marguerite spending much of the day in bed on account not only of poor health and low spirits, but also, he thought, because his presence disturbed her. Clothilde too was perpetually anxious, hoping for word from Michel, wherever he was, serving in what Lannes thought of as the legion of the damned. And if the boy should survive the war, and return home, what awaited him? Ignominy, arrest, imprisonment, a trial for treason, even perhaps the firing squad. He couldn't speak of these fears to his daughter, and so they no longer had the early morning conversations he had valued. There was nothing to talk about because the subject that oppressed them both was forbidden, by tacit and shameful agreement.

It was a beautiful spring morning with only a few wispy clouds high in the sky, and the sense that it would be the first hot day of the year. He had taken Marguerite a cup of tea and some bread and a scrape of butter from their meagre ration, and she had murmured thanks and turned away from him. He washed last night's dishes, swept the kitchen floor, sat at the table, lit a cigarette, and saw emptiness stretch before him. He picked up his blackthorn stick.

*   *   *

The bookshop in the rue des Remparts had been closed for months now. As Henri said, 'I simply no longer have the heart.' That was how many in Bordeaux felt about everything. The war had turned, there was no question about that. Rumours of an Anglo-American invasion were rife, but the Occupation was more severe than ever, food shortages too. Nobody spoke of the Resistance, though many knew that there had been numerous arrests and imprisonments in the early months of the year. Some of those picked up by the German and Vichy Security Services had succumbed to torture, and – doubtless – given information which led to more arrests, deportations or executions. But whatever people knew or suspected there was nothing to say because there was nothing which it was safe to say. And of course there were many committed to Vichy who viewed the prospect of invasion and 'Liberation' with misgivings, even fear.

It was a couple of minutes before Henri answered Lannes' ring. He was unshaven, he had lost more weight and his trousers sagged, but at least his breath, when they embraced, no longer stank of wine. Music sounded as they climbed the stairs to the apartment above the shop: the 'Pilgrim's Chorus' from *Tannhäuser* on the gramophone.

'I wonder if Wagner still comforts Hitler,' Henri said.

'How's Miriam?'

'Weaker and in more pain. She's sure it's cancer, like her sister, but what can one do?'

'That doctor you said you thought you could trust?'

'In the end I didn't dare. Finding a doctor willing – and brave enough – to treat a Jewish woman? And even if I had, what in the circumstances could he have done?'

'Something to relieve the pain at least. Morphine?'

'Which is certainly in short supply. Besides, Miriam wouldn't hear of it. For my sake, she said. If it was known that I had given her refuge . . . it's an appalling situation. I'm utterly at a loss, Jean. And you have troubles yourself.'

'Nothing comparable.'

Nothing comparable indeed, because if he survived the coming months he might expect to be reinstated when the Germans had gone, Vichy had finally collapsed, and France was liberated. Bracal, the examining magistrate with whom he had worked on the Peniel case, had made that clear when he apologised for having been unable to prevent his suspension.

'It may even be well for you to be out of things meanwhile,' he had said. 'And since you're suspended rather than dismissed, your salary will still be paid of course.'

As indeed it was. The State might be crumbling but the bureaucratic machinery continued to work, and the salaries of officials, policemen and teachers were paid, even on time.

'There's no word of the boys, I suppose,' Henri said.

'None. But then there can't be.'

'And how do you fill your days?'

'With difficulty.'

There was silence but for the whirring of the record on the turntable.

That's how it is, Lannes thought. The music stops, but the record continues its revolutions.

'I'll ask around,' he said. 'See if I can find a doctor we can trust. There must be one, surely. Say nothing to Miriam meanwhile. If I find one we'll bring him here without warning her. Meanwhile, would she like a visit from me?'

*   *   *

It would have been distressing to see her. He knew that, and had been relieved when Henri came back down the stairs to say that she was asleep and that he hadn't cared to wake her since untroubled sleep was rare and precious. Relieved, but also ashamed to feel like that, and now, as he sat in the sunshine on the terrace of the Café Régent in the Place Gambetta, with the swifts and swallows wheeling and diving above him as they went about their urgent and mysterious business, he wondered if Miriam had not wanted to be seen by him as she was or had perhaps simply felt too ill and weak for company and so had asked Henri to make some excuse. It was quite possible. Wasn't it how he might have behaved himself in similar circumstances?

It was midday. The hours stretched out, empty, ahead of him, and he couldn't even bring himself to pick up his glass of beer. It wasn't that there was nothing he wanted to do. There was of course, he couldn't pretend otherwise, but it was three years now that he had been denying himself Yvette, and this wasn't going to change, no matter how often and how vividly he pictured her stretched out all but naked in her mean room in the Pension Bernadotte. The image disturbed his sleepless nights. It disturbed him now. He knew she would welcome him. She had made that clear often enough, even saying – jokingly but nevertheless, he thought, sincerely – that for him there would be no charge. 'And not only because a lot of girls are ready to give it free to a flic, but because I really like you and have a lot to be grateful to you for.' Which might be true. He liked to think it was true. Nevertheless he would be using her to staunch his loneliness, for consolation, even if he did indeed, to be honest, feel affection for her too, as well as the desire he was ashamed of. I'm not much of a man, he thought, but I have to cling to what there is. Even picturing Yvette's legs was some sort of a betrayal of Marguerite, and would surely disgust Clothilde if she knew of it. There were moments when he envied a man like Edmond de Grimaud who took women as he found them and discarded them carelessly. Then he remembered that Edmond's son, Maurice, had once implied that his father had come to hate the English wife who had left him and resented what he saw of her in Maurice himself – Maurice whom Miriam had called 'a sweet boy' and who was Dominique's closest friend. Would they be able to extricate themselves from the mess that was Vichy when the collapse came, and did Dominique still intend to study for the priesthood? He might have spoken of this to his mother, and he didn't doubt that Marguerite nursed such a hope. But what would be the position of the Church, whose bishops had almost unanimously approved Vichy, in the New France to be reborn after the war?

He was rescued – for the moment – from these troubling thoughts by the sight of young René Martin crossing the square toward the café. They shook hands. René said he had hoped he would find him there, and Lannes realised that since his suspension he had formed the habits of a pensioner who gives meaning to empty days by falling into a comforting routine: the prescribed walk, the hours spent at first this café and then that one, the time trickled away sitting on a bench watching a game of boules. And it would have been so easy to include in that rhythm an afternoon hour in the Pension Bernadotte.

'The Alsatian was asking after you,' René said.

Lannes knew that the Alsatian, which was how they all referred to Commissaire Schnyder, the head of the police judiciaire, hadn't lifted so much as a finger to defend him when word came from Vichy that he was to be suspended while under investigation for it had never been quite clear what. There had been complaints from the Boches by way of the most recent German liaison officer, a sour-faced young man from the Sudetenland. At their first meeting he had tapped his forefinger on Lannes' dossier, and said, 'There are things here that I don't like, superintendent.'

'Oh yes?' Lannes had said then, and now said again to young René.

He didn't actually blame the Alsatian who was really quite amiable. A man is what he is and he had long ago realised that Schnyder was determined to survive, however things turned out.

'He said you used to do him a private service and hopes you still feel able to do so. I don't know what he meant but I said I would pass the message on.'

'Cigars,' Lannes said. 'Havana cigars. I've a black market connection. Tell him not to worry.'

And why not? If he survived, the day might come when they would work together again, for he was sure that whatever sort of regime succeeded Vichy, there would be no indelible black marks on Schnyder's record.

'How are things?' he said. 'With you, René, and with our old bull-terrier?' – which was of course what they called his second-in command, Inspector Moncerre.

'They're not good. We don't know where we are or what we should be doing, and as for the bull-terrier, he's drinking too much and his troubles with his wife are worse than ever. Just the other day he said, "I should strangle the bitch." '

'He won't,' Lannes said. 'It's an old refrain and he'd be lost without her.'

Which might, or might not, have been true.

'It wasn't however on account of the Alsatian,' René said, 'that I came in search of you today. I don't jump to do what he wants, you understand, because' – he paused and blushed, looking even younger than he was – 'because it annoyed me that he didn't stand up for you, even if I know him well enough not to have expected that he would. It's because I took a telephone message for you this morning. From someone called the Comte de St-Hilaire. I don't know who he is, but he said you would. He didn't know of your suspension – I thought I was required to tell him – but he said this was irrelevant , since it wasn't, strictly speaking, a police matter he wanted to discuss with you. He would be grateful if you would call on him. I said I would pass the word on to you. That was all, I think. Did I do right?'

II

Lannes moved more slowly, leaning hard on his stick, as he turned into the Allées de Tourny. Stendhal had once called it the most beautiful street in France, and it might indeed be so, even now, but it unnerved him. If he hadn't been a policeman he would most probably never have entered any of these houses, certainly not by the front door. By his age, with fifty in sight, he should have rid himself of this sense of social inferiority. As a Radical and free thinker he despised it. But there it was: ultimately you are what you feel, not what you think; sentiments can be changed less easily than opinions. He had reason to respect the Comte de St-Hilaire, even to believe that the respect was reciprocated. They had done each other services, the Count by facilitating the boys' escape from Occupied France to join de Gaulle, Lannes by what he knew to be an unprofessional act, a dereliction of duty, for which he felt no regret. Nevertheless he hesitated before approaching his house and ringing the bell.

The butler showed him into the salon and said he would inform the Count of his arrival. As on his previous visits Lannes admired the comforting simplicity of a little Courbet still-life of bread, fruit and a jug of wine. There was also a Fragonard of nymphs bathing which he remembered the actress Adrienne Jauzion praising. It wasn't to his taste, but it struck him now that the nymph drawing herself up from the pool in the bottom left of the canvas had a look of Yvette, the same smile at once innocent and knowing – deceptively innocent, disturbingly knowing.

St-Hilaire entered. They shook hands as they hadn't done on previous occasions when Lannes had come on official business. He wore an English tweed suit which hung loose on him, for he had lost weight in the two years since Lannes last saw him. His face was more deeply lined and he moved as if he no longer had full trust in his legs. The butler returned with wine, claret from the Count's vineyard.

'I am sorry to hear of your troubles,' the Count said. 'But, as I said to your young inspector, it's not precisely a police matter that I wish to speak of. Or not yet, anyhow. At least I don't think so. In any case I am obliged to you for responding so quickly.'

'I have time on my hands,' Lannes said, 'on account of what you tactfully call my troubles.'

He was tempted to add that he didn't often get the chance to drink such good wine. But the Count would take the quality of the wine for granted – he had probably never drunk vin ordinaire in his life.

'I'm in some perplexity,' St-Hilaire said.

He paused and took a cigar from the box on the occasional table beside his chair.

'I think you prefer cigarettes? Yes? Then please smoke. My doctor has advised me to give up cigars. But, at my age, breaking the habit of a lifetime? It's ridiculous.'

Nevertheless his hands shook as he clipped the end off the cigar and held a match to it.

Yes, Lannes thought, he's not the man he was. He tapped out a Gauloise from a crumpled packet and lit it. There was a great stillness in the high-ceilinged room, as if life hung suspended, and for a few minutes neither spoke as smoke drifted upwards.

'I am not in the habit of asking favours,' St-Hilaire said.

Doubtless this was true. Such things would have been more often sought from him.

'I have a cousin I'm fond of, an elderly lady. In fact she's a few years younger than me, but it is as if she has made herself older, perhaps because her life has been an unhappy one. Her husband was killed in the first weeks of our war – I say "our", superintendent, because, as I remember, you were at Verdun. Her only son was no good, a wastrel who ran through much of the family fortune. He went to the bad and nobody knows what has become of him. My cousin was distressed of course, but brought up his only child, a daughter whom she adores. She never speaks of her son now. Perhaps she feels guilty because she spoiled him. I don't know. No matter. It's the daughter – that is, my cousin's granddaughter, who is now giving cause for concern. That's putting it mildly, an understatement, I'm afraid.'

The Count paused, laid down his cigar, removed the monocle, letting it dangle on a black silk ribbon, and dabbed his temples with a handkerchief scented with eau de cologne.

Lannes waited; patiently, as he had so often waited in the course of an interrogation or while a victim or witness to a crime struggled to make sense of a horror they had never previously imagined. Any good policeman knows that silence is hard to endure and will often bring better results than questioning.

'She's not beautiful,' St-Hilaire said. 'Not even pretty. A plain child and a shy one, perhaps young for her age, which is, I should say, only nineteen. My cousin used to call her "my little novice", though, so far as I know, she has never shown any sign of having a vocation for the religious life. Nevertheless she is a girl who has had, endured I should say, unhappy experiences. Her grandmother reared her with great tenderness, though you may say that in these times it's wrong to bring up a child in seclusion and to try to shield her from all the realities of the world. I don't know. Love often takes the wrong path at any fork in the road. You'll have seen examples, I've no doubt.'

Clothilde. Michel. If only she had never met the boy.

He cleared his throat, sipped wine, and lit a second cigarette.

'And so?'

'So she formed an unsuitable attachment and has now disappeared.'

The Count knew very little of the man. He was middle-aged, in his late thirties or early forties, and called himself an art-dealer. Which indeed he might well be, but whether a reputable one or not was another matter. Nobody knew how the girl – Marie-Adelaide – had met him. At an exhibition perhaps. He might even have picked her up in the street, for she was sufficiently naïve for that to have been possible, responding, shyly at first perhaps, to a friendly word. No matter. It was shocking. The girl was besotted. Her grandmother had come on letters written to her which she had concealed in a drawer. The count couldn't say what was in them – but his cousin had been horrified. She had spoken to the girl about the unsuitability of any relationship with the man, without, apparently, mentioning the letters. And now the girl had left home, overnight, a week ago, taking almost nothing with her, and there had been no communication since. She had simply vanished. It was strange, alarming, inexplicable to the grandmother. She needed help. Might Lannes be kind enough to offer it, make enquiries, see what there was to learn about the man and search for the girl? St-Hilaire would be in his debt.

There would be no debt – it might so easily have been Clothilde. He would call on the Count's cousin.

'What of the girl's mother?' Lannes said. 'You spoke of her father – no good, you said – but said nothing about the mother. Is she alive? Did she play no part in her daughter's upbringing?'

'None at all. I confess I know little about her, and certainly never met her. She was a dancer, I believe, in the chorus-line at nightspots patronised by tourists. Something like that. The marriage didn't last. So far as I know she has never shown an interest in her daughter, and hasn't been heard of for years.'

St-Hilaire rose stiffly and poured them each a second glass of wine.

'And your charming son and his friend, the little Jewish boy whose name I forget?'

'Léon. No, we have heard nothing. Perhaps when the Americans arrive . . . '

'Which won't be long now, I think.'

'Not long,' Lannes said, 'but the months till then . . . '

There was no need to spell it out.

'I agree,' the Count said. 'They'll be the most bitter of all. Germany has lost the war, there's no question about that, but they'll fight to the end. The madman in Berlin won't imitate the Marshal in 1940 and ask for an Armistice, which I suppose wouldn't in any case be granted, now that the Allies have, stupidly in my opinion, demanded unconditional surrender.'

'Perhaps,' Lannes said, recalling his conversations with Lieutenant Schuerle, the East Prussian who had been the previous officer responsible for liaison with the PJ, 'someone will remove him.'

'Unlikely, surely. Only senior officers, generals, could do that, and they have their tradition of blind obedience. *Kadavergehorsam* – corpse-obedience – they call it, as I remember. But I pray that your Alain is safe, he impressed me, and his friend – Léon, did you say? – wherever they are. As for the third of them, my godson, little Jérôme, I listen occasionally to Radio London, as I suppose you do yourself, and I have heard him speak. Unexpectedly well. The Gaullists found the right role for him – he's no fighter, poor boy. I trust they did so also for your son and his friend.'

III

The girl mopped his brow with a cloth soaked in vinegar, and held a mug to his lips.

'It's wine sweetened with honey, what Maman says you need.'

Alain sipped. His throat hurt when he swallowed and there were sharp pains in his head. He didn't know where he was and had never seen the girl before. Her hands were cool, also rough. He should speak, ask questions, but when she took the mug away, his eyes closed and he fell back into sleep

She sat and watched him. Once his whole body seemed to twitch. Then he called out 'no, please, no, don't please' and sweat started on his brow. She stroked his cheek. She could hear her mother banging pots in the kitchen and a goose honking in the yard. Dusty sunlight streaking through the window lay on the boy's face.

*   *   *

Children's voices, cries and laughter, rose from the Place Contrescarpe. Léon put the book aside and, though knowing he was going to be late, couldn't bring himself to get up and dress. It was essentially silly, and yet it fascinated him, the idea behind it, of a portrait that changes for the worse while the original remains pure, innocent and beautiful. Chardy had pressed it on him. 'You are my Dorian,' he said. 'You fascinate me. I still after all this time can't imagine what you are like and what you do when I am not with you. You are so secretive, my dear.' No doubt it was only because Léon had denied him so much of what he demanded that he spoke in this manner. Not always, of course; at other times he called him a little bitch, a cock-tease, a parasite, unworthy of his attention and of the affection he offered. Then Léon would sigh and say 'all right, I'll get out of your life if that's how you feel about me' which, if it didn't reduce Chardy to tears, had him in obvious distress.

It was a ridiculous relationship, and yet Léon couldn't break it off, not only because it provided cover of a sort by giving him a recognised role, but also because without it, now, since the network had been broken, there was only fear. He still didn't understand why the Gestapo hadn't come for him. Was it possible that the girl who acted as his liaison, conveying the messages to be transmitted to London and passing on those he received, had withstood torture or had died without speaking? And yet she had been watched. Someone must have observed the meetings at which they pretended to be lovers. He couldn't hear steps mounting the stairs to this apartment without finding himself trembling. And London had gone dead on him, that was strangest of all. Perhaps they believed he had been arrested in the round-up and was now in a camp or more likely dead. His own attempts to re-establish communication had all failed. So he was now in limbo.

The children in the square sounded happy. He ran his hands down his thighs.

It took him three attempts to knot his bow-tie to his satisfaction.

*   *   *

The Marshal still took his walk every day before lunch and was cheered by schoolchildren assembled for that purpose. He wasn't in uniform today, but wore a black suit and the kind of Homburg hat which, before the war, they had called an Anthony Eden. His complexion was as pink as a rose, and when Dominique and Maurice saluted him, they were rewarded with a flash of the astonishing blue eyes which, with the snowy moustache, had regularly had loyal journalists comparing him to an Ancient Gaul.

'Doesn't he know it's all but over?' Dominique said. 'Can he really be as complacent and untroubled as he looks?'

'He's confident he is still France,' Maurice said. 'And perhaps he is. I mean really that, whatever the outcome, he will always represent many people's idea of France.'

'I don't know,' Dominique said. 'There will be so many eager to humiliate and punish the poor man if only to pretend they never revered him.'

*   *   *

Michel lay back on his bunk, his right hand between his legs. Clothilde's letter had taken two months to reach him here in the wastes of this plain which stretched eastwards forever. She said what she always said, that she loved him for always, would wait for him for always, no matter what, and wanted to cover his face with kisses. Yes, he thought, and remembered how once at that café in the Place de l'Ancienne Comédie a trickle of strawberry ice-cream had escaped the corner of her mouth, and he had leaned across the little table and licked it off, steadying himself, deliciously, with his hand on her thigh. But it was all so far away, and days passed when he didn't think of her, and there were others when he had to take out the photograph he kept in the breast pocket of his shirt to be able to picture her face.

'A letter from your girl?'

He looked up to see his corporal smiling.

'She'll be fortunate if she ever sees you again, and, if by happy chance she does, you won't be the boy who went away.'

The corporal, Baron Jean de Flambard, who before the war had worked, spasmodically, as a publicity agent for film companies, doing most of his business in the bars around the Champs-Élysées, had made himself Michel's mentor, having been, he said, just like him in his own springtime, mad for girls and adventure in dark places. Michel responded: the baron had the glamour of audacious failure.

Now he ruffled Michel's hair, and said, 'I've a book for you to read. It will tell you why we are fools to be where we are. If only Little Adolf had read it. The Comte de Ségur's memoir of 1812. It'll prepare you, my dear, for the worst we'll experience. Last winter was bad. Next one? Well, we'll be lucky to survive it, or unlucky as the case may be.'

* * *

The light went out and Jérôme left the studio in a hurry. The broadcast had gone well, he was sure of that, and his superiors were pleased with him. One had even told him the General approved of his work. Praise was welcome, even if you didn't quite believe what they said to you. Meanwhile there was a party in Charlotte Street to go to, in the scruffy office of the little magazine that had published his poem, a French text with an English refrain – 'And the ebbing tide bore all my hopes away' – he'd had to ask Max for the English verb that translated *baisser*.

There were still days he was ashamed to be here safe in London. That was really the theme of the poem. He had made a success, a little success, of not doing what he had hoped to do, and when the Liberation came and he returned to France with whatever glamour attached itself to his service with the Free French, he would feel a fraud.

He stopped off at the Duke of Argyll to collect the sailor-boy, Freddie, who had never been to a literary party before, was keen to go and would probably be bored. But it didn't matter so long as he came back with him afterwards.

IV

Lannes couldn't believe that fresh air was ever admitted to the salon of the apartment in the rue d'Aviau, only a few doors from the *hôtel particulier* of the Comte de Grimaud, that house which, as old Marthe had told him, had seen so much evil. But there was no such sense of corruption here, only sadness, a feeling of waste, of life ebbing away. Even the stuffed birds in the glass case seemed to be moulting. The room was spotlessly clean, and yet you couldn't escape the impression that a layer of dust covered everything and that there should be cobwebs in the corners of the window-panes. He could imagine the shy young girl brought up there longing to escape in order to experience she wouldn't know what.

Madame d'Herblay was embarrassed by his presence. It was probable she had never spoken to a policeman before, certainly not in this apartment which was completely feminine. He wouldn't have been surprised to be told that the modest and gentle land-scapes, of which there were at least a dozen on the walls, were her own work, painted in her now distant youth.

'I don't know that there is anything you can do,' she said. She spoke so quietly that Lannes had to strain to hear the words. 'But I had no one to turn to but my cousin, the Comte de St-Hilaire. I have always relied on him for advice, you understand. And I was quite at a loss. She is such a good girl you see.'

'I've a daughter myself,' Lannes said, to give her confidence. 'Do you know where Marie-Adelaide met this man – I'm afraid I don't know his name?'

'He calls himself Mabire, Aurélien Mabire.' She touched her cheek which was paper-soft and wrinkled. 'But whether that is truly his name, I don't know. I know so little about him, and certainly not how my poor girl became acquainted with him. The truth is, superintendent, I am at a loss.'

'Now that I have a name I can at least find out if he is known to us, if he has a record.'

He wondered if St-Hilaire had told her he had been suspended.

Probably not, and in any case it didn't matter since he was acting unofficially. He could rely on young René to see if they had a dossier on anyone called Mabire. It certainly wasn't improbable that there was one. The sort of man capable of enticing a young girl from her family home is quite likely to have attracted the attention of the law.

'Monsieur le Comte said he believed he was an art-dealer, or gave out that he was,' he said. 'If so it shouldn't be difficult to find out about him. And I gather there are some letters.'

Mention of them caused her to lower her eyes and blush.

'They are terrible,' she said. 'I don't know how my poor girl could bring herself to read them.'

Or leave them behind, he thought. That was the strange thing.

'What of her father?' he said. 'Does he know about this?'

'I haven't spoken to my son for seven years. He has done nothing for his daughter. He has scarcely seen her since she was a little girl.'

For the first time a note of decision sounded in her voice.

*   *   *

As soon as he was out in the street Lannes lit a cigarette; he hadn't dared to ask if he might smoke in that apartment in which he supposed it was likely that no man except perhaps St-Hilaire had set foot for years. And the Count wouldn't have lit one of his cigars there either, he was sure of that – any more than the sun, now shining brightly out of a cloudless sky, was ever admitted to that shuttered salon. Perhaps it was not so strange after all that the girl had left the letters behind. A gesture of defiance: you've bottled me up, but look, I've found a life for myself. He could understand that, no matter how shy and reserved she might be. And the letters which he had been so reluctantly given and which he had stuffed into his pocket might not be so terrible, no matter how shocking they seemed to the grandmother. That didn't mean it wouldn't indeed turn out to be a dirty business. Nevertheless it cheered him up. It was something to do.

He turned into a bar, ordered an Armagnac and asked for a *jeton* for the telephone.

'René?'

'Yes, chief. What can I do for you?'

'If you have nothing pressing, you might meet me for lunch.'

'Nothing that can't be put aside.'

'Chez Fernand then. One o'clock.'

He picked up his glass and settled himself at a corner table to read the letters. There were only four, each written on a single sheet of cheap notepaper such as a café provides for its clients. They were ordinary enough, the kind of thing a boy might write to a girl he was in love with, what Michel, he thought with a spasm of distaste, might have written to Clothilde. Yes, but this writer, Mabire, who signed himself 'your devoted Aurélien' was reportedly a man in middle-age. It was only this that made them unsuitable. But he learned nothing from them.

V

Though Fernand had been his friend since they were young boys, Lannes hadn't been to his brasserie since his suspension. It was a place associated for years with lunches with Moncerre, René Martin and other inspectors during which they mulled over whatever case they were currently engaged in, and so it had been a sort of adjunct to the office. Now he was greeted by Jacques, the oldest of Fernand's several illegitimate children, who said his father would be sorry to have missed him; he was in bed suffering from a heavy cold which had turned into influenza.

'But he'll be up and about again soon,' Jacques said, 'probably before he should, you know what he's like. Actually we're short-staffed, so it's fortunate we're not busy today.'

Indeed fewer than half the tables were occupied. That was unusual. Then Lannes realised that there were no Germans there, for the first time since 1940.

'Yes,' Jacques said, 'and when they do come now, they tend to go heavy on the brandy rather than the champagne. The word is they're preparing to pull out, but I don't know as I believe it. How many will you be?'

'A table for two's enough. In that corner perhaps, well away from that fellow.'

He indicated the advocate Labiche whom he detested.

'You're in luck,' Jacques said. 'We've got your favourite blanquette de veau. And a bottle of good dry Graves? Fine.'

It wasn't like young René to be late. Lannes looked at his watch and realised he was early himself. That was what happened when you were idle.

Jacques uncorked the wine and poured a glass.

'Can we have a word in private before you go?'

'Of course.'

Lannes lit a Gauloise, and sipped his wine which was fresh as the spring morning. Labiche glanced in his direction, then turned away. He looked as sure of himself as ever; yet, as a member of the Commission set up in 1940 to deal with what they called 'the Jewish Question', he should surely be feeling a cold wind on the back of his neck. Of course like many he might have persuaded himself that any Anglo-American landing was likely to be repelled. He was now joined by a priest.

Young René arrived, full of apologies for keeping him waiting, not, he said, that he had been engaged on anything urgent.

'I don't know why it is, but we've very little to do. It's as if we're in a state of suspended animation. The Alsatian's taken to spending no more than a couple of hours in the office, and this morning he hasn't even put in an appearance. What can I help you with, chief?'

Lannes explained, added, 'You realise of course that as things are I'm not entitled to ask you to do this. Nevertheless I'd be grateful if you can find out anything about this chap Mabire, if we've had dealings with him. And I'd also like to know if we have anything on one Jean-Pierre d'Herblay, though I don't even know if he is in Bordeaux, or when he was last here. I've really nothing to go on, you understand.'

'Of course, I'm delighted,' René said. 'No matter how things are at present, you're still the chief.'

He blushed, which he had always done when embarrassed, as he was now, Lannes thought, to have expressed his feelings so openly.

'If there's anything on either of them I'll find it. And how, if I may ask, are Madame Lannes and Mademoiselle Clothilde?'

He blushed again. Lannes had long been aware that the boy fancied Clothilde but had never nerved himself to speak of his feelings. If only he had done so, a couple of years ago indeed, before she had met Michel. He would have been much more suitable, even though Marguerite might not have thought so. Michel was well-bred, of good family, and had charming manners. René's widowed mother had gone out cleaning and indeed continued to do so, despite his efforts; he had told Lannes he had urged her to give up the work since he now earned enough to support her. She had refused, saying he should be saving for the day he married and in any case she enjoyed her work and her old ladies relied on her, besides keeping her amused. They can't really do anything for themselves, she used to say, not ever having had to do so.

'I'll check through the hotel *fiches* too,' René said. 'Just in case they are still in Bordeaux and staying in a hotel or pension.'

*　　*　　*

After René had left, all eagerness to be doing something for him again, Lannes sat over an Armagnac and the cup of coffee Jacques had brought even though both knew the ersatz stuff tasting of chicory was scarcely drinkable, and smoked as the brasserie emptied. Then, to his surprise, the priest who had been lunching with Labiche returned a few minutes after leaving with the advocate and approached his table.

'May I join you, superintendent?'

'As you like.'

Lannes stubbed out his cigarette. The priest smoothed his soutane over his backside and sat down.

'We've never met,' he said, 'but I know you by reputation, and I understand that you have been charged with a private investigation. This surprises you, that I know of it?'

'If you say so.'

'Madame d'Herblay is one of my parishioners. Naturally she has confided in me in her distress. So when I saw you here, I thought it expedient we should speak.'

Lannes picked up his glass, rolled the brandy round in it, made no reply. The priest placed his hands on the table. There was sweat on his forehead and his fingers were very white and pudgy. They tapped out a little tattoo.

'Marie-Adelaide is a sweet child,' he said. 'It's a sad business. Have you made any progress?'

'None at all. But then it was only this morning that I saw Madame d'Herblay. So I'm surprised that you already know she has asked me to look into the matter.'

'If I can be of any help.'

'Do you know anything of this Aurélien Mabire?'

'The name is familiar, but it's only a name. I can't put a face to it.'

'In that case, Father . . . '

'Paul. Father Paul.'

'I can't see that you can be of any assistance. The gentleman you were lunching with . . . '

'The advocate?'

'Has a certain reputation,' Lannes said.

He almost added, but a girl of nineteen is too old for him.

'He's a distinguished citizen of Bordeaux,' the priest said. 'But you must know that, superintendent. I call you that though I understand you have been suspended.'

'Did Labiche tell you that?'

'He mentioned it, and I wondered if Madame d'Herblay was aware of your position when she sought your help.'

'It's irrelevant,' Lannes said.

'It's been suggested to me that the business is more complicated than it may appear to you.'

'Suggested by Monsieur Labiche?'

'That's as may be. I was merely asked to pass on the message. When you lift a stone you never know what may be revealed underneath it. Especially in times like this.'

The priest mopped his brow with a white-spotted blue hand-kerchief.

'I know nothing myself,' he said, getting to his feet. 'But I've done what I was asked to do.'

It had been a puzzling conversation. Lannes couldn't make head or tail of it. First, Madame d'Herblay had evidently told the priest that he would be searching for her granddaughter even before she had asked or commissioned him to do so, and the priest had seemed concerned about the girl. Then he had in effect warned him off, and hadn't denied that it was the advocate who had deputed him to do so, while being nevertheless in a sweat of embarrassment or even fear. But what on earth was Labiche's connection to the girl's disappearance, elopement, whatever, which appeared to have been entirely voluntary? It must surely be something to do with the man Mabire, rather than the girl.

The restaurant was now empty. Jacques came over, the bottle of Armagnac in his hand. He sat down and poured them each a drink. He looked worried and it struck Lannes that he was no longer a boy, but a young man. Was that how Alain would look when he returned, as Lannes forced himself to believe he would, some day, when this was over and France was liberated?

'It's Father,' Jacques said. 'I'm worried about him. He's on edge, and I don't know what he's up to. He disappears for hours and won't say where he's been.'

'A woman?'

'That's not something he usually makes a secret of. You must know that as his oldest friend.'

'It's a worrying time for all of us.'

The reply was inadequate. He knew that.

'He won't speak to me,' Jacques said, 'except of course to discuss menus and staff problems of which I don't mind telling you we have plenty. But he's not himself, I've never known him like this. I think he might open up to you.'

There had been no secrets between them when they were boys. But that was long ago. In middle age you rarely exchanged confidences with others. It occurred to Lannes that it must be at least ten years since he and Fernand had spent an evening together, engaged in the sort of conversation in which anything and everything can be said. As we grow older we are no longer willing to reveal ourselves to others. There is too much we are ashamed of; it's a mistake to think the young are more vulnerable, for they can still believe themselves capable of controlling the future.

'When he comes in in the morning,' Jacques said, 'I can tell he hasn't slept well.'

'That's not unusual, after a certain age. I don't sleep well myself.'

'But will you speak to him. Like I say, I think he might open up to you. Otherwise I'm at a loss.'

He agreed of course. How could he not? Jacques' anxiety was evident and he had to admit that his curiosity was aroused. Nobody he knew had ever seemed as comfortable in himself as Fernand; it was one of the things that had made him a rock-like presence in Lannes' life. He had always been there, from the days when as boys they crouched in hides by the pond on his grandfather's farm , guns at the ready as they waited for the evening flight of ducks.

VI

Afternoons were the worst time, nowhere to go and nothing to do. Marguerite certainly wouldn't want him back in the apartment because his presence there would deepen the gulf of silence that divided them. It was hard to remember that there had been a time when they talked about everything, except his work of course. She had never wanted to know about that and he had preferred that she shouldn't. It should be good to think he now had something to work on, and yet he still felt strangely detached. Was finding this silly girl important? She was nineteen and had taken off, of her own volition it seemed, with a middle-aged man who might after all be sincerely in love with her. Meanwhile, to put things in perspective, it was a beautiful afternoon in May, rumours of an Anglo-American invasion buzzed around him, and the Resistance, whatever it might exactly be, was engaged in what was already almost a civil war with what remained of Vichy, notably the Milice, that paramilitary body made up, so far as he could tell, of thugs, ne'er-do-wells, young men who had joined up to avoid being sent to Germany as labourers, and, he supposed, a number of anti-Communist zealots, natural Fascists many of them. Then there was also the auxiliary police force, generally known – and feared – as the French Gestapo. Yet, sitting in the sunshine with a glass of beer on the terrace of the

Café Régent, he shrugged his shoulders at all of it. He was a superfluous man. Perhaps he was going mad? What other explanation could there be for his indifference? For, more immediately, his reluctance to do as he had promised young Jacques, and seek out Fernand to find out what was wrong with him? Fernand had done well out of the Occupation, like countless others. Was he afraid this would now be held against him? Yet he couldn't imagine Fernand afraid, or indeed ashamed. He could hardly have barred Germans from his brasserie or refused to serve them. Certainly there was a time of retribution coming. Many would suffer, some deservedly, like the advocate Labiche he hoped, others too for less reason: Yvette who had gone with Germans, engaging in what they were already calling 'horizontal collaboration', and the rent boy Karim, guilty of the same crime. Yet everyone had in a sense collaborated, sleeping as it were unavoidably in German arms. Almost nobody was innocent including himself, Moncerre and young René, and all those other officials who had done their duty to the French State. Collaboration had been enjoined on all of them, and some like his own Dominique and his friend young Maurice had engaged in it enthusiastically, certain that they were doing good work with the deprived city boys entrusted to their care. How would they stand when accounts came to be settled? Was anyone, except those like Alain, Léon and little Jérôme who had escaped France to join the Gaullists, free of guilt? And where were they now? Were they indeed still alive? It was more than two years since they had had word of Alain. The thought appalled him: all the youth of France had been betrayed, one way or another.

He finished his beer, got up and walked away.

*   *   *

Mériadeck slept in the sunshine, but, whereas in the years before the war women would have brought chairs on to the pavement to enjoy the weather, the streets were now all but deserted. The deportation of the Jews had sucked the life out of the quarter.

Old Mangeot in shirtsleeves and braces sat behind the reception desk in the Pension Bernadotte, a half-drunk bottle of beer by his right hand and an extinguished half-smoked cigarette stuck to his lower lip. A bluebottle buzzed round the naked bulb that hung above him.

'You're in luck, superintendent,' he said, 'for I take it you've come to see Yvette, since I've done nothing that might concern you, and she's in her room and alone without company for once. I've no doubt she'll welcome yours.'

Lannes knocked on Yvette's door, and, without waiting for an answer, turned the handle and entered. She lay stretched out on the bed, as he had so often imagined her, wearing a cream-coloured blouse, half-unbuttoned, and black knickers.

'Stranger,' she said, and, smooth as a cat, was off the bed, put her arms round him and kissed him. She made to force her tongue into his mouth, but he disengaged her arms, saying, 'No, Yvette.' He sat down on the only chair and she sighed, took a bottle of white wine from a bucket where it stood in water that was no longer cold, poured them each a squat tumbler, and handed him one.

'If you don't want what I offer,' she said, 'why are you here? Not that I'm not pleased to see you.'

Why indeed was he there? Not surely only to refuse what she so willingly offered and what he knew – she knew – he wanted so badly? He had thought about it so often, so urgently as he walked through the sad streets of Mériadeck, in the sunshine that seemed a reproach to the misery there, or a mockery of it, rather than a summer promise of better days, and yet, now that she was standing in front of him, her lovely legs parted, and he had only to reach out his hand to draw her to him, he knew that he was indeed going to say, 'It's no good, Yvette, you know it's no good, you know why it's no good.'

She leaned forward and stroked his cheek.

'You poor man,' she said. 'Don't you know it wouldn't matter? It's only natural after all.'

When he made no reply, she returned to the bed, glass in hand and sat there, the upper half of her body upright and her legs tucked under her bottom.

They sat and looked at each other, and, because he feared what she might read in his eyes, he said, 'It would matter too much.'

'Lots of married men come here because they say their wives

don't understand them. You're different, I think. You come because she understands you too well.'

'You may be right,' he said, 'but that's not why I'm here today. Anyway, who wants to be understood? Who can bear to be thoroughly known? But I haven't come to discuss such things. Do you happen to know of a man called Mabire? Aurélien Mabire?'

'Most of my visitors don't give me their true name or any name at all. You're the exception. But in any case it doesn't ring any bells. Who is he?'

'I don't know. Said to be an art dealer. He's a middle-aged man who has apparently run off with a young girl.'

'How young?'

'Nineteen, I'm told.'

'Nineteen. And so? Old enough to know what she's doing. I was fifteen when I left home.'

'Nineteen,' he said. 'But young for her age, it seems.'

He lit a cigarette, passed it to Yvette, then another for himself. The cat that had no name but Cat and had belonged to the old Jewish tailor who had killed himself emerged from under the bed and leapt on to Yvette's lap, where it lay purring as she scratched it behind the ear.

'Not like me then,' she said.

'I don't know about that,' Lannes said.

'What do you mean?'

'I don't know. Is your mother still alive?'

'Oh yes, it'll take more than a war to see her off.'

'You should go home to her.'

'That's a good one. What makes you think she'd have me? I'm a disgrace to the family. And my father would beat me – again – if I so much as showed my face. You don't know my story, super-intendent, and I'm not going to tell it you. But take my word for it. Home is a place I'm not welcome. Why anyway?'

'Because,' Lannes said, 'when the Germans have gone – and that won't be long now – things are likely to be difficult for girls like you, difficult and unpleasant.'

'Then you'll just have to protect me, won't you?'

'I may not be able to.'

VII

The metal plate read: 'Family Pension – Moderate Prices' with, below, the promise of hot and cold water and showers. It was a small two-storey building in a narrow street behind the Gare St-Jean. The brickwork, unusual in Bordeaux, was dirty yellow, and, even in the sunshine the place gave off an air of squalor and, he thought, misery. It seemed an unlikely place for Aurélien Mabire to be holed up in, especially in the company of a young girl of good family. But René Martin had been certain.

'He is known to us, chief, and he did indeed used to be an art dealer. That's how he came to our notice, according to his dossier, handling works of art of what they called 'dubious provenance'. I don't know the details. He was never charged, but a year later, his gallery was closed. That was in 1937. We don't have a photograph of him, I don't know why. He's been registered as living in the Pension Smitt for two years now, with no known means of support. He's a shady customer, there's no doubt about that. Do you want us to take a look at him? The bull-terrier's quite eager.'

'There's no crime,' Lannes said, 'since the girl left home of her own accord. I'll have a word with him myself, first anyway.'

The truth was he was curious and also happy to have something to do. In any case it was likely that neither Madame d'Herblay nor the Comte de St-Hilaire himself would want the investigation to be made official and Marie-Adelaide's name to appear in police records.

The reception desk was deserted. There was a smell of dust mingled with the sickly odour that came from a vase of withered carnations standing in water that had been left unchanged for too long. A clock ticked loudly. Otherwise silence, broken only by the rattle of a train from the tracks that ran behind the house. There was a little hand-bell on the desk. Its tinkle was high-pitched but faint. The clock was half an hour slow, and there was a long interval between each tick as if it was struggling not to fall further behind. Lannes rang the bell again, and this time the door behind the desk opened and a woman came through. Her hair, dark and streaked with grey, hung in rats' tails. She wore a flower-printed housecoat and carpet slippers on her feet.

'We're full,' she said. 'No vacancies. So you can bugger off.'

Her breath stank of white wine, and the assurance of her words was contradicted by the dead tone of her voice. Lannes had the impression of a woman who had seen and survived more of life than she cared for.

'I'm not looking for a room,' he said.

'So bugger off.'

'Aurélien Mabire,' he said.

'Never heard of him.'

'That's strange. He's registered as living here.'

'So you're a flic. I'd have spotted you sooner but I'm not feeling myself today. You can still bugger off,' she said, and plumped down on the chair behind the desk. She opened a drawer, took out a packet of Gauloises. Her hands shook so violently that she missed the tip of the cigarette and lit the underside.

'I told him to bugger off too,' she said.

'Would a drink help?'

He took a quarter-bottle of Armagnac from his inside breast pocket.

'It might go to the right place. There's glasses in the cupboard behind you.'

She downed hers in one, shuddered, and held out the glass for a refill.

'So you told him to bugger off? Why?'

She drew on her cigarette and took a sip of the second brandy. Her nails were cracked.

'Because of the girl,' she said. 'I wasn't having the girl here. He's my brother and I've let him live here rent free because of that, but I didn't like having the girl here. I don't know why he brought her. There was something up and I didn't like it. Aurélien's a queer, always has been, well, that's just how it was and there's nothing to be done about that, some men are and I've no time for them. To tell you the truth it disgusts me, what they do, whatever that is, I don't like to think about it, but he's my brother, my little brother

34

and I've always looked out for him, which hasn't been easy, I tell you, you know how it is I expect, you being a flic. So I knew from the first there was something up. She was in love with him, I could see that, because you don't keep a pension for twenty years without learning what's what, when I say in love, I mean she had the hots for him, stupid girl.'

'Did they share a room.'

She sniffed loudly, and held out her glass again.

'This is good brandy,' she said. 'Well, yes they did, but what went on in bed I can't imagine. Well, I don't care to, though it wasn't much I dare say. She's an innocent, that girl, I wondered even if she wasn't retarded in some way, which is another reason I didn't like having her here. I've a horror of idiots. When I questioned my brother, he said it wasn't what it seemed and I wasn't to worry. So I knew he was up to something, it's a relief really to speak of it. And then when that toad appeared, I'd had enough.'

Lannes passed her a cigarette, lighting it for her, though she might have managed to do this for herself now that the brandy had steadied her and her hands had stopped shaking. He took one for himself, drew the smoke into his lungs, breathed out, and said, 'The toad, tell me about the toad.'

'That's what he looked like. They say a toad's eyes are like jewels, don't they? He looked at me as if I was dirt, you could see this wasn't his sort of place, though I keep it as decent as I can. He told me to fetch Aurélien and when he appeared he spoke to him like he was dirt too, and told him to bring out the girl. He eyed her up and down like she was a young heifer in the market – I was brought up on a farm, though you mightn't think so to see me now, and I know that look. Then they went off together, all three of them, and later Aurélien came back on his own and when I asked him about the girl he said it was no business of mine. That's when I told him to leave, I didn't like the sound of it all. He told me I was a fool and didn't know what I was speaking of. But I saw him off all the same. That's good liquor, I'll have another spot if I may.'

'Help yourself. Had you seen the toad before?'

'Never in my life, and don't want to see him again. But Aurélien said he was his lawyer, and that he was in his debt. That's all I know and I tell you it's more than I want to know, but if Aurélien's in trouble with you lot it won't be the first time as I expect you know, and I fear it won't be the last. He's my little brother that I cared for and brought up when our mother died and then my father was killed at Chemin-les-Dames in the last war. They wanted to put the boy in an orphanage but I wasn't having that, so my husband and I became his legal guardians and a lot of trouble he brought us both. He's always been trouble but he's my brother nevertheless.'

Her voice tailed away. A tear trickled from her left eye and she dabbed at it with a dirty handkerchief. There was silence except for the slow tick of the clock. It was the dead hour of the afternoon and it was difficult to realise that when he stepped out of the pension, he would step into sunshine.

'Do you know where he'll have gone to?'

'How should I? To his own kind perhaps.'

'By which you mean?'

'You know what I mean.'

She dabbed her eyes again, and lifted her glass.

'He's not a bad man, just weak and not half as clever as he's always thought he is. And he's always been soft, when he was only little the pigs we reared used to frighten him and he would run to me for protection. Protection from pigs, I ask you. It's the girl you're looking for, isn't it? He won't have harmed her, you can be sure of that. We did our best for him, my husband and me, and I've continued to do my best since I was widowed. But it's no good, I know that. He's no good, poor bugger.'

She pressed the glass to her flat breast as if it was a baby to be protected.

'Do you have a photograph of him?'

She pulled a drawer in the desk open, shuffled around in it, and came up with a photograph.

'It's not recent. He used to be such a pretty boy.'

He heard pain in her voice, pain and the fear of more to come.

VIII

Outside in the street he felt soiled by her misery. He didn't like the feeling, it wasn't how you should respond to a woman who had been beaten down by life. But there it was. She deserved pity. Perhaps her brother did too, he didn't know. But he was like so many who had come his way, a man who had gone from one failed venture to another, and this time, cultivating a girl who meant nothing to him under instructions he was sure of the lawyer – 'the toad' – who treated him with contempt, he hadn't known where to take her except to the pension run by the sister who had been a mother to him. Had he at first pretended that he had changed his ways, and really was in love with the girl? If he had he couldn't deceive her. Perhaps he was the sort of man who couldn't deceive anyone, except, he supposed, that innocent and ignorant girl. He looked at the photograph. She had said it wasn't recent and that he used to be such a pretty boy. His hair was receding and he had the kind of mouth that makes promises too easily. You can't tell anything really from a face; it's not an exact science. Still this wasn't one he would ever trust; it was a face made for excuses.

And the toad – the lawyer – it must, given the priest's warning, be Labiche. Well, he couldn't approach him, and not only because too much had passed between them. You've been suspended, the lawyer would say, get out of my office, you've no right to be here. And indeed he wouldn't have.

He couldn't think Labiche wanted the girl for himself, for he wouldn't have used a creature like Mabire if that was the case. Moreover, as he'd already said, she was too old. He remembered that photograph of the advocate on a couch with a naked girl of eleven or twelve, and how Labiche had torn the print in pieces and the contempt in his voice as he said 'this means nothing'. To be a good policeman you must be capable of inhabiting the Other. He couldn't in Labiche's case. He recognised the egoism which allowed men to lust for what is properly forbidden and dismiss the prohibition as something that didn't apply to them. He'd encountered it too often in a certain type of criminal. Nevertheless it still puzzled him that men like Labiche could suppose they were entitled to whatever they wanted. He thought of Sigi – the old Comte de Grimaud's bastard and, perhaps, murderer, Michel's idol and mentor, damn him – and how he talked so complacently of the division of the world into Slaves and Masters – *Herren-Moral und Sklaven-Moral* – and of how he and Labiche . . . he banged his stick against a lamp-post and spat into the gutter. If Mabire was what his sister said he was it shouldn't be too difficult to find out more about him . . .

*   *   *

There was a bead curtain hanging over the door of the bar that used to be called 'The Wet Flag' – in English – but had been renamed Chez Jules in the early days of the Occupation. He pushed his way through it, out of the sunshine.

Jules was at the bar, leaning on his elbows and, as so often, fingering the wart on his cheek. The place was otherwise deserted except for an elderly man in a creased and shabby grey linen suit who looked up as Lannes entered, but didn't remove his arm from around the shoulders of a curly-headed boy, and a couple of other boys loitering by the pinball machines.

'You're quiet,' Lannes said.

'I like it that way.'

'No Boches?'

'I'm waiting for the Americans. Do you think they'll come?'

'How can I say?'

Jules sighed, took a bottle of Armagnac and two glasses from the shelf, poured out a couple of drinks, and passed one to Lannes.

'If you're looking for Karim . . . ' he said.

'What makes you think I might be?'

'No offence meant. I know you've done him a good turn, more than one indeed. Not that I'm implying anything, you understand. But I've been keeping my nose clean as you recommended on a previous visit. So it's natural to wonder if that was the reason for your call. He was grateful to you, you know, on his own account and that of his old bag of a mother. She's dead, as it happens, at the end of last year, drink of course, and I've not seen the lad for weeks, months even . . . '

'I didn't know,' Lannes said. 'He was fond of her, I think, in a way.'

'There's no accounting for tastes.'

'Well, you're in a position to know that.'

Lannes took the photograph of Aurélien Mabire from his pocket. 'Know this chap?'

Jules fingered his wart again.

'Can't say I do. Not one of my customers. Far as I remember and my memory's good, has to be in my line.'

'Are you sure?'

'I don't want trouble. That comes often enough without going to look for it. So when I say he's not one of my customers, you can believe me. I stick my head out for nobody. All the same I won't say that there may not be something familiar about him, and since you've come here to ask about him, it's obvious that you think he is of what we politely call a certain persuasion. The doc over there might know, he's got a wide acquaintance. Or of course the boy with him, though, as you can see, he's not been about long. No more than sixteen I'd say to look at him.'

Lannes turned towards the couple sitting under a cinema poster advertising *Morocco* with Marlene Dietrich and Gary Cooper.

'What are they drinking?' he said.

'A plum brandy for the doc and orangeade for the boy.'

Lannes took out his wallet.

Jules said, 'For you, superintendent , it's on the house. Just to show willing, you understand. The first round anyway.'

'Bring them over then, please.'

He approached the table, pulled out a chair and sat down.

'Lannes,' he said. 'Superintendent in the PJ, currently suspended. Which means I'm not entitled to question you, but nevertheless hope you will be kind enough to answer me.'

'How commendably frank. Naturally it will be a pleasure to oblige. I have always tried to be on good terms with the police. Allow me to introduce myself in turn: Alfred Solomons, doctor of medicine, retired.' He passed Lannes a card. 'Retired of my own choice, I may say, though, as you will understand, I would in any case in these unhappy times be prohibited from continuing to practise, on account of my family name. And this is Miki, of whose family name I am ignorant. Our acquaintance is recent, but won't, I hope, prove brief.'

He leant across and pinched the boy's ear.

Jules brought over the drinks and, without a word, retired again behind the bar.

'So how can I help you, superintendent?'

Lannes lit a cigarette, and laid the photograph of Mabire on the table. Dr Solomons glanced at it, took some coins from his pocket and handed them to the boy.

'Go and play Babyfoot with one of your mates over there.'

He picked up the photograph, but his eyes followed the boy across the room.

'I know something about you, superintendent,' he said. 'We have friends in common, acquaintances anyway. The old tailor, Ephraim Kurz, spoke of you as an honest man. And then there's young Karim. I know something of what you have done for him, and would go so far as to say he is even fond of you.' He smiled. 'I don't imply anything by that,' he said. 'Nevertheless it's unusual, isn't it, given what you both are.'

Lannes remembered how the boy, lying on his bed with only a towel wrapped round him in that filthy apartment with his drunken slattern of a mother in the next room, had offered himself to him, and when Lannes had said 'don't be silly' or something like that, had laughed and said it was worth trying, 'any time you change your mind' – though both had known that day wouldn't arrive.

'The photograph?' he said.

Dr Solomons put a nicotine-stained finger on it.

'I'm not respectable, superintendent. I used to be, but . . . ' He lifted his finger, spread his hand, palm upward, and, as it were, waved the past away. 'And perhaps you yourself are no longer respectable either, in the opinion of your superiors anyway, seeing as you have been suspended. But then – again perhaps – given the times we live in – that is a mark of distinction, reason indeed for me to respect you. So it may be that I should trust you. I observe that

Jules treats you with respect. Moreover, it's unlike him to stand anyone a drink.'

'He's a cautious man.'

'As we should all be things being as they are. But now I'm too old, seventy-six last month, to be careful. So . . . '

He gestured towards the Babyfoot table and the boy Miki who was leaning over it presenting neatly-formed buttocks to his gaze.

'So,' he said again, 'I'm old and all too aware of the cruel joke that God plays.'

'And what's that.'

'Simply that sexual desire outlives one's ability to inspire it in others. So one has to pay, in cash and the contempt of others.'

He put his finger on the photograph again.

'Poor Aurélien,' he said. 'Such a pretty boy twenty years ago. What sort of mess has he got himself into now?'

Lannes explained. Dr Solomons smiled.

'Have you considered that he might be sincere, or think himself sincere? Sincerely in love? Turning away, in disgust perhaps from what he is? His life has been a catastrophe. Why not change direction?'

'Is that likely?'

'How can I tell? We are all capable of the strangest developments or of course of the strangest self-deception.'

'Nevertheless,' Lannes said.

He paused and lit a cigarette.

There was silence but for the rattle from the Babyfoot table. Jules behind the bar wiped glasses that were already clean.

'Do you know the advocate Labiche?' Lannes said. 'He's involved in this, I don't know just how.'

'In that case . . . '

He turned his thumb down, like a Roman emperor.

'Poor Aurélien,' he said again.

'I need to speak to him. If you have the means of getting a message to him, I'd be grateful. And it would be in his best interest. You can understand that, I'm sure.'

'You really are suspended, superintendent?'

'I am. I have no powers of arrest. This truly is a private matter. As

I told you, I've been asked to find the girl. By her grandmother. All she wants is to have Marie-Adelaide home. So I'd be grateful to you.'

Dr Solomons picked up his glass of plum brandy and drained it.

'I'll do as you ask,' he said.

Lannes stubbed out his cigarette, lit another, looked the doctor in the face and saw that he was smiling. He read amusement, even irony, in the smile, and this encouraged him.

'You say you no longer practise medicine.'

'But naturally. Even if I was ten years younger, I couldn't. It would be forbidden as you know.'

'Sometimes what's forbidden can still be done.'

'If you say so.'

Lannes drew in smoke, got up and crossed to the bar for an Armagnac for himself and a plum brandy for the doctor. This time he paid for the drinks and brought them back to the table.

'Strange world,' he said. 'You're forbidden to practise medicine, and I'm forbidden to be a policeman. Nevertheless I'm investigating a case and . . . I'm going to trust you, doctor. Trust you as a man and a doctor.'

Lannes fingered his glass. Dr Solomons raised his and took a little sip.

'Trust?' he said. 'There's a word that's out of fashion.'

'Nevertheless,' Lannes said again. 'I've a friend, a Jewish woman. She's in hiding, needless to say. She's also very ill, perhaps dying. I'm afraid it's cancer, though of course I'm not competent to say. That's just my suspicion, you understand. The friend in whose apartment she is staying hasn't been able to find a doctor, hasn't dared indeed, for reasons you'll appreciate. Would you see her? Possibly give her something at least to alleviate the pain. Morphine, I suppose?'

Dr Solomons smiled.

'You ask a lot, superintendent, superintendent suspended.'

'You may even know her,' Lannes said. 'Since you mentioned the old tailor. She's some sort of connection, I can't recall what exactly.'

The bead curtain was swung aside. Three young men entered. They wore the uniform of the Milice, the paramilitary police

42

auxiliary force recruited by the dying regime to counter the Resistance. One with the insignia of an officer marched up to the bar and struck Jules hard on the face.

'Scum,' he said, 'corrupter of French youth.'

He turned round, pointed at Miki and said, 'That's the one. Grab him.'

The boy tried to make a run for it, was seized by one of the miliciens who twisted his arm behind his back so violently that Miki yelped in pain. The other milicien punched him in the mouth and blood spurted from his lips.

Jules ducked behind the bar and came up pointing a Luger at the officer.

'Tell your men to let the boy alone and get out all three of you before I blow a hole in your face.'

Lannes got up, very slowly, and approached the bar.

'Put it away, Jules. We don't want any shooting. It's not necessary.'

Jules lowered the gun but kept hold of it.

'I don't allow trouble here,' he said.

'No,' Lannes said. 'There'll be no need for trouble.'

He turned to the officer who, he now saw, was little more than a boy himself, no older that Dominique. He produced his badge.

'Lannes,' he said. 'Superintendent in the police judiciaire. I think there's some misunderstanding. What do you want with the boy?'

'The little rat's been running messages for those swine of the Resistance.'

Lannes took him by the elbow and shepherded him to the corner of the room.

'As I said, a misunderstanding. Not your fault of course. You've been misled. Well, that's not surprising. We live in confusing times. As it happens, however, the boy is one of my agents, an informer spying on a Resistance group on my instructions. They've come to trust him and the proof that they do is the information – the inaccurate information – that has been laid against him and brought you here.'

'You use creatures like that, degenerates that prostitute themselves for money?'

'It's a wicked world, my friend. We use all sorts. How do you think he made the acquaintance of a particular Resistance leader and was able to supply us with information? Pillow-talk, it's called. So, be a good chap, tell your boys to let him go, and we'll all have a drink and pretend that this little incident never happened. You wouldn't want me to have to lay a complaint against you for interfering with an officer of the French State in the pursuit of his duty, would you? And I've no desire to have to do that. As proof of my good intentions, I don't know your name and I'm not even going to ask what it is.'

The officer hesitated, looked Lannes in the eye, then saluted.

'Paul Lagisquon, lieutenant in the Milice, at your service, sir. I'm not ashamed to have my name known.'

'And why should you be? You have my respect, lieutenant.'

Lagisquon ordered his men to release the boy.

'Don't even give him the kicking the little tart deserves,' he said. 'But we won't accept your offer of a drink, sir. I wouldn't let my lips touch a glass the customers of this bar have drunk from.'

He saluted again, clicked his heels and led his men out, his head held high.

Silence followed him. The bead curtain thrust violently aside swung gently in the air. Jules put the Luger out of sight below the bar counter. Miki wiped the blood from his mouth and the tears from his eyes. He was still shaking. Dr Solomons led him through to the toilet.

'A nasty moment,' Jules said.

'It would have been nastier if you had pulled the trigger.'

'I don't allow people to insult me in my own bar.'

'I'd have thought you'd be used to it by now. Give me another Armagnac, please.'

'This one is on the house, and I'll join you. Don't think I'm not grateful, superintendent.'

'There may be more incidents like this.'

'I can look after myself.'

'Oh yes?' Lannes said. 'If I was you, I'd close the bar till the Americans arrive.'

'You think they will.'

'They have to. Or the English. If it's the English there'll be lots of demand for what you have on offer. I don't know about the Americans. There may be fewer among them.'

Dr Solomons returned from the toilet. He had cleaned up Miki's face but the boy's lips were still quivering.

'You should keep him out of sight, doctor. I won't be around another time.'

'No. What a world we've survived into.'

'The thing to do is survive it.'

'We're grateful to you. If you hadn't been here . . . well, it doesn't bear thinking on.'

He picked up his glass.

'I needed that,' he said.

Then he took Lannes aside and, lowering his voice, said, 'I'll see about Aurélien and I'll do what I can for your friend. It should be possible. Morphine, I mean.'

'Tomorrow?'

'If I can.'

'I'll be at the bar in the rue de la Vieille Tour in the afternoon. Three o'clock.'

IX

Maxim's was crowded as ever. There were German officers there, Frenchmen in dinner-jackets and Society women in evening gowns from, Léon supposed, the best couturiers. Waiters glided between the tables with bottles of champagne and trays piled with dishes such as no ordinary Parisian had seen for four years, such indeed as most of them had probably never eaten. There was a buzzing babble of conversation and smoke rose from cigars and cigarettes. Chardy took hold of Léon's elbow between his thumb and fore-finger to steer him across the room, and Léon knew that he held him in this way to demonstrate his ownership, to show him off as his boy. Well, he couldn't deny that he was that, in a sense anyway. Chardy protected him. He'd have been at a loss without him, and he had come to realise that Chardy felt affection for him as well as everything else. All the same he couldn't avoid the thought that it was disgusting and shameful to be here, even though something in him responded to the seedy glamour of this scene that nevertheless represented everything that he had joined the Free French to fight against.

They were led to a table at the back of the room. There were four people there and four empty places. Léon found himself between a blonde woman and an unoccupied chair. The waiter filled his glass with champagne. Chardy began talking about his new novel; he was making a sales pitch to a film producer. His tone was arrogant, as if he would be conferring a favour by allowing his masterpiece to be made into a movie. The blonde crumbled a bread roll. She leaned over and said in an undertone, 'I don't think your friend is making a good impression. Are you a writer yourself?' 'Not much of one,' he said. 'Just his boy then?' He felt himself blushing.

'I'm not being critical,' she said. 'We all have to live as best we can these days. I'm a kept woman myself. I suppose I'd be dead if I wasn't.' She laid her hand on his and pressed it. 'Drink your champagne,' she said.

*   *   *

Alain rolled off the girl and lay back in the hay. He almost said 'I needed that' but checked himself. It would sound as if she was merely a convenience, though she was indeed that, or as if what they had done together was for him only a physical necessity. It was that too of course, but he shouldn't leave her with the idea it was nothing more, since he might never see her again now that he had recovered and was ready to leave the farm.

'I have to go,' he said. 'You understand that, don't you.'

She sat up and pulled her knickers up from her ankles and rolled her dress down. She sniffed, twice, and he realised she was crying. He put his arm round her and kissed her on the lips.

'It's not that I want to leave you. It's just what I have to do.'

'I don't want to know about it. I don't want to know anything. Will I see you again?'

He kissed her a second time, gently. It was true what he said, that he didn't want to go. He was afraid to go, and lying here with her in the hay, with her milky breath on his lips, he knew this was also what mattered, real life. It's what we're fighting to restore, he thought. But he couldn't promise anything. He couldn't give her that lying assurance. He had to go, find his unit again. He couldn't live with himself if he didn't.

*   *   *

Descending from the train Dominique could see no sign of François. He felt a tremor of fear, even though both his ticket and his pass were in order, and when he approached the barrier he was allowed through without question. Nevertheless the sight of half a dozen German military policemen scrutinising the departing passengers quickened his sense of alarm. I mustn't do anything to attract their attention, he thought. I look respectable, there's nothing to be afraid of. But he couldn't fail to be conscious of what he was carrying in his briefcase. He wasn't made for this, Alain would have strolled past them with an air of unconcern he couldn't match. He wanted a cigarette, but he was afraid his hands would shake as he lit it and he would look guilty.

It was a relief to be free of the station. His instructions were clear. If François wasn't on the platform, he was to go to the Café Voltaire in the Boulevard Maréchal Soult. Better not to ask for directions. In any case he had the town map in his head. But he badly needed to pee. Nerves, nothing but nerves. He went into the first café, ordered a lemonade and paid for it, went down the stairs to the toilet to relieve himself and found he was still trembling. Someone had scrawled the Cross of Lorraine on the wall and written 'Laval is only a cunt' beside it. Another hand had added, 'And what's de Gaulle then?' He left without drinking his lemonade and wondered if this was a mistake.

François was sitting at a table on the terrace. Dominique didn't recognise him at once. He had grown a moustache and was wearing a tweed suit with plus-four trousers. He looked like a country squire or, rather, an actor playing a squire.

'The Gestapo were at the station,' he said. 'So I thought it safer not to go in. Not that I've any reason to think they were looking

47

for me. My cover's secure. I'm Jacques Morland, a commercial traveller in cosmetics. I've got a case of samples to prove it. Pleased to see you anyway. You got the papers without trouble?'

Dominique patted his briefcase. Again, he thought, this isn't my sort of thing. François enjoys this game of nerves, I wish I could.

'It won't be long now,' François said. 'It really won't. But the next months are the most dangerous. Look after yourself. And leave the briefcase with me – there's nothing of your own in it, I suppose?'

'Nothing.'

It would be a relief to be rid of it.

'What you're doing now won't be forgotten,' François said. 'I assure you of that.'

He made it sound as if he personally would pin a decoration on his chest. Then he remembered that he had been shown a photograph of François receiving the 'Francisque' from the Marshal himself.

* * *

Freddie , the sailor-boy, slipped out of bed and stood in front of the smeared and cracked mirror admiring himself. Jérôme turned over to look at him. There was certainly much to admire, 'Nice as pie, aren't I?' as Freddie himself said. Now he pulled on his baggy Royal Navy regulation underpants and looked ordinary, even for a moment absurd. The singlet followed. He picked up his trousers and turned round.

'Like what you see, Froggie?'

'Not the pants.'

'What's under them's all right though, intit?'

'I wish you weren't going.'

'We've had fun, haven't we?' Freddie said. 'But now fun's over. King and Country call. I'll be all right, you know. As my old woman says, it's the good die young, not a limb of Satan like you, Fred. You'll go to see her, won't you, when I'm away, carrying the troops to liberate your belle France?'

'Will she want me to?'

'Course she will. She likes you.'

'Does she know what we do, what we get up to?'

'Course she does. The old woman wasn't born yesterday, and you don't grow up in the East End without knowing what's what – 'sides if what she says is true it was her own old man, my granddad, who was the first to give her a taste of how's your father, her and her brother, my uncle Alf, too. Catholic tastes, he had, the old bugger. So she's not one to be shocked. Just take her a spot of gin when you call, not your red rotgut, though she'd swig that too if there was nothing else.'

Freddie was fully dressed now. He snapped to attention in front of the mirror and saluted.

'Able Seaman Spinks reporting for duty.'

He sat on the bed, and thrust his hand under the covers between Jérôme's legs.

'Bit of reporting for duty here too, that's nice. Know what the old woman says? I'm glad you've got that nice French boy, she says. If it wasn't for him that Ethel Briggs would have had you putting a bun in her oven and screaming for a marriage licence just so's she could collect the widow's pension if you don't come back. That's what she says. But don't you worry about me. I'm coming back, no question. Remember your promise. When we've sent Jerry packing and little Adolf's done for, you're going to show me Gay Paree, the Folies Bergère and all that whatever. Now I'm off. Don't do anything I wouldn't do.'

He leaned over and kissed Jérôme's cheek.

'Mind you, that leaves you a lot of scope.'

The door closed behind him. Jérôme listened to his steps clattering down the stairs. He looked at his watch. Only an hour till he had to be in the office, to speak to the Youth of France, tell them the day of Liberation was approaching, while Freddie was on his way to carry the troops that would – how had he put it? – send Jerry packing. He wondered if Alain, wherever he might be, might be listening in. And Léon too, with whom he'd learned the Service had lost all contact months ago and who might now be dead.

*   *   *

'So you've had enough?' Baron Jean said.

Michel looked away. This wasn't what he had signed up for, guarding a miserable collection of stinking Jews, escorting them to a concentration camp.

'They don't trust us, do they, the Boches I mean?'

'War's war,' de Flambard said. 'There's no end of dirty jobs.'

'And this is one of the dirtiest. I came to fight the Bolsheviks.'

'So you did. So did I.'

The baron passed him a bottle of schnapps.

'Take a drink. Take a good drink. This present job's better done drunk, just a little drunk. But don't fret yourself. There'll be plenty of fighting yet. We've joined the losing side, you know. They'll need every man they've got before this is over.'

He leaned over and picked a louse out of Michel's hair.

'You'll have every chance,' he said, 'to be a hero yet, my son.'

X

The sun shone out of a cloudless sky. Lannes sat at a table outside the bar in the rue de la Vieille Tour with a glass of beer untouched in front of him. He had no desire to drink, no desire to do anything. A pigeon pecked around his feet. There were fewer pigeons in Bordeaux than in the days before the war. Boys trapped them and took them home for their mothers to cook, not that there could be much eating on these city birds. But you could make a broth with them, women said. Rationing was more severe than ever. The doctor was late. It didn't matter. He had nothing to do but kill time. They were all killing time, waiting. If the first months of the war had been a phoney war, the *drôle de guerre*, they were now living in a phoney peace, a *drôle de paix*. That morning, in the kitchen, he and Clothilde had tuned in as he did every day now to Radio London. The speaker had been stern, warning all those who had collaborated with the Boches that the day of reckoning was drawing near. There would be nowhere, he had said, for collaborators to hide. But who hadn't collaborated? Many who were now in the Resistance had done so, even the Communists who hadn't lifted a finger or a voice against the Occupation till Hitler had committed the folly of invading the Soviet Union. And were the Communists in the Resistance now fighting for Stalin or for France?

Dominique, his gentle and honourable Dominique, he was a collaborator in the eyes of the Resistance, working for Vichy along with his friend, young Maurice, trying by his account, which he didn't dispute, to give these boys from the poor quarters of the cities a better life, or at least show them the way to such a life. Were they to be condemned for that? Vichy was disreputable. That was, he had come to realise, undeniable. It had attracted scoundrels, like Labiche and Sigi de Grimaud, but not all who had adhered to Vichy were scoundrels. The idea was ridiculous. Some were merely fools, like his brother-in-law Albert. And there were others he couldn't be certain of. Maurice's father, Edmond de Grimaud, for instance, a minister in the Vichy government till he was dismissed a few months ago. He was certainly no fool, and perhaps no more than half a scoundrel. In any case he himself had long been in Edmond's debt. And the Alsatian, who sat so firmly on the fence that his buttocks were creased, what was he but a diligent time-server resolved to survive no matter how? He couldn't despise him. In truth he couldn't suppose he was entitled to despise anyone. As for the Marshal himself, he felt little but pity for the old man who had undoubtedly done his duty as he conceived it. If he had flown to Algiers in November '42 at the time of the American invasion, wouldn't they have received him with open arms? Wouldn't the French there have cheered him – to the rafters, as the saying went? Wouldn't he when the day of Liberation came have returned to Paris in triumph, even as it were on a white horse? But he had, as he put it, made a gift of his person to the French people, promised to share their suffering – even if his own could only have been mental or perhaps spiritual – and remained in place, powerless now, only a symbol of Lannes didn't know what. A broken and divided France, he supposed.

For there had been an idealistic side to Vichy, at first. How could he deny that since it was represented by Dominique and Maurice? Might they perhaps in years to come look back on the time of the Marshal with tender nostalgia?

And that young lieutenant in the Milice, wasn't he in his way a patriot? Liberty, the Girondin Madame Roland had said, as they carried her to the guillotine, what crimes are committed in your name! Patriotism too, patriotism likewise.

He picked up his glass of beer and, as he did so, saw Dr Solomons approach carrying a medical bag, perhaps for the first time in years.

He stood up. They shook hands. He attracted the attention of the waiter and ordered a plum brandy for the doctor.

'So?' he said.

'So I am here as promised. That was a nasty moment yesterday. It was fortunate you were there.'

'Is the boy all right?'

'All right but very frightened. He had indeed . . . '

'I don't want to know,' Lannes said. 'It's better you say nothing about it.'

'You don't care for the Resistance?'

'There's more than one kind of resistance, and I don't care for Frenchmen killing Frenchmen.'

'But it's happening and will continue to happen, and, as Miki himself says, it's better to be on the winning side. Which of course he wouldn't have been if you hadn't been there yesterday, superintendent.'

'Superintendent suspended, and, if that young lieutenant should find out that I am indeed suspended, or when, perhaps I should say when, he learns that, well I need only say that you should remind the boy of this probability, and tell him to keep out of sight. You also perhaps.'

'And yet I'm meeting you here, openly in the city.'

'So you are, and perhaps I shouldn't have put you at risk.'

'My dear superintendent – suspended – I've been at risk for years. And I'm an old man, though one, I confess, who is nevertheless still afraid of death.'

He raised his glass.

'Your health, superintendent suspended.'

'And yours, doctor suspended.'

'So we understand each other, or at least each other's position.'

'You can still smile?' Lannes said.

'And why not? I'm a Jew, a member of a race that over the centuries has had only two defences against hardship, misfortune, and persecution. Our religious faith, as God's chosen people, a faith I have never shared, and humour, Jewish humour which sees light on the dark side of things. It's been the defence that has kept us going. Once I was a distinguished man, attending some of the best families in Bordeaux. Now I live in disgrace and, as you have seen, in thrall to what the respectable world regards as vice. But I'm still alive, superintendent suspended, still alive. Perhaps that's something of which I should be ashamed, given the fate that has befallen so many of my race. The old tailor, Ephraim Kurz, killed himself, didn't he? That surprised me.'

'I think,' Lannes said, 'it was the last act of self-assertion of which he felt capable. So: Aurélien Mabire?'

'Poor Aurélien. Such a pretty boy once, but a weak man always. And now you suggest he's in the clutches of the advocate Labiche.'

'You know him?'

'Only by reputation, which is not good. He would never employ a Jew, not even as his physician. But I know enough of him to have sympathy with Aurélien, whatever he has done. And this girl you are looking for, she's of good family, I take it.'

'Yes,' Lannes said. 'But that's not the point.'

'There must be money involved.'

'Perhaps. Do you know where Aurélien is to be found?'

The doctor lifted his glass and drained it.

'Can you spare a cigarette?' he said.

Lannes pushed the packet of Gauloises towards him and then lit one for himself. For a moment neither spoke. The doctor drew on his cigarette and sighed.

At last, 'It's difficult,' he said. 'We haven't spoken for years. We quarrelled. He thought it was my fault. Perhaps it was. I was arrogant, demanding, possessive, jealous. So I feel guilty, I wouldn't want to get him into trouble.'

'He's there already. It's a question perhaps of getting him out of it. I don't believe he has been acting of his own volition. He's a pawn, no more than that, I think. And in any case I'm sure Labiche took the girl away from him. I hope Aurélien can tell me why.'

'And you really are suspended? You have no power of arrest?'

'None.'

'And your colleagues or former colleagues?'

'Have nothing to do with it. This isn't a police matter. I'm acting only on behalf of the girl's family. If Aurélien answers my questions, that, I hope, will be the end of it, as far as he is concerned.'

Dr Solomons stubbed out his cigarette.

'Very well,' he said. 'You have after all done me a service. That poor boy, Miki, I hate to think what would have become of him if you hadn't been there – and if that stupid Jules had pulled the trigger. The man you want to speak to is a Russian, a White Russian who calls himself Count Peter, though whether he is entitled to do so I don't know. He runs a gymnasium, popular with the sons of the wealthy and well-born. Perhaps you have already come across him? I believe he served time in the Foreign Legion. He and Aurélien. I'm sure I don't need to elaborate. If anyone can lead you to him, it will be the Russian. And now . . . ' he got to his feet and picked up his bag, 'let me resume my profession. Take me to your friend. If it is, as you fear, cancer, I have to tell you there is nothing I can do, except alleviate her pain. I've brought a supply of morphine. Don't please ask me how I came by it. But I'll require payment, I'm afraid. Of course you may be wrong. Cancer is difficult to diagnose.'

XI

Dr Solomons hadn't of course, as he had warned, been able to diagnose anything. He had examined Miriam, while Henri hovered beside him and Lannes waited below, with Toto, Henri's little French bulldog, snuffling at his feet. It might, the doctor said, when they descended, be cancer; it might not. It might be her gall-bladder; it might not. She should be in hospital but he realised this was impossible. Perhaps when they were liberated? The sooner the better of course. Meanwhile he had given her morphine, as requested, to dull the pain, and he left instructions with Henri as to the dose and frequency of administration. 'There's a danger she will become addicted,' he said, 'but it's improbable. That would require a higher dose, more morphine than I could obtain.' Yes, he was sorry, he would require payment, but only for the drug, not for the consultation. And he would call again if they wished, though, sadly, there was nothing really that he could do.

'A good man, I think,' Henri said when he had shown the doctor out. 'I'm grateful to you, Jean, for finding him. I have felt so useless and guilty for being useless. And how are you yourself, Jean?'

'I feel the same as you.'

'And yet,' Henri said, 'the nightmare is surely approaching its end. It can't be long now, and, as Dr Solomons said, we can get Miriam into hospital.'

'I hope so.'

There was no point in speaking about his fears. Of course Liberation would be welcome – to see the Germans march out, perhaps even, preferably, in orderly fashion, without the need for an insurrection and street-fighting. And yet, what would follow? No doubt his suspension would be lifted but, back at work, what would he be faced with? He thought of that lieutenant in the Milice who had so proudly given him his name – which, for the moment, he couldn't recall. Was it innate viciousness that had prompted him to attach himself to a cause that any reasonable person could see was now doomed? Or patriotism – perverted patriotism if you like? He remembered the contempt with which the lieutenant had regarded the boy Miki, a contempt that he supposed nine out of ten, or more than that, ninety-nine out of a hundred, of the respectable citizens of Bordeaux would share. If Lannes hadn't lied to him, he would have taken the boy away, to be beaten up, tortured perhaps, and then shot in a cellar. That was the sort of thing the Milice did. It was revolting, but would the Resistance behave differently? Wouldn't they exact an equally brutal revenge? And Lannes found, admitted to himself, that he had a strange respect for that young lieutenant who had committed himself to his cause. Perhaps because he knew himself to be incapable of any comparable commitment to anything, except, he thought, his vague and useless idea of what he called decency.

'I must go,' he said. 'Give Miriam my respects. I only hope the doctor's visit has been of some service. At least she'll be in less pain now.'

'I'm grateful to you, Jean, and so will Miriam be. I scarcely dare ask if you have any news of the boys, of Alain and Léon.'

'None at all.'

'I think of them often. I even pray for them though I have no belief in prayers. Silly, isn't it? But I became fond of Léon while he worked for me. I saw what poor Gaston loved in him even though that side of Gaston's life had always dismayed me. Even disgusted me if I am honest. I'll see you out, lock up after you. It's a comfort, I find, to be behind a locked door.'

They passed through the dark and musty shop where that mad spook who called himself Félix had raped Léon and compelled him to consent to be used as bait for the German liaison officer Schussmann,

'Are you going home now?' Henri said. 'Give my respects, please, my affectionate respects, to Marguerite. It's too long since I saw her.'

'Of course,' Lannes said. 'When it's over you must come to dinner.'

Empty words, but why not?

The air was still soft and warm when he stepped into the rue des Remparts where the advocate Labiche had once accosted him and asked, sneeringly, if he had been visiting his 'pretty little Jew-boy'.

It was too early to go home, to be met with silence. Clothilde wouldn't be back yet; there had been talk of a visit to the cinema with a girlfriend. He should make that promised call on Fernand, find out what was troubling him. He turned into a bar, asked to use the telephone and rang the number of his friend's apartment in the rue du Port St-Pierre. No reply. Why is it that the sound of a telephone ringing in an empty house can be so sad?

Meanwhile there was the old Russian to be seen. Lannes knew a bit about him. At the age of fourteen or so Alain had gone to his gymnasium in an old building behind the Marché des Capucins, gone together with his friend Philippe whom Lannes disliked. Then he'd stopped, saying he just didn't like it, it wasn't for him, not his kind of place, and Lannes hadn't inquired further. But Clothilde's Michel had later been a regular there, and when he joined the Legion of French Volunteers against Bolshevism, the old Russian had called on Michel's grandfather, the Professor, apparently in distress and uttering threats against Sigi de Grimaud whose influence had led Michel astray. Lannes remembered the Professor's words: 'He said he loved Michel with a pure love, which may of course be true.' And he had said that the Russian's impassioned speech, full of self-recrimination, was like something out of Dostoevsky whose novels Lannes had never read.

The door was open and a little passage led into the gym. There was a boxing ring at one end and the usual pieces of equipment, mats on the floor, a wooden horse, ropes dangling from the rafters. But there was a layer of dust over everything and Lannes had the impression that the old Russian's pupils – if that was what he called them – had deserted him. A couple of posters advertising boxing matches had half-detached themselves from the boards to which they were pinned, and dangled loose.

There was a light beyond a doorway at the end of the room and he approached it.

The old Russian was sitting on a stool in front of a stove on top of which stood a samovar. He wore a shabby grey suit and a dirty silk muffler round his neck. He looked up as Lannes entered. His eyes were red-rimmed and the tips of his moustache stained yellow. He held a glass of tea in his hand and there was a cigarette in the corner of his mouth.

'Mr Policeman,' he said. 'I remember you. You brought your son here once. It didn't take. He disliked the discipline that is necessary. And now here you are again. Is he dead? Forgive me for asking bluntly, but so many are.'

Lannes found a chair and sat down. The Russian returned his gaze to the stove. Its door was open but there was no fire and the ashes were grey.

'I don't know,' Lannes said. 'I hope he isn't, but I don't know.'

'So many are,' the Russian said again. 'I should be dead myself, but it seems the Lord isn't ready for me. And there is something I still have to do.'

'Sigi's in Paris, when I last heard,' Lannes said. 'Others will take care of him. It's not your responsibility.'

'You know about my vow?'

'Naturally.'

'The hand of the Lord is raised against the evil-doer and I am his instrument.'

'Michel isn't dead,' Lannes said. 'My daughter who loves him tells me she would know if he was. Do you believe that?'

'I don't know. Some days I believe nothing. Some days I believe everything. I have prayed to the Virgin to protect the boy. My love for Michel was pure. I have lived a long time, often wickedly, but that love was pure, I assure you. In my old age I believe in goodness, in virtue. The man you call Sigi believes only in power, he sold his soul to the Devil long ago. That is why I must fulfil my vow. Do you think I am mad?'

Lannes lit a cigarette.

'Not mad,' he said, 'miserable, wretched, all that, but not mad.'

'You are wrong. One has to be mad today. How else can one live in this world?'

'I don't know. Is Aurélien mad?'

'No. That is why he is afraid. Only the truly mad can escape fear.'

'Where is he?'

'Through there, in his cupboard. Asleep on his mattress. He sleeps most of the time because he is afraid, afraid of the day, afraid of the night. Go speak to him. I loved him once. That love was impure. It is why he is here. But I can do nothing for him because he is afraid. Nor can the Virgin. Go speak to him and take him away. He is already in prison in his own mind, so you can do him no further harm. There is no place for him here. I told him that, but he only wept. Take him away, Mr Policeman. Leave me alone in my madness. Leave me with my vow and my dream of revenge. It will better for Aurélien if you take him away.'

The man was indeed stretched out on a dirty mattress, but he was fully dressed in a high-necked jersey and thin trousers. Perhaps the voices had awoken him, for when he became aware of Lannes standing over him, he sat up and rubbed his eyes.

'I'm a policeman, Aurélien. I'm taking you away. Count Peter doesn't want you here any more, and we have to talk. So get up, please.'

The man pushed himself half-upright so that his back was against the wall.

'You'll hit me if I get up. I know what the police are like, and I can't stand being hit. And I promise, I did nothing to the girl, I never even touched her, I swear.'

'I know you didn't. And nobody's going to hit you. In any case this isn't a police matter, though I am a policeman. It's private business, and even if you had touched the girl – which, yes, I repeat, I believe you didn't – she's not a minor, but we have to talk. We'll go to your sister's pension, it's not far, and talk there. And give you something to eat. When did you last eat?'

'My sister's?'

'Your sister's. She's the only person who cares for you, Aurélien, the only one who cares whether you're alive or dead.'

'That's not true,' Aurélien said. 'I've been threatened with death.'

'You can tell me about that at your sister's. Come on.'

XII

The door of the Pension Smitt was locked or bolted. Lannes rang the bell, knocked hard on the wood, and waited. Aurélien propped himself against the wall. It had taken them a long time to get there, though the distance wasn't far. Aurélien had stopped twice, saying he couldn't go on, couldn't face his sister, wanted to die. But these were only words. His resistance was feeble, his will broken.

At last the door opened.

'Oh, it's you again.'

'I've brought him back to you,' Lannes said. 'You may not want him, but it's the only place for him. He's in a bad way as you can see. I doubt if he has eaten since you threw him out. I have to talk to him, but he needs something to eat. Have you any food in the house?'

'Food,' she said, as if the word was strange to her, but she stood

59

aside to let them in. She put out a hand and touched her brother, lightly, on the cheek.

'There might be an egg,' she said.

'Anything,' Lannes said, 'and a bottle of wine. Here, I'll pay for it.'

She took the note without a word and stuffed it into the pocket of the same flowered housecoat she had been wearing on his previous visit. Then she turned and led them into a little room where, in more prosperous times, she had doubtless served coffee and croissants or slices of bread and jam to her guests and lodgers. The shutters were closed and the room was lit only by a single low-wattage bulb dangling from the ceiling.

Aurélien sat at one of the little tables and buried his head in his hands. His sister, muttering unintelligibly, shuffled away in her carpet slippers. Lannes lit a cigarette. The smell in the room was horrible, as if there might be a dead rat decomposing under the floorboards. He waited. There was no point starting till she had brought her brother something to eat and drink. He had smoked three cigarettes before she returned.

'The egg was bad,' she said, 'you can't trust them in the market nowadays, but there's some hard cheese. And bread.'

She put the plate on the table, alongside a litre bottle of vin ordinaire and a couple of smeared tumblers.

'You'd better tell him what he wants to know,' she said, 'and then perhaps he'll leave us alone. I told him the last time he was here it's not my fault you are what you are.'

Lannes filled the glasses, pushed one towards Aurélien, and said, 'Drink and eat. There's no hurry. I've all the time in the world. But I'm not going away and you're going to talk. You know that really. I'm not going to hit you. I told you I wouldn't, but we're staying here until you've told me everything. I know you're afraid of Labiche. Well, that's natural. I don't blame you for that. Why did he want the girl?'

Aurélien shuddered and shook his head, but he stretched out his hand to the glass and made to lift it, paused, and said, 'I can't.' Lannes picked it up, held it out to him and said, again, 'Drink.' This time Aurélien managed to take a mouthful, swallowed it, and leaned back in the chair. Sweat stood out on his brow.

'That's better,' Lannes said. 'We've all the time in the world,' he said again. 'It's a strange business, isn't it? You're a queer, you've never fancied women, and Labiche is a pervert whose taste is for under-age girls, little girls who haven't reached the age of puberty. Marie-Adelaide's nineteen and yet you make her acquaintance, write love-letters to her – I've read them by the way, she left them behind for her grandmother to find – you persuade her to come away with you and bring her here to the pension your sister keeps. You can see why I'm puzzled?'

Aurélien made no reply, but this time he lifted the glass himself and emptied it.

'You shared a room with the girl,' Lannes said, 'and I wonder what you talked about. Did she still think you were in love with her?'

'No,' Aurélien said, 'it wasn't that. It wasn't ever like that. You've got it all wrong. I really did like her, she was sweet and innocent. No, that's not true. She was sweet, but she wasn't innocent, though I believed she was. But she liked me, she really did, and, as for me, well, what can I say? I hoped, yes hoped. You don't know what it's like to be me, to be what I am, what I've always been. You think I like being what I am, what you call a queer? That I haven't always wanted to be normal? That I'm not ashamed?'

He paused and for the first time lifted his head and looked Lannes in the face.

'Ashamed,' he said again, dwelling on the word. 'You despise me, don't you, for being what I am?'

'No,' Lannes said, 'I don't despise you. I've met many worse men than you, and I didn't despise them either.'

He lit a cigarette, passed it to Aurélien, and lit another for himself. 'Go on,' he said, 'continue, please.'

'She was unhappy. I liked that, not because I'm cruel, you understand, but because I responded to it. Do you understand that? She felt confined by her grandmother who watched everything she did. That's what she said, it was like being a prisoner. That was what we had in common, I see that now. But it was no good, she was sweet, but it was no good. It wasn't me she wanted.'

'You're going too fast,' Lannes said. 'Let's go back a bit. How did you meet her and where does Labiche come in?'

'Labiche? Why do you think her grandmother kept her so close, as a prisoner as she said? I didn't know that then of course when he introduced me to her at a gallery private view. Don't ask me how she came to be there, in view of what she said about how her grandmother watched over her, because I don't know. I was an art dealer, you know, so it was natural for me to be there, and he was my lawyer who had, I confess, got me out of trouble in the past. So when he saw her there, he told me to approach her and make up to her. It seemed strange, I thought at first it was just for his amusement but I did as he suggested and, as I say, I found I really liked her. It wasn't me who suggested we should be together, it was her idea. I don't expect you to believe me,' he drank some more wine, 'because I'm accustomed to people not believing me, but that's how it was. It excited me, I admit that, to be wanted by a girl, it had never happened to me before. I'm sorry, I need a pee.'

He looked better when he came back. He had washed his face and his hands were no longer shaking. Lannes wasn't surprised. He had been here often before; there are moments when a policeman becomes a priest or psychoanalyst, offering, providing, the relief of confession which is welcome whether the terror of condemnation is lifted or still hangs heavy.

'So you realised you weren't the man she wanted,' he said. 'That must have disappointed you?'

'Yes of course it did, but when it came to the point it didn't surprise me.'

'What do you mean by that?'

'Well I couldn't do what I thought she wanted, and so it was good to find that really she didn't want it from me, that I was only a sort of excuse. Do you see what I mean?'

'I think so,' Lannes said. 'Let's go back to Labiche. You say at first you thought it was just for his amusement that he suggested you approach the girl, but it wasn't that, was it? He had seduced her when she was a little girl? Yes?'

'Yes.'

'But she's too old for him now?'

'Yes.'

'And he came here, and you both went away with him, and then you returned alone, without the girl. Yes?'

'Yes.'

'This puzzles me,' Lannes said. 'Wasn't she horrified to meet him again? It would be only natural if she was.'

'You might think so, but she wasn't. She was excited.'

'By Labiche? That doesn't make sense to me.'

'Not by Labiche. Whatever you suppose or think natural, she was indifferent to him. That may, as you say, make no sense to you, but it's how it was. It was what he promised that excited her.'

'And what was that?'

'To take her to her father.'

'Her father?'

'Yes. She talked about him at night, every night. He was the one she wanted, the only person, as she said, that she had ever loved, and she hadn't seen him for years, seven years, not since she was twelve, and even then only in secret because his mother, her grandmother, had cut him off and forbidden him to see his daughter. He was a friend of Labiche and Labiche was acting on his behalf. He wanted her back and this made her happy. So she said goodbye to me with a smile on her face.'

'And then you collapsed? Why was that, Aurélien?'

'For two reasons. First because I realised I will always be what I am and I wanted to kill myself, but know I don't have the courage to do so. And, second, because I am afraid of Labiche. I know this doesn't make sense, because if he does what he threatened to do if I talked, I might get what I want and be dead. But two things that separately don't make sense nevertheless reduced me to the state you found me in.'

'And now?'

'Now? I don't know. I'm sure of nothing. I suppose my sister will look after me, as she always has. Unless you . . . '

'I've nothing to charge you with,' Lannes said. 'You may have been a fool, deceiving yourself, but you're not a criminal. As for your sister, I can see that she's an unhappy woman herself. Perhaps it's your turn to look after her, Aurélien, now that you've unburdened yourself. So eat the bread and cheese she brought you. And leave

Labiche to me. I assure you, his time's running out. Not because of this, certainly, but because the world is shifting.'

XIII

Well, he didn't doubt the truth of what the wretched Aurélien had told him. So he had solved the mystery, such as it was, even if he hadn't found the girl, and could report to St-Hilaire. That might be enough. He hoped it would be, for he had no wish to confront Labiche himself. As for his last words to Aurélien, the world might indeed be shifting, the Allies' invasion couldn't be long off and it was clear Germany was losing the war on the Eastern Front, but Labiche? Perhaps he would indeed be arrested and put on trial as a collaborator and organiser of the deportation of the Bordeaux Jews. But he was resourceful. He had friends, men of influence, who would doubtless speak up for him, and there were surely others of whom he knew much to their discredit who would pull strings on his behalf in return for a promise of silence. Lannes was still enough of an old Radical to be sceptical about the likelihood of punishment being meted out to the rich or the well-born and well-connected, no matter what they might be guilty of. It was the little people of no importance who would suffer for their collaboration. A picture of Yvette being rabbled and humiliated came horribly to mind.

He mounted the stairs to their apartment. How sad to be reluctant to come home at the end of the day. How long was it since Marguerite had greeted him with a smile? How long since they had talked easily together? It was almost a relief to hear his brother-in-law Albert's voice when he opened the door. Even Albert's conversation which always irritated and often depressed him was preferable to chilly silence. Now he shook hands with him and told him he was welcome as he always was, the lie, which was less of a lie today, coming easily to his lips. Once Alain, who detested his uncle, had charged him, angrily, with hypocrisy because he tolerated Albert's opinions and didn't argue with him, and he had replied only that family was family and it was necessary to maintain civil relations. Alain had glowered and said he believed in honesty and plain speaking, and in any case he saw no reason to treat repulsive opinions with respect, no matter who uttered them. He loved Alain's commitment, but said it was a question of good manners too, and moreover he shouldn't upset his mother.

'Isn't Clothilde home? Her film must have finished hours ago.'

'No,' Marguerite said, 'she's spending the night with her friend Marie-Louise. They're having a party for her name-day. You would remember if you paid as much attention to your family as you do to your work, or to whatever you now do outside your home where it seems you prefer not to be. Your friend, that Moncerre, telephoned. He wants to see you, he didn't say why and of course I didn't ask. Meanwhile, if it's of any interest to you, my mother is ill again. They've taken her to hospital. Albert and I have just been to visit her. She said to give you her regards, as she always does, I can't think why since you never go to see her yourself.'

'I'm sorry,' Lannes said. 'What is it? Is it serious?'

'They don't know. There are tests to be done. Albert, I'm exhausted. I'm going to bed. Thank you for being with me. I dare say Jean will entertain you, as best he can.'

Entertainment wasn't what Lannes associated with his brother-in-law. Since he had had a glass of that bad wine at the Pension Smitt, he took a bottle of marc from the cabinet, if only to get the taste out of his mouth. Albert accepted a glass and filled his pipe.

'How ill is she?'

'Palpitations of the heart,' Albert said. 'I don't think it's serious, you know what she's like. But Marguerite worries. She's worried about you too, Jean.'

'Did she say so?'

'Not precisely, not in so many words. But I can tell.' He drew on his pipe. 'This suspension. I haven't enquired about the reason, but you'll understand that it causes her anxiety.'

'They're difficult times,' Lannes said.

'Soon to be better. I have it on good authority that the Germans are confident that they will throw the Anglo-Saxons back into the sea. Breaching the Atlantic Wall, that's a formidable task. And they're undoubtedly ready for them. You'll see. When the invasion has been defeated, these rats of the Resistance will crawl back into their holes.'

'You think so?'

'I have it on good authority, as I say. And then I hope this suspension of yours will be lifted and things can return to normality. Is there any word of a visit from Dominique? It would do his grandmother good to see him. As she says, she doesn't have favourites, but you know she dotes on him.'

'He's a lovable boy. But there's no word of a visit.'

'I'm told they think well of him in Vichy. He has won golden opinions, that's what I hear. Golden opinions. You must be proud of him.'

'I'm proud of all three of the children,' Lannes said.

It was true, even though it often occurred to him that to express pride in your children was to claim credit that you had really perhaps done nothing to deserve.

'Clothilde is of course charming,' Albert said.

The evening dragged on in desultory fashion. They had never been easy together, and now there were so many subjects to be avoided, Alain most of all. And of course the coming months. Lannes wondered if Albert could really be as complacent as he seemed. Didn't he realise that Vichy was now no more than the ghost of a government, that, if the Boches did indeed defeat the Americans and British as he supposed they would, the Occupation would only be intensified and a new even more pro-German, authentically fascist administration would be put in place. Even Laval's days would be numbered, his collaboration deemed insufficient, half-hearted, with too many reservations.

At last Albert heaved himself to his feet and said he must be off.

'I'll enquire what can be done to have your suspension lifted,' he said. 'It would be one less worry for Marguerite.'

The words were futile, for he had no influence. Perhaps the pretence made him feel good.

When he had gone, Lannes took the dirty glasses through to the kitchen. There was a sheet of paper on the table, held down by a salt-cellar. He picked it up. The single, typewritten line read: *Ask your husband about his whore at the Pension Bernadotte.*

He folded the paper and put it in the inside pocket of his jacket.

XIV

Moncerre wouldn't have admitted it, but he was jealous of Lannes. Irritated by him often too. They had worked well together for years. In many respects their abilities complemented each other. But Lannes' tendency always to see both sides of a case or argument was infuriating. Moreover, Moncerre, whose own marriage was unhappy, even stormy, envied what he regarded as Lannes' happy family life. He had no children himself, and always insisted he didn't want any. Nevertheless to be a husband and not a father was in some way to be inferior, incomplete anyway. In truth he would have loved to have a son who looked up to him as a heroic figure. He might have adopted young René Martin as a substitute, but it had been evident from the day he was transferred to the PJ and joined their team that René had eyes only for Lannes. So Moncerre teased him, sometimes cruelly, and in response René took pleasure in disagreeing with him when they were discussing a case. To make matters worse Lannes was likely to take René's side, and Moncerre found himself the odd one out.

It would be too much to say that Lannes' suspension was welcome to him, but it certainly wasn't displeasing. It gave him an opportunity to prove his worth, and he had indeed cleared up a couple of cases successfully. All the same his nerves were on edge and, as René had told Lannes, he was drinking too much and was often incapable of doing any work in the morning until he had steadied himself with a quarter-litre of red wine or a couple of bottles of beer. And now there was a new development which worried him and tested his loyalty.

The day before yesterday he had been visited by an officer of the Milice asking to speak with Superintendent Lannes. Moncerre had explained that he was currently unavailable; it was clear that the man didn't know of Lannes' suspension. Moncerre had asked how he himself might help.

'I doubt if that's possible,' the officer said, nevertheless taking a seat on the other side of the desk. He introduced himself as Captain Fracasse and said, 'Our work is difficult enough.'

'I've no doubt it is,' Moncerre said, lighting his pipe and wondering what all this was about.

'More than difficult if we are denied co-operation by other organs of the State.'

'Quite so,' Moncerre said.

'Not only denied co-operation, but actively obstructed. You understand that we are charged with the elimination of these traitors who call themselves the Resistance. This is why I must speak to Superintendent Lannes. Will you please tell him to get in touch with me. Here is my card with the telephone number to ring. I'll expect a call within twenty-four hours. Otherwise I shall have take action such as I would wish to avoid.'

*   *   *

'Fracasse won't be his real name,' Lannes said. '*Le Capitaine Fracasse* was a nineteenth-century novel. By Gautier, as I remember. I think he was a mercenary or soldier of fortune, perhaps in the Thirty Years War. I haven't read it since I was a schoolboy.'

It was ten in the morning. They were in the Café des Arts, Cours de la Marne, one of Lannes' favourite bars. The old waiter, Marcel, had brought him an Armagnac and a cup of bad coffee without having to be asked. Lannes took a mouthful of the brandy and tipped the rest into the coffee.

'What's that got to do with it?' Moncerre said.

His eyes were red-rimmed and he looked away and called to Marcel to bring him another quarter-litre.

'I didn't say anything,' he said, 'beyond assuring him that I'd pass the message on. But it's obviously trouble.'

Was there a note of satisfaction in his voice?

'I think I've a right to be told. As it is, I felt like a fool. Obviously I didn't tell him you are suspended from duty, though I've no doubt he's likely to find out that you are.'

'Yes,' Lannes said. 'I suppose he will.'

'So what's it all about?'

'I'm not sure that you want to know,' Lannes said. 'I think it's better that you shouldn't. Then you're not involved.'

'That's typical,' Moncerre said.

'What do you mean?'

'Typical of you. You keep your cards so close to your chest that they stick there. "I think it's better that you shouldn't know" – is that the way to speak to me? We've worked together for years, I think of you as a mate, but when it's an important question, you freeze up.'

'It's for your sake.'

'Don't you trust me? I bet if it was young René who'd been asked to pass on the message, you'd tell him what it was about.'

'No I wouldn't. I certainly wouldn't.'

He drank his coffee and lit a cigarette. Was he being unfair to the bull-terrier? Didn't he in fact trust him and wasn't Moncerre justified in feeling aggrieved?

'All right,' he said, and recounted the incident in Chez Jules.

'You're a fool,' Moncerre said. 'It's a real mess.'

'So it is. That's why I said it was better you knew nothing about it. And I suggest that you still don't, that you haven't seen me to pass the message on. That won't surprise him when he learns that I'm suspended.'

'He'd still want to know why I didn't tell him.'

'Oh, you can always plead loyalty,' Lannes said, '*esprit de corps*. How's work, anyway?'

'No problems I can't deal with,' Moncerre said.

'That's good. I'm glad to hear it.'

*   *   *

When Moncerre had left him, saying with some satisfaction that he had work to do even if Lannes didn't, he fingered the sheet of paper in his inside pocket. It was like Marguerite to have said nothing, merely leaving it for him to find. She had been asleep when he joined her in bed, her face turned towards the wall. He had let his hand rest lightly on her thigh as he had so often done, tenderly and lovingly. Had he hoped for a response, hoped to hear her give a little sigh and ease herself towards him?

It was a time of anonymous letters, denunciations. They had been inundated with them in the PJ ever since the early days of the Occupation. Many were trivial, if malicious: the writer had a neighbour engaged in the black market. Others were more serious: the authorities should know that Madame X was sleeping with German soldiers. More recently there had been accusations of harbouring Jews or of involvement in the Resistance. He had been in the habit of ignoring them, and disobeyed the requirement to file all such communications. The wastepaper basket was the place for them. But this was different. He couldn't just stow it away in a corner of his mind and pretend that it had never been delivered. That's what he would have done of course if he had intercepted it. But Marguerite had read it. He could tell her it was a lie, Yvette wasn't his whore. This would be true. He didn't think of her like that. But he had committed adultery in his imagination; he was indeed, as he sat at the café table smoking a cigarette, picturing Yvette offering herself to him. It came to him that if – when? – she did so again, he might . . .

He turned away from the image of what would so desirably follow. But why should he continue to say no, since he couldn't hope that Marguerite would believe that he hadn't done what he was accused of doing? Why not go straight to the Pension Bernadotte?

He didn't of course. He retained that much self-respect. Instead, he sat for some time, scarcely even thinking, sat like a boxer on his stool in the interval after a round in which he has taken a pummelling and doesn't know if he can answer the bell. Then, reckoning that Moncerre wouldn't have returned to the office yet, he rang the PJ, had himself put through to René Martin, and asked him to meet him that afternoon in Gustave's bar behind the Gare St-Jean.

Moncerre's information was worrying too. He couldn't suppose that the Milice, this Captain Fracasse, whatever his real name might be, or the young lieutenant himself , wouldn't soon learn that he had been suspended and hadn't therefore been entitled to interfere with the lieutenant in the course of his duty. He would doubtless be suspected of being in the Resistance himself, all the more suspect, perhaps, as a frequenter, they would suppose, of a disreputable bar.

Well, there were things to be cleared up, and it came to him that he might not have much time. He didn't know much about the Milice and how they operated. He had preferred not to. But they certainly had little regard for due process of law.

He stepped outside. It was a surprise to find that the sun was shining and that the buildings glistened after overnight rain. House-wives were returning from doing their marketing; they had to be out early before the shops and stalls were cleaned out. There were pretty girls in summer dresses, and a priest hurrying, head down, perhaps because he was in danger of being late for a Mass he was due to celebrate. Two policemen approached. One was smoking a cigarette which he transferred to his left hand when he recognised Lannes in order to be able to salute him. How much longer would he be greeted like that? It took him only a few minutes to reach the rue du Port St-Pierre through streets that he had known since he was a child. Yet everything seemed different and he looked round a couple of times to see if he was being followed. It was a ridiculous idea, but he couldn't shake it off. He already felt like an outlaw in his own city, like so many whom he had himself hunted down. The props of his identity were being kicked away.

Fernand was at home. If he was surprised to see Lannes, that was natural enough – Lannes couldn't remember when they had last talked anywhere but in his friend's brasserie. And if he seemed also embarrassed, this certainly wasn't on account of the presence of a young woman, even though she was wearing only a bra and panties. She was a big girl with badly-dyed blonde hair, and when she smiled in greeting you could see that there was a wide gap between her front teeth. Fernand patted her on the bottom and told her to go and make them coffee, or, rather, 'what passes for coffee'.

'What brings you here, Jean? Not of course that I'm not pleased to see you, but it's a surprise.'

'I'm sorry to interrupt. A new girl?'

'New enough for me not to be tired of her. You look troubled.'

'Do I? Troublesome times. What about you?'

'I'm all right.'

'Are you? Jacques told me you had had flu or a bad cold you couldn't shake off.'

'He's like a mother hen, young Jacques. Fusses over me. I'm fine.'

'Actually,' Lannes said, 'he's worried about you. Not only about your health. He said you weren't yourself.'

'Which of us is these days? I'm all right. You don't look so good yourself, troubled as I say.'

'Yes,' Lannes said, 'I'm in difficulties. I've been suspended from duty and acting as if I wasn't. So . . . '

'So you're in the soup. How's Marguerite? How's she taking it?'

'She's worried. Naturally.'

'I never criticise my friends' wives, not to their face anyway.'

'So don't.'

'Well, I know she doesn't like me, thinks I'm a bad influence. As if I've ever managed to influence you.'

The girl came through with a coffee pot and two cups on a tray.

'I hope you don't take sugar,' she said, 'we're out of it.'

Lannes registered the pronoun and wondered if the girl had actually managed to move in on a basis that was at least semi-permanent. Fernand patted her on the bottom again, and said, 'Go back to bed, sweetheart. I'll join you when we're through.'

As the door closed behind her, he opened a bottle of marc and put a slug in both cups.

'She's all right, you know. A real peach. Great in bed, likes it both ways, up the arse pleases her most. Am I embarrassing you, Jean?'

Lannes smiled. Fernand was quite right, he knew him too well. Lannes' attitude to women had always amused him. For Fernand they were there to be used. It was, he insisted, what they really wanted. He accused Lannes of putting them on a pedestal where, he always said, they weren't comfortable. Perhaps it was true, but he couldn't be other than he was. He had always been sorry for women, living in a world made by men and ordered by men. No woman would have led France and Europe into this terrible war, or his own, earlier one, either. But for the moment he knew that Fernand was speaking in this way to distract him from asking more searchingly whether young Jacques had reason for the anxiety he had expressed.

'So Jacques has nothing to worry about? Is that right? Everything's fine and dandy with you?'

'Absolutely,' Fernand said.

And yet Lannes didn't believe him. It wasn't only on account of his new girl that he was here at home at this hour of the morning and keeping away from the brasserie.

'Labiche was in your place when I had lunch there the other day. He's one of your regulars, isn't he? He's a bastard. You know that of course and I've often wondered why you don't throw him out, tell him he's barred.'

'That would be clever, wouldn't it?' Fernand said, 'considering the position he's held these last years. He's not short of influence. I'd probably find I was being closed down on account of transgressing this regulation or that one. Besides, I sell food and drink. I don't make moral judgements. I can't afford to. I used to think you couldn't either. So, yes, I put up with Labiche, it's been in my interest to do so.'

Lannes looked his old friend in the eye. Fernand met his gaze steadily.

'You don't need to worry about me, Jean. I've got everything under control.'

'I hope you have. More than I can say for myself. More, I sometimes think, than any of us can say for ourselves.'

'And now,' Fernand said, 'that slut will be getting impatient. So, if you don't mind . . . oh, and here's a box of cigars for your boss if you're still on speaking terms with him. That's all right, pay me later.'

*　　*　　*

Gustave greeted him with a warm handshake. He had been grateful to Lannes ever since his son had got into trouble over a botched burglary. Lannes had arrested him, given him a good talking to, and, Gustave said, straightened him out. Now the boy was married and had recently become a father.

'A beautiful wee girl,' Gustave said. 'Are you a grandfather yet yourself? No? I recommend it, I really do. The wife and I dote on the little one.'

He gave Lannes an Armagnac and refused payment.

'We'll never forget what you've done for us.'

Young René arrived with apologies for being late.

'You're not late. I'm early. I always seem to be early now. What are you drinking, René?'

'A beer, thank you. I've been dashing all over town, and it's given me a thirst.'

'Fine. May we use your back room, Gustave?'

'Of course, and you won't have eaten. I can't offer much, but the wife'll make you a sandwich.'

Settled at the table in the back room, they spoke only trivialities at first, René as always asked politely about Lannes' family, especially Clothilde, and Lannes responded by asking if René's mother was well.

'Work all right?'

'We all miss you. Even the Alsatian said he hoped your suspension might soon be lifted. Oh and he asked about his cigars again.'

Lannes handed over the box.

'Give him these, but I'm afraid there's no chance of me returning to work soon. Quite the contrary. So you'll have to make do with the bull-terrier. Are you getting on all right with him?'

'It could be worse. Nevertheless, the sooner you're back the happier I'll be.'

'That may be some time yet.'

Gustave came in with two glasses of beer and a plate of baguettes filled with cheese and salad.

'It's not much I'm afraid but the best we have. I hope your appetite's good.'

'Thank you. It'll be fine.'

Lannes hesitated. He knew what he wanted to say but was reluctant to speak the words. He trusted René absolutely, more anyway than he trusted Moncerre. He had no doubt that René would do whatever was asked, but was he entitled to involve him? Was it even fair? Moreover he would have to explain what he would have preferred not to speak of.

'You remember Yvette, that girl in the Pension Bernadotte?'

He wasn't surprised to see René blush. He had always blushed easily, to his considerable embarrassment, and Lannes recalled that Yvette had described him as 'quite a dish'. Perhaps she had invited

74

him into her bed and he had been alarmed. Or might he have accepted?

Lannes pushed the plate across the table to René. He had no appetite himself. Instead he lit a cigarette. Meanwhile he waited till René had finished eating.

'My wife's had an anonymous letter.'

'How horrible! You mean about that girl?'

'About her, yes.'

'What do you want me to do?'

'I'm not entitled to ask you to do anything. Since I'm suspended, I certainly can't give you orders.'

'That's irrelevant. You're the chief, whatever. Besides in these times, well, it seems to me that normal rules don't apply.'

'That's not all,' Lannes said. 'There's something else you should know before you commit yourself. I saw the bull-terrier this morning. He had a visit yesterday from an officer in the Milice, looking for me.'

He related the incident at Chez Jules.

'You see that when they discover I'm suspended, they'll come looking for me again and I've no doubt I'll be arrested. Given what one hears of the Milice, that wouldn't be pleasant, and it might not stop merely at arrest. I don't need to spell it out. So I'm going to have to disappear off the map, if I can. I've an idea about that. But there are other matters to be attended to. First, the anonymous letter. I wouldn't be surprised if Yvette has had one too. I want you to go to see her, keep an eye on her. All right?'

'Of course, chief.'

'Then there's another thing. I suspect that the letter came from Labiche. Aurélien Mabire, whom you found for me, was working for him. I've interfered in his little game. This is just the sort of nasty response he would make. Now, when we were investigating his brother's murder – that murder in which he said he took no interest – you made the acquaintance of one of his clerks. I forget his name.'

'Jacques Bernard.'

'Look him up again, would you? Cultivate him, pump him, find out everything he knows about his boss's activities. What sort of chap was he?'

'Very young, a bit wet, scared to death of Labiche.'

'Good. See if you can make him more scared of us. Speak of the Liberation which isn't far off and of the likely consequences for collaborators like his boss.'

'I'll suggest he's in that boat himself. How do I keep in touch with you, chief?'

'I don't know yet. I'll call you. There's a couple of other matters I have to see to first, and I don't know how much time I have.'

'Does the bull-terrier know about all this?'

'Only what I've told you about his visit from the Milice. I don't think he needs to know more. On the other hand he's your boss now. So if you feel you . . . '

'Certainly not. After all, this is unofficial, isn't it? So I don't see that it concerns him.'

'I'm very grateful to you.'

René blushed again, as he always did when Lannes praised him.

'You've nothing to be grateful for. Not after all you've done for me.'

When René left, Lannes asked Gustave if he might use his telephone. St-Hilaire's butler answered. Lannes asked if the Count was at home and said that, if convenient, he would call on him later in the afternoon. It was convenient; the Count would be delighted to see him.

XV

'What can you tell me about Madame d'Herblay's son?'

St-Hilaire sighed and seemed to examine the ash on his cigar. Apparently deciding it wasn't about to fall off of its own accord, he put the cigar between his lips and drew deeply on it.

'You see,' Lannes said, 'none of it makes sense to me. Assuming I've been told the truth, why employ an unreliable fellow like Aurélien Mabire? And where does the advocate Labiche come into it? It seems – again if Mabire isn't lying – that the girl, Marie-Adelaide, is devoted to her father, or at least to her idea of him. So why not approach her directly?'

St-Hilaire tapped his cigar on the ashtray, got to his feet and crossed the room to look out of the window.

'Such a beautiful afternoon,' he said. 'I'm grateful to you, superintendent. My cousin will be grateful to you also.'

'With little reason,' Lannes said. 'I haven't found the girl. Indeed you might say she's more lost than ever since I've established she isn't now with Mabire. Moreover what I've learned of the girl's history – her earlier experience – I won't say relationship – with Labiche is, I suppose, something that Madame d'Herblay would rather I didn't know.'

'Undoubtedly.'

With his back still to Lannes, the Count said, 'I owe you an apology. I was – how should I put it? – reticent, or as you might say economical with the truth when we spoke last. I gave you to understand that Marie-Adelaide was an innocent. Evidently, as you have discovered, this wasn't exactly the case.'

'The father too? So that's why no action was taken?'

St-Hilaire returned to his chair.

'Had I been consulted at the time, I would have advised my cousin to call in the police. Perhaps she would have shrunk from doing so. She was horrified by the thought of a public scandal. So, instead, she bought her son off, increasing his allowance on condition that he signed a paper relinquishing all rights over his daughter and promising to have no future contact with her. I learned of this only a few years later when he was in prison.'

'You didn't tell me he had a police record.'

'It seemed unnecessary. It was a short sentence, eighteen months, as I recall, and the crime was political. Jean-Pierre d'Herblay was a Cagoulard charged as an accessory to the bombing of the offices of the employers' federation. Doubtless you remember the case?'

Lannes did of course. The Cagoule had been – no doubt still was, in some form anyway – a secret society of the extreme quasi-Fascist Right which had murdered two Italian Socialists, refugees from Fascist Italy, to oblige Mussolini, and more importantly had embarked on a campaign of bombing and other acts of terrorism. Its targets had been men and organisations on the Right in the hope that the Communists would be held responsible for the outrages. The Cagoule's broader aim had been to discredit the institutions of the parliamentary Republic. Because so many on what was known as the constitutional Right, politicians, business magnates, senior officers in the army and princes of the Church, had connections with members of the Cagoule, itself financed, it was believed, by certain great industrialists terrified of Communism, who were at least in sympathy with its aims, if not its methods, investigation of the organisation had been little more than perfunctory. In 1940, as Lannes knew, many Cagoulards had welcomed Vichy and found positions of importance there. Others were said to be among the leaders of the Parisian Fascists who despised Vichy as lukewarm and would have had France join Germany in the war against Bolshevism.

'I've heard it suggested,' he said, 'that there are even Cagoulards among the Gaullists in London. Do you think that possible?'

St-Hilaire smiled.

'Why not? The men of the Cagoule believed themselves to be patriots, and, as we know, patriotism wears many faces. Besides General de Gaulle himself is a man of the Right. I knew his father slightly, an admirable man, a school-teacher or lecturer, a devout Catholic and a monarchist, one of those, I think, who continued to believe Dreyfus guilty of spying for Germany long after it was obvious and established, you would have thought, beyond any reasonable doubt that the unfortunate Alsatian Jew was innocent, believed it even after he had been brought back to France, exonerated and reinstalled in the army.'

'After so many years on Devil's Island,' Lannes said.

'Quite so.'

Lannes lit a cigarette. How deep and prolonged were the divisions in France! He had always known that. Nevertheless it was a surprise to discover how easily so many managed to bridge them, maintaining friendships across the divide, friendships that transcended political differences. He wondered if Labiche was also a Cagoulard like the young d'Herblay. If so, mightn't he have friends among the Gaullists who would be in a position to offer him protection after the Liberation and might indeed be eager, or at least willing, to do so?

'I haven't found the girl,' he said again, 'and I'm bound to tell you that I may not be able to be of any further assistance.'

St-Hilaire made no reply, drew on his cigar, and waited.

'You knew I've been suspended from duty. Since this wasn't, as you said, a police matter and Madame d'Herblay was determined it shouldn't be that, I saw no reason not to act on her behalf, carrying out an unofficial investigation.'

'We were both grateful to you. But things are different now? Am I entitled to ask what has changed?'

'Simply that I'm no longer only suspended. I'm in danger of being arrested.'

'My dear fellow . . . ' St-Hilaire raised an eyebrow.

'It's not,' Lannes said, 'that I've done anything discreditable, or nothing, that is, that I consider discreditable. But I've fallen foul of the Milice, am accused, or will be accused, of obstructing an officer of that patriotic body in the pursuit of his duty. Since I actually did so, I have no defence, and since I have no wish to find myself in one of the Milice's prisons – or perhaps a German one, in the hands of the Gestapo – I'm going to have to try to disappear from the scene, go underground as it were. So I can't continue to search for Marie-Adelaide. I'm sorry and must ask you to convey my apologies to your cousin. I'll add only that I don't think any harm – any new harm – will come to the girl. I shouldn't be surprised if her father, wherever he may be, is badly in need of money, and that your cousin will receive some sort of ransom request. That's just my suspicion which may be quite mistaken.'

St-Hilaire stood up. He offered Lannes his hand.

'What you say distresses me. I've formed a high regard for you, superintendent, and ask only if I may be of any help.'

'Thank you, but I already know where I'm going. Perhaps after the Liberation, things will be different. Meanwhile the fewer people who know my whereabouts the better.'

It was only when he was out of the house, and walking away that he wondered if his last sentence hadn't been ungracious, might even have been interpreted as an expression of distrust. He hadn't intended it that way. But it was a time when distrust was every-where.

XVI

Clothilde was happy. She hugged and kissed Lannes as soon as he entered the apartment. She had had a card from Michel, from where she didn't know, nor when it had been written, for he had omitted to date it. But he was alive – or had been, Lannes thought – and he sent her love and a thousand kisses. So one day the war would be over, he would return and they would be married. There was nothing to say to this, no possible response except to be happy that she was for the moment happy. Moreover she chattered merrily throughout the meal – a cassoulet of beans with some stringy pork – chattered as if unaware of the constraint between her parents. It was something to be thankful for.

Nevertheless the silence had to be broken, Marguerite retired first as had become her habit. Clothilde followed. Lannes sat and smoked and pretended to read until he was sure their daughter would be asleep. Then he went to join his wife.

His delay had been cowardly. He knew that. It was as if he had spun a coin. Heads or tails? Asleep or awake? Talk now or in the morning? Better of course to get it over with in what had been for so long the intimacy of the bedroom, the intimacy of the night when it is so often easier to say what has to be said in a conversation that nevertheless you still hope can be postponed, even when you know it has become unavoidable.

Her breathing told him she was awake. He sat on the edge of the bed, sought her hand in the dark and pressed it. She said nothing but didn't pull it away. It was, he knew, a conversation she had shrunk from also but which it might be she too recognised as necessary. If they couldn't speak now, he thought, they might never do so again. And if she didn't believe him . . .

'You were right to leave the letter for me,' he said. 'Now we've both had time to think about it. It's malicious of course. You'll realise that, I'm sure. We've been snowed under with such letters ever since the Occupation began, people taking revenge for whatever reason on their neighbours . . . '

He paused. There was no answering pressure from the hand he held.

'That's irrelevant , of course,' he said. 'I realise that. You want to know if there's any truth in what it implies.'

Truth, he thought, what a slippery word. He hesitated. The silence enfolded them.

'We once promised,' he said, 'we would never lie to each other. A difficult promise for anyone to keep. The truth can be so hurtful.'

Tenderness can so easily provoke deception. Why – how even – should you tell someone you love what will only distress them? It had always been his habit to keep bad news to himself. It wasn't an admirable habit; he knew that.

'The girl's called Yvette,' he said. 'She's not my mistress. But, yes, she's attractive, and she's young, not much older than Clothilde, the same age perhaps as Dominique. She was a witness in a murder case, that's how I met her, and then she was assaulted by one of the suspects and came to my office, in distress and afraid.'

'And she's a prostitute?' Marguerite said.

'Yes, she's a prostitute.'

He pressed her hand again.

'That disgusts me. You know it disgusts me.'

'Yes,' he said. 'I know that. It disgusts most women, I think.'

'But not men?'

'Some men, yes. Others, no.'

Dominique, he thought, would be in the first category, Alain, he suspected, in the second, Henri in one, Fernand in the other. He held his wife's hand and pictured Yvette inviting him to her bed, and waited for Marguerite to speak.

'You like her,' she said. 'I can hear it in your voice. Is she pretty?'

'Yes, she's pretty, she's attractive, and I like her, despite what she does, but that's all. She's not my mistress. She's never been that and . . . '

He was about to say, and she never will be, but found he couldn't.

'Is it because of me, because I've not been what I used to be for so long, that you go to her?'

'I don't go to her, not in the sense you mean. I've visited the

Pension where she lives, several times, as your anonymous letter-writer whoever he or she is might tell you because chance made me in some way feel responsible for her, as I feel responsible for many people whom I find in trouble or difficulties. But I've never been unfaithful to you, never.'

Except in my imagination, he didn't add.

'I can't prove anything. You can't prove a negative. I can only ask you to believe me.'

'Why should I? When you never say anything to me beyond what is necessary?'

'Because I love you.'

'Do you?'

'You know I do.'

She withdrew her hand.

'I know nothing,' she said. 'I've never been able to trust you, Jean, since you encouraged Alain to go away and leave me without a word from either of you. You broke my trust then. You made me miserable and unhappy and I don't believe that broken trust can be repaired.'

'Please,' he said, 'please try. There's something else I must tell you. It means I am going to have to disappear, go into hiding, perhaps for only a few days, perhaps for longer, perhaps even till the Liberation.'

He told her why, and found she was in tears.

'It'll be all right,' he said, 'I'm sure it will be all right.'

'But if it isn't?'

He leaned over and kissed her on the lips.

'If it isn't, it isn't,' he said. 'But I'm sure it will be.'

He took her in his arms and kissed her again. This time she responded. Later they made love, for the first time in three years.

'I'll leave first thing in the morning,' he said. 'It's better you don't know where I am.'

'You're not going to her? Your Yvette?'

'No, I'm not. Young René Martin is working with me. He'll keep in touch with you. I won't telephone. It's not safe. It will almost certainly be tapped.'

XVII

It was the softest of summer nights. There was still a touch of gold over the peaks of the mountains to the East, but a milky haze covered the stars. Dominique and Maurice lay stretched out on the rough upland grass. Most of the boys in the troop they had led into the hills were already asleep; they had marched some thirty-five or nearer forty kilometres that day.

'We won't be doing this much longer,' Maurice said. 'In fact it wouldn't surprise me if this was the last expedition. Apart from anything else, it's clear that a lot of boys now evade the call-up. I can't blame them. They know Vichy's finished. Do you think we've wasted our time?'

'I don't know. Some of the boys have benefited. Surely. But you're right, it's all but over.'

'What then?'

'I don't know. It's hard to imagine a post-war world. What it'll be like, I mean.'

Neither wanted to say what was in both their minds: that Dominique, having joined François' network of ex-prisoners-of-war, and having therefore participated to some degree in the Resistance, would be accepted as one of the victors, despite his work for Vichy, whereas Maurice . . .

He had turned down the chance offered him, and not only because he hadn't himself served in the army in 1940, and wasn't therefore a veteran of the prison camp, but also because he felt that to accept would be some sort of betrayal of his father – that father who for the first time in his life approved of him. He might have added that in any case he neither liked nor trusted François. It was a measure of the strength of the bond between them that neither had allowed the divergent paths they had taken to disturb their friendship. So, when Maurice now asked 'what exactly does François ask of you?' Dominique didn't suppose that he was fishing for information that might compromise him, or which Maurice might use to his own advantage.

'I'm only a messenger boy, really,' he said. 'A go-between, carrying false papers, identity cards even passports, which François' friend in the ministry supplies to the network. And the remarkable thing is that this friend is quite high up in the ministry and does this simply because he admires François, even though he is loyal to Vichy himself. It's really odd. You should hear how he speaks about François, he really thinks he's wonderful. You might say he dotes on him.'

Maurice said, 'Perhaps he's a queer, in love with him.'

'Well, he's not likely to get much satisfaction,' Dominique said. 'François chases any skirt in sight. The last time I made a handover, he couldn't wait to be rid of me, not because of security but because he said he had a date with a brunette, and added that in these dangerous times you should never let the chance of a good lay slip by. I was really quite embarrassed.'

Maurice turned over to lie on his back.

'It's beginning to look like rain. Do you think his network achieves anything of value?'

'I don't know,' Dominique said. 'I'm the messenger boy, as I said. Sometimes I think the point for François is simply to be known to have formed it and been in the Resistance. He's very intelligent, you know and has political ambitions. He once said to me, "The only problem is deciding which party to join after the Liberation." His own family are all on the Right, I think, which is partly why he was made so welcome in Vichy, but he suspects the future may be Socialist. And there's another thing I'm sure of which is that he neither likes nor trusts de Gaulle. He met him in Algeria and it's evident they didn't get on. Or so I gathered.'

'Do you like him?'

'I'm impressed by him. I like listening to him. But like him? Not really. He's a cold fish, I think. Not that it matters.'

'As you say, it's so hard to imagine what sort of France will emerge. Or what will become of us?'

'As to that,' Dominique said, 'if all goes right, you'll marry my sister and be my brother-in-law.'

'She's in love with that boy, Michel. That was only too evident the last time we were in Bordeaux.'

'He's no good,' Dominique said. 'It's a terrible thing to say, but it would be better if he never returns from Russia or wherever they're fighting.'

*   *   *

Léon sat on a chair by the bedside of the blonde woman he had met at that dinner in Maxim's. She had invited him to call.

'I'm living in a nursing home,' she said, 'for reasons too boring to explain.'

The room was full of flowers, brought by admirers, he supposed. She asked him to open a bottle of champagne which was sitting in a metal bucket full of water that might have been ice when it was placed there.

'We have to grab such pleasures as we can,' she said, 'don't you think so? *Mignonne, allons voir si la rose* and all that.'

Her accent puzzled him. Her French was fluent, grammatically correct, and she had told him her estranged husband was a Norman aristocrat, either a vicomte or a baron, he couldn't remember which. Perhaps she was Belgian or Dutch. He picked up a photograph of a young man seated in a racing-car; he wore goggles and a silk muffler round his neck.

'Is this your husband?'

'Certainly not. Poor Robert doesn't even drive, he's too nervous. It's just a friend. If you must know, the one who supplied the champagne we're drinking. Tell me about yourself.'

'There's nothing to tell, really.'

'I know what that means these days. It means there's too much to tell. I didn't greatly care for your friend by the way, and I had the impression you don't like him much yourself. That puzzled me since he so obviously behaved as if he owned you.'

'Was that why you asked me to call on you?'

'Not really. I was just curious. But don't worry. We all have things to hide these days, things not to be spoken about. I have myself.'

He had the impression she was laughing at him. She lay back on her pillows, her hair falling over her shoulders, and smiled. For a moment he wondered if she was part of the organisation and had been sent to find him, charged to discover why he had lost contact with London six months ago now, and even perhaps to arrange for him to be reactivated. The idea excited him. It would clear him of the guilt he felt. Her accent might after all be English?

'Or perhaps I just took a fancy to you,' she said. 'That wouldn't be unreasonable, would it? You're a pretty boy.'

'Even though you decided I was so obviously Chardy's?'

'Oh that,' she said, as if it was of no account.

This excited him too. He had never made love to a woman, scarcely felt the desire, never met one who wanted him, as Gaston and Schussmann had and Chardy now did, and as he wanted Alain. Why not be frank? Why not say, I've been in love for four years now with a boy who only likes girls? So you see my position's hopeless, and if you want me . . .

'What are you doing in Paris?' she said. 'I can tell you're not Parisian.'

'Trying to survive.'

'Like the rest of us,' she said, and held her hand out to him.

*   *   *

'They despise us,' Michel said. 'That's why we've been landed with this filthy job, guarding these stinking Jews. I don't blame them. These SS men are real soldiers, war heroes.'

'So they'd have us believe,' his corporal, the Baron, said. 'Some of them may even be telling the truth, though I wouldn't count on it.'

'I'm stinking and itching all over from these filthy lice. The filthy Jews pass them on. What do they do with the Jews anyway?'

'You don't want to know, laddie.'

'Don't I? And the gypsies, the stinking gypsies. Did you ever fuck a gypsy, corp?'

'Certainly. She was a singer at Le Chat Noir. Perfectly clean, I assure you.'

'When are we going to see action?'

'*Pazienza*, dear boy. There are worse things than being alive, you know. Even today, even here, especially here.'

*   *   *

The men from the Resistance group were late. Alain had twice gone to the door of the barn and stood there listening for the noise of a motor, as if by stepping outside he could will it to arrive. But there was only the silence of the summer night, not even the cry of an owl. He had never been so aware of silence; he hadn't thought of it as an almost palpable presence.

'They should have been here two hours ago,' Fabrice said. 'How long do we give them?'

Nobody answered. Everyone, Alain thought, shared the same fear, born of the awareness, or at least the apprehension, that something had gone wrong.

'The local boys, the village team, don't trust us much anyway,' Olivier said.

'You can't blame them. Trust is in short supply everywhere.'

Olivier was new. He had been parachuted in only three weeks ago, to take over after the Gestapo had picked up Raoul. It was the first time Alain had worked with him.

'They'll come,' Olivier said. 'They need the money and the guns.'

What worried Alain was that, by his own admission, Olivier didn't know the country, didn't indeed know France. He was an Algerian *colon* whose military service had all been in Africa and the Levant. No doubt he was tough, tough as the leathery yellow skin of his face. But he was too confident, too sure of himself, so much as that he was breaking the first rule of the trade: if your contact doesn't keep the rendezvous, you bugger off. You don't sit round waiting. Alain knew. He'd been in France eighteen months now, had been wounded twice and each time been lucky to escape arrest; and it always happened when you let your guard slip and played it by ear rather than obeying instructions and following the rules. He wanted to say this; he should speak out. But from the first meeting with his new chief, Olivier had treated him as if he was a recruit wet behind the ears. He had looked at him with the condescension of a forty-year-old captain who had been decorated in the war against the Rif. If Alain told him they should get out, now, while they could, Olivier would give him that superior smile and ask him if he was windy. Well, he was windy; he was windy because he knew how things were.

'They're not professionals,' Olivier said. 'Amateurs are never good time-keepers. We'll give them another hour. It won't be dawn for two hours at least. We'll have lots of time to make ourselves scarce if they don't turn up. But they will. I'm sure they will.'

He opened his silver cigarette-case, took one for himself, and passed the case round.

'Don't say I'm not generous, boys. I'll say one thing for the English. They make the best cigarettes in the world. These are Player's, none better. General de Gaulle himself has taken to smoking them, you know. That says something, because he's not fond of the Anglo-Saxons. Nor am I, come to that.'

In the distance, from the valley below, they heard the sound of a motor.

'Told you so,' Olivier said.

'There's something wrong,' Alain said. 'I think there's more than one car coming.'

*   *   *

Sir Edwin Pringle, MP, slipped his hand under the tablecloth, and squeezed Jérôme's thigh. Jérôme let it lie there. He didn't think Sir Pringle would go further, not in the Ritz Grill, not much further anyway. It was a hot night. One of the windows was open and the scent of cut grass and blossom wafted in from Green Park.

'Max is entitled to be late,' Sir Edwin said. 'Now that he's a hero, flying bomber-crew over Germany. Who would have thought it of our little American dancer? Not, between you and me, that I am in favour of area bombing, even of Berlin. I've had so many happy times there. Berlin in the twenties was sheer heaven, you know. I get in trouble for saying it, but really this war was unnecessary. And to find ourselves in alliance with the Bolsheviks, supping with the Devil, I call it. I'm a very rich man, you know. Of course Winston's convinced himself that Stalin is his chum. I don't believe it for a moment. And you are still broadcasting, are you?'

His hand moved up Jérôme's leg.

'Yes,' Jérôme said. 'We're all waiting anxiously for the day. I don't suppose you . . . '

'My dear, I'll know no sooner than anyone else. I'm quite out of favour, you know. Even in my own party. All because I remained loyal to poor Neville, and because I still insist that Munich was justified. If he hadn't bought us a year's grace, we would have lost this terrible war. We had no Spitfires then, you know. Of course Winston won't have it. You know what they used to say in Italy: *Mussolini ha sempre ragione* – Mussolini is always right. Of course he wasn't, poor idiot, but that's what Winston thinks of himself – *ha sempre ragione*. The man's a megalomaniac, you know, just as bad as your General. So poor old me is out in the cold. Ah, here's Max . . . I was just saying you're entitled to be late, my dear.'

'I'm lucky to be here at all,' Max said, leaning over to kiss Sir Edwin on the cheek, an action which had the happy consequence of ridding Jérôme of their host's attentions. 'Last night . . . I can't tell you. It was sheer hell. I was terrified out of my tiny wits. Nevertheless the boy did his duty. Is that champagne, Edwin? Goody goody, I never felt more in need. Bless you. Love you too, Jérôme.'

XVIII

Lannes was woken by Madame Smitt bringing him a cup of dreadful coffee. Even though it was only three days since he had established himself in her Pension, which no longer seemed to function as that, a routine was already forming. In a little she would bring him a jug of hot water so that he could wash and shave. Then she would go out to do her marketing which she was now more able to do because of the notes he had given her and which she had accepted without counting them and without any word of thanks. She hadn't enquired either why he had come to her door asking for a room for a few days or perhaps weeks, he couldn't tell. Likewise she hadn't remarked on the fact that he had neither put so much as a foot outside the door nor asked to use the telephone. Her lack of curiosity seemed to be total. When she returned from her marketing, she shut herself away in the kitchen beyond the reception desk, and remained there till noon when she brought him a bowl of soup. By that time of the day she was in carpet-slippers again and her breath was sour with white wine. She put the soup on the table without a word, and shuffled away.

Aurélien didn't leave his bedroom till the afternoon. On the first day he looked horrified to see Lannes sitting at the table. It was evident his sister hadn't warned him he was there, and this too was a mark of her indifference to everything and perhaps of her reliance on white wine to deaden feeling. But now Aurélien had also grown accustomed to Lannes' presence. As soon as he understood that he hadn't come there to arrest him, or even to interrogate him again, he tried to pretend that the superintendent was merely a chance fellow-guest in the Pension. And so he sat in the same room as him and played Patience by the hour. Lannes might be waiting for something, he didn't know and it was no concern of his. And in his turn Lannes seemed content to do nothing, to live for a few days in limbo, divorced from life. Actually he wasn't content. The truth was, he thought, that he was exhausted. He remembered a great-uncle, his peasant grandfather's elder brother, a widower, who spent hours without moving or talking in his cabin in Les Landes and who, when asked how he was, would say in the peasant patois that he was 'just fair done'.

'Red six on black seven,' he said. 'You're not concentrating on your game, Aurélien.'

'Let me be. I don't need your advice. I don't like being interfered with.'

'That's natural,' Lannes said. 'Where do you think Labiche took the girl?'

'How should I know? By that time I was pleased merely to be rid of her. She bored me, if you must know.'

'Did Labiche pay you well?'

'That's none of your business.'

'I don't suppose he paid you anything at all, really. You're afraid of him, aren't you?'

Aurélien collected his cards formed them into a pack, shuffled it, and began to deal them out again.

'Why should I be?' he said.

Lannes lit a cigarette and pushed the packet across the table.

'Take one. Why should you be? Why shouldn't you? A lot of people are afraid of Labiche. He has influence and power and doesn't care how he uses it. That can be frightening. I'm a bit scared of him myself if you must know.'

It's true, he thought. Malevolence is frightening, because you don't know how far it may reach.

Patience, he thought. When you don't know what to do, you do nothing and wait to see which card is turned up. Like Aurélien he was killing time. People all over France were killing time, waiting for the day of Liberation, some eager to be able to walk through their home city without seeing a German soldier, others merely for the return of a normality in which nevertheless they might scarcely be able to believe, so long was it since they had known it. There were women who longed for the return of their husbands or boy-friends, and others who were afraid of what their man would find and of how he might have changed. Was anyone, Lannes thought, the same person he had been in 1940? And of course there were many, thousands of them, who must lie awake thinking of the retribution that they might suffer, suffer often only because they had made the wrong choice or had continued to do what they believed to be their duty.

Had Marguerite believed him? He had no idea. She had wept when he said goodbye and made to kiss her, but she had turned her head away. Was she weeping because he was in danger, or for the end of their marriage?

XIX

When Jacques Bernard emerged at lunchtime from Labiche's office René Martin let him turn the corner before he came up behind him and took hold of his arm.

'Remember me, Jacques?' he said. 'Off to lunch, are you? I'll join you if I may. Do you still eat in the same place? A brasserie in the Cours du Chapeau Rouge, wasn't it? Fine by me.'

'I don't suppose I can prevent you,' the clerk said.

In the brasserie Jacques Bernard made for what was obviously his usual table at the back of the room. There was a slightly stained napkin on the side-plate and a half-empty bottle of vin ordinaire placed there in waiting for him. Without being asked, the waiter brought him bread and soup, and René said, 'For me too, and a glass of beer, just a demi. You were quite helpful to us a couple of years ago. I hope you are going to be helpful again.'

'I don't know what you're talking about. You were investigating a death then, a murder you said.'

'So we were, and I didn't let your boss know that you had helped us because you were obviously afraid of him. You said he was a holy terror, I made a note of the expression. But you evidently satisfy him because you're still in the job. This soup's rather good, isn't it?'

René smiled.

'This is just a friendly chat, no more than that. Well, it might be a bit more. It might be a warning, I suppose. You see, we're interested in Labiche. Well, a lot of people are going to be interested in him in the months to come. You're intelligent, Jacques, so I don't need to spell out why. You must have wondered whether you'll have a job when things change. I suppose Labiche is making arrangements for himself, perhaps moving money abroad, that sort of thing. As an insurance against the worst, I suppose.'

'I wouldn't know anything about that.'

'No, of course, you wouldn't. You're only a very junior clerk, aren't you? Or that's what I remember you telling me.'

The waiter approached bearing the soup tureen.

'More soup, Jacques? More soup, monsieur? I'd advise it because I wouldn't recommend the plat du jour, scrag end of mutton from a sheep that must have been almost as old as the Marshal himself. I wouldn't feed it to my dog, if I had a dog, that is.'

'You're obviously popular here,' René said. 'They look after you. That's nice, that's always nice. Is it because you work for Labiche?'

Jacques dipped a crust of bread in the soup and sucked it.

'It's not like that,' he said, 'it's not a bit like that. The patron is a sort of cousin of my father's. That's all. Not that that gets me a reduction in the price. I only wish it did.'

'That's natural. We all feel the pinch these days, don't we? But you see, there's something that puzzled me when we last talked.

You told me that you had had to leave school early because your father was a prisoner of war, and your mother needed a wage coming in from you, and then that you were only a sort of dogsbody in Labiche's office, running messages for him. But you eat here every day, and it certainly isn't cheap, even if they are reduced to serving scrag end of old mutton. And this looks like a new suit you're wearing, nice piece of cloth too. So I can't help wondering if Labiche employs you for some other work, spying on people perhaps. Unless of course you're blackmailing him, and I've no doubt there's occasion for that.'

'Blackmailing the boss? You must be joking. Nobody who tried that trick would last long?'

'No, I suppose he wouldn't. Indeed it wouldn't surprise me if anyone who attempted to put the black on him was fished out of the Garonne soon afterwards. So how do you get the money that enables you to live as you obviously do? That's a question that might interest some of my colleagues in another department. We in the PJ are easy-going about little peculations and the like. But there are other matters we take more seriously, and anything that concerns your boss is one of them. For instance – I don't mind telling you this, though you must regard it as a confidence – just at the moment, I'm investigating him on account of the disappearance of a girl. You wouldn't know anything about that, would you?'

'No, nothing. You must believe me.'

'Then there's a priest, name of Father Paul, I think. Know anything about him?'

'I've seen him with Monsieur Labiche. I think perhaps he's his confessor.'

'A full-time job I'd call that,' René said. 'So how do you earn your extra money? You can't tell me that you bought this suit out of a junior clerk's wage. And don't try to persuade me you saved up for it.'

The young man, who still looked as if he wasn't yet old enough to shave, and indeed had only a pale down on his cheeks and chin, shook his head. René who hated bullying felt a moment of pity – Jacques Bernard was so obviously terrified of Labiche. If René hadn't understood that in some way Lannes' future, even his safety, was at stake, he might have let the wretched boy off the hook.

Instead, he said, 'Look, it's obvious you have something to tell me and I realise that you are reluctant, but we can do this two ways. I'm asking you nicely, without threats, and you can answer me here. Or, if you prefer, you can accompany me back to the station and I'll hand you over to my immediate superior, a senior inspector. We call him the bull-terrier because when he gets his teeth into a suspect he doesn't let go. That's your choice. Which is it to be?'

'I've done nothing wrong. I promise. You have to believe me. I'm only a messenger boy, I told you. I've been a fool, I realise that, but I couldn't afford to lose my job. What Monsieur Labiche needs – what he likes – is information. About people. He says knowledge is power and I'm sometimes asked to collect it. About Father Paul, for instance, yes, I think he's his confessor like I say, but I'm also sure Monsieur Labiche has a hold on him. And about another man. I was sent to ask a prostitute about him. I didn't know he was a policeman and I was terrified when I found he was. I've been living in fear, it's almost a relief to speak to you, you must believe me.'

'And what did the tart tell you?'

René spoke with deliberate roughness.

'She told me to get the hell out. Monsieur Labiche smiled when I reported that.'

'I see,' René said.

He saw all too well, and it frightened him too.

'And Father Paul? You say Labiche has a hold on him.'

'Yes.'

'Go on.'

The waiter approached to take their plates away.

'Are you all right, Jacques? This gentleman's not troubling you, is he?'

'Not at all,' René said. 'We're just having a friendly conversation. You might bring us some coffee and the bill.'

The waiter looked doubtful, but collected their plates and turned away.

'There you are,' René said. 'Now if I'd told him I'm a policeman that would really have embarrassed you. So Father Paul?'

'He likes boys. Like many priests. It disgusts me. Well, one of them was blackmailing him, or so he said, and I expect it's true. Why wouldn't it be? So I was sent to bring him to Monsieur Labiche's office with the promise of a settlement.'

'When was this?'

'Day before yesterday.'

'And did he come, accompany you back?'

'Why wouldn't he, with the promise of money?'

'And what happened then?'

'How should I know? I was disgusted, I tell you. That sort of thing, it makes my flesh crawl. A priest and an Arab boy because that's what he looked like. It's repulsive even to think about it.'

'So you delivered him to Labiche. What happened then?'

'How should I know? I'd done my duty, what I was asked to do. And I tell you, it didn't please me to think that somebody I knew might have seen me in the street with that creature.'

'No,' René said. 'I don't suppose it did. You disgust me rather yourself, Jacques.'

XX

The Alsatian hadn't appeared in the office for three days. Moncerre was missing too. Drunk or nursing a bad hangover, René thought. The letter was addressed to the Alsatian, but the address was in printed capitals and this made René suspicious. He would later say that he had some sort of intuition. If Madame Lannes had been sent that anonymous letter about the girl in the Pension Bernadotte, then mightn't a similar one be addressed to the Alsatian? So he opened it, and when he read it was pleased that he had done so, and horrified by what he read: *I suggest you ask Superintendent Lannes about his Arab catamite.*

It wasn't a message for anyone else to read, he was sure of that. So he struck a match, held it to the edge of the paper and was about to burn it when he had second thoughts. It was evidence and he was trained to respect evidence, even on occasions when it might be prudent to conceal it. So he folded the letter and put it in the inside breast-pocket of his jacket. Then he sat back and found that he was sweating.

It was vile, nonsense, vile nonsense.

The previous afternoon Yvette had sighed – theatrically – and murmured 'if only' when he told her about the first anonymous letter.

'He's been kind to me,' she said. 'And he treats me with respect which is not how I'm commonly treated. And I can see that he's unhappy and anxious. But there's been nothing doing. I offered him what I'm sure his wife isn't giving him and what I've no doubt he wanted. But he still said no, and what's more he turned me down in a manner that didn't offend me because I understood that if things had been different he'd willingly have got into my bed. But there it is. Things are as they are. I sound quite a philosopher, don't I?'

She lay back on her bed.

'Usually it's insulting for a girl to be turned down, even if she's a tart, but, like I say, I wasn't offended. He's in trouble, isn't he?'

'I'm afraid he is.'

'I mean, this letter's really nasty, isn't it. To send lies like that to his wife.'

And now, very evidently, it was worse. René couldn't doubt that, not after his conversation with Labiche's clerk. The letter was a lie of course. He had no reason to suppose Lannes had ever met this Arab boy, but equally it was likely that the boy who had been blackmailing a priest had now been bought off by the lawyer and would be paid to support these allegations. Well, by intercepting the letter, he had thwarted this attempt to blacken the super-intendent's reputation, for the time being anyway. But should he tell him about it? Yes, of course. He had to give him the letter. It would be insulting not to do so. The chief wasn't a man who had to be protected from bad news.

It was raining for the first time in days and there was a cold Atlantic wind blowing up the Garonne and stripping the last of the cherry blossom from the trees in the Place de la Cathédrale. René who had set out for work that morning without a raincoat or umbrella found himself shivering. He stepped into the gutter to allow two old women, black-dressed widows, to have the pavement, and found that his right foot was wet. He had forgotten that his mother had told him to wear a different pair of shoes this morning and she would take these ones to the cobbler to be re-soled.

He had to bang several times on the door of the Pension Smitt before it was opened. The old woman said she had no rooms available, it was no longer a pension and she should have had the sign removed, but he shook the rain from his hair and said he wasn't looking for a room but had come to speak to the superintendent.

Lannes was reading when the old woman showed René in, with some muttering about people causing a disturbance where they weren't wanted. He laid the book – a Simenon novel – aside, and told René he looked like a drowned rat.

'It doesn't matter,' René said.

'Nevertheless you're in danger of catching a chill. Would you please make him a grog, Madame?'

The old woman shuffled off and they could hear her still grumbling as she made her way to the kitchen.

'So, you've news of some kind. Did you manage to see Yvette? Is she all right?'

'Yes, and indignant on your behalf when I told her about the letter sent to Madame Lannes. But that's not why I'm here, not exactly.'

He took the paper from his packet and handed it to Lannes.

'This came addressed to the Alsatian. He wasn't in the office this morning. So I took the liberty of intercepting it. I'm glad I did, because, well I don't need to say why. They're trying to destroy you, aren't they? You see, I did as you asked and spoke to Labiche's young clerk.'

When Lannes made no reply, but turned the letter over in his hands, René recounted his conversation with Jacques Bernard.

'It's all connected, isn't it, but I don't see what it's all about. Is it just malice?'

'It's certainly that, but there may be more to it. Labiche, as you told his clerk, is in a dangerous position himself. So perhaps he's striking out blindly.'

Actually Lannes couldn't believe this was the case. Labiche was a lawyer, therefore a bargainer, a man always ready to deal. He might want to destroy him, he might also want to have a hold on him which might afford him protection himself.

'I have to speak to the boy,' he said. 'No, it's better that you aren't involved in it, René.'

'You know him then?'

'He's come my way more than once. You remember Schussmann, the German liaison officer who shot himself? And then there was that Vichy spook who called himself Félix. He was killed in what we officially described as mysterious circumstances. Actually they weren't so mysterious, at least I knew all about it, but the man had become what his superiors called a loose cannon, and the investigation was closed down. Conveniently enough, I have to say. A senior spook was happy to be rid of him. I know this one only by the code-name Fabien. I think I need to speak to him again. Judge Bracal knows something about him. So does the Alsatian, but Bracal is more likely to be helpful. He's a good man, or I believe he is. There aren't many you can be sure of. So, René, please go to Bracal. Tell him everything as far as you know it, and ask him if he can arrange for me to meet Fabien. Meanwhile I'll root out the boy, and have a word with him. Give me something to do rather than just sitting here, envying Maigret' – he indicated the book he had discarded – 'for finding it so easy to solve cases. Meanwhile, I'll look up the boy. He's not a bad kid, but a bloody nuisance every time I've had anything to do with him. I need to know just how his little conversation with Labiche went.'

XXI

The stairs were as dirty as on his previous visits, and there were cobwebs hanging from the walls. Nasty smells of cooking-fat and stale air; dry rot too, he thought. It should have been condemned years ago but it would probably still be standing and in this same sordid condition when most of its residents were dead. He knocked on the door and remembered how the old woman, Karim's mother, who wasn't in fact old, but aged by drink and poverty and disappointment, had taken several minutes to answer it, shuffling towards the door in carpet slippers with holes in the toe, and wearing a filthy housecoat held together by safety-pins. This time, however, his knock was answered at once.

Karim's mouth hung open when he recognised Lannes, who pushed past him into the middle of the room in case the boy was tempted to try to shut the door against him.

'Expecting someone else, were you?'

Karim nodded. He was wearing only sky-blue shorts which revealed most of his thighs and a sleeveless singlet.

'A client?'

'Yes, I thought he'd arrived early. They do sometimes.'

'Get impatient, do they?'

'Sometimes.'

'Understandable. Who is it? Father Paul?'

The smile which had appeared when Lannes said 'understandable' vanished so quickly that he might only have imagined it.

'No, no, not him. What do you know about Father Paul?'

'More than enough,' Lannes said. 'Take a seat, Karim, we've some talking to do. You've cleaned the place up, I see. Daresay your clients prefer it, unless they're the kind who get turned on by squalor. Jules told me about your mother. I was sorry to hear it. Miss her, do you?'

To his surprise, Karim's lips quivered and his eyes filled with tears.

'She was a right old cow,' he said, 'but . . . '

'Yes,' Lannes said. 'There's nobody now for whom, despite everything, whatever you do, you're the most important person in the world. Nobody for whom you're still a little boy. Sit down, I said, and tell me what you've been up to.'

'I don't know what you want to know.'

He stretched out on a broken-backed couch, trying to look at his ease.

'You're in my debt,' Lannes said, 'you owe me. Remember Félix. Well, of course you do, you couldn't have forgotten what he did to you, raped you, didn't he, beat you up, and then what happened

99

to him. I covered up for you, for you and your old mother. Remember?'

Karim lowered his head and began to scratch the inside of his thigh.

'Look at me,' Lannes said. 'I cleared up the mess you were in, didn't I? Got rid of the body, protected you. Not for the first time either. The Gestapo wanted you, searched for you after that poor fool Schussmann shot himself, and I helped you then too, got you out of Bordeaux, into safety. You haven't forgotten that, have you? I remember how terrified you were when I spoke of the Gestapo. I don't blame you for that. They are terrifying. You wouldn't have lasted long if they'd got hold of you, a rent-boy like you, half-Arab, looking Arab. It doesn't bear thinking of . . . '

'I offered . . . '

'Oh yes, you offered yourself to me. Fair enough, but not my thing, as you knew. You did know, didn't you? A boy like you? Bound to know if you've made a hit.'

Karim looked up and gave a half-smile, a shy one in which Lannes read mischief.

'It was worth trying. Besides, what else could I offer?'

'What else indeed? So how do you explain this, Karim?'

He handed him the paper young René had given him.

'Who have you been telling lies to?'

'It's not like that,' Karim said. 'Honest, it isn't.'

Lannes lit a cigarette and passed it over to the boy, then lit one for himself.

'Let's start with Father Paul. The word is you were blackmailing him. Easy game, I suppose you thought. A priest who frequents rent-boys. He wouldn't want that known, would he?'

'It wasn't like that at all. Sure, he came here a couple of times. Someone told him about me, he said, told him I was good. Which I am, superintendent, which I am. But then I told him, that's your lot.'

'Why?'

'Because I didn't like what he wanted. I won't do just anything, you know. I'm not depraved.'

'I'll take your word for it. Go on.'

'What about? What do you want to know?'

'Tell me about the lawyer. He sent his clerk to fetch you. Why? Tell me about him. Tell me about the advocate Labiche.'

'You know him? He's a horror, he scared me shitless.'

'Go on. Tell. Tell me everything.'

It took the boy a long time. He couldn't look Lannes in the face and he kept alternately picking at his thigh and stroking it. But, with hesitations and false starts, he told the story.

The clerk had come to fetch him, come with a promise – there was a rich man wanted him. OK, fine, he was used to that, happy about that. Why not? It was natural, his business. But the clerk was scared stiff himself, or maybe he was just ill-at-ease. It was obvious he didn't like what he was doing, and didn't like him either. He wouldn't walk close to him, as if he was pretending they weren't together. It was pathetic, but actually it also amused him. The more the clerk was embarrassed, the more he camped it up, swaying his hips and speaking to him in a fluting pansy voice which some of his clients, he had to say, really went for. 'You know, some like their boys to be a bit effeminate, and I'm happy to play up to them. So I did that to this chap because it amused me to embarrass him. And anyway, that's part of me, of what I am. I'm not ashamed of it, you know.'

Lannes remembered how Karim's mother had once been an exotic dancer, though it was hard to believe it when you looked at what she had become, and how, when he asked for a trunk in which they might remove Félix's body, Karim had produced one full of her old dresses and costumes, and then that, in a curiously tender moment, he had spoken of the days when they would both, the boy and his mother, dress up in her stage costumes and dance together in a dream of what might have been and for him might yet be.

'Some men want a girly-boy, others the boy next door and others a young tough from the back-streets whom they like to think has a criminal record. I'm usually happy to oblige.'

For a moment he looked pleased with himself, forgetting his fear.

'I'm sure you're good at it,' Lannes said. 'Go on.'

The clerk took him to a first-floor apartment overlooking the

Place de l'Ancienne Comédie, richly furnished, a lot of gilt, velvet and fine paintings. Good money, he thought. But then three men came in, and this made him anxious.

'Some boys don't mind that,' he said, 'but for me it's just one to one, and I was about to say "no thanks" when one of them, a big bruiser with a cauliflower ear, came up and punched me hard and low in the belly. I doubled up and fell down, and heard one of them laugh. The bruiser pulled me up by the hair and flung me into a chair. That's just a taster, he said, as I was still fighting for breath. But one of the other two said, "That's enough for now, Fritz, he's got the message, I'm sure." '

'Describe him,' Lannes said. 'The one who spoke.'

'Short, broad, balding, a mouth turned down at the corners. He was wearing a double-breasted suit and a silk shirt.'

'You took all that in, even after that punch?'

'Not then. I'd time later, enough time, too much time. He spoke very quietly and that made it worse.'

The description, as Lannes expected, fitted Labiche, and so he said, 'That's the advocate. I don't think I'm going to like your story. He's as nasty a piece of work as anyone I've come across in years. And the third man?'

'He was tall, fair-haired, thinning, though, and he didn't speak much. In fact he looked like he didn't want to be there. It was the one in the double-breasted suit, Labiche you say, did all the talking.'

'Go on . . . '

'I don't like to. He spoke to me like I was dirt, like that Félix indeed.'

He pulled his knees up, with his hands round them, and buried his head.

'Go on. You have to.'

Lannes felt sorry for the boy. He could picture the scene. It disgusted him, as cruelty always did, but he had to know the worst.

'He said Father Paul had told him I was blackmailing him and I could go to prison for that. I wouldn't enjoy it, I knew, didn't I, what they did to boys like me in prison. I said I wasn't blackmailing Father Paul, and he laughed. Your word against a priest's, who would they believe? But it wasn't true and anyway I didn't believe

Father Paul would dare. My word against his, certainly, but it wouldn't do him any good, would it. You'd still go to prison, he said, but you don't have to. I'll make a bargain with you. Just sign this paper and we'll forget about it. Easy for you. So sign it. What does it say? I asked. It's just a confession, he said. A confession of what? There's a policeman, he said, a senior policeman, you know who I mean, don't you? This little paper – all it consists of is an admission that he's paid you for sex a number of times, first when you were still under-age. Sign it and you're free to leave, nothing will happen to you. No, I said, it's not true. Then the one they called Fritz grabbed me by the hair again and smacked me hard, first one cheek, then the other. Give me five minutes with the little rat, he said. There's no need for that, his chief said, he'll see sense, he'll sign. If you don't, he turned to me, it won't be the prison I spoke of. It'll be worse. My friend here – he indicated the tall man – is an officer in the Milice, a captain. He doesn't care for your policeman friend any more than I do, and the Milice? They don't like boys like you, degenerates they call them. They despise them. They like beating them up, not that it would stop at a beating. If you're stupid and obstinate, I'll give you to him. Suspected of working for the Resistance, wouldn't that be it, captain. Yes, it would, he said – first time he'd spoken. And you don't bother with a trial, do you? No point, we just shoot the little bastards. So there you are, your choice is simple, Labiche said. And then he laughed, not that I would call it a choice, not really. Fritz pulled me up and over to the table. A pen was put in my hand. I signed. I'm sorry. But what else could I do?'

'What else indeed?'

Lannes couldn't blame the boy. Given that choice, there was no other way he could have expected, or required, him to act. Confess to a lie or choose death? How many would have made a different decision? Dominique and Alain, he thought, Dominique from principle, Alain on account of his natural obduracy, his bloody-mindedness. But Léon and little Jérôme? He had no idea. There is so often a time when courage fails. Or Clothilde's Michel? Perhaps.

Karim looked up, his mouth open, tears in his eyes.

'I'm sorry, truly sorry. Can you forgive me?'

'Big word, forgiveness,' Lannes said. 'I don't like big words. You've only done what people all over France have been doing for the last four years, submitting to reality, to things as they are. You're no worse than most of us. Dry your tears, you've a client coming.'

'You despise me too, don't you?'

'Why should I do that? You've come up against a force you couldn't resist. Like so many of us. I think they'll leave you alone now.'

On the stairs he met a middle-aged man in a light summer suit.

'He's all ready and waiting for you,' Lannes said. 'Nice boy. Enjoy yourself.'

XXII

René was nervous about approaching Bracal. He had never spoken to him and indeed because of his junior rank he had never had any dealings with the instructing judge in any case under investigation. That was normally the superintendent's responsibility, or Moncerre's, now that Lannes was suspended. Moreover he distrusted these gentlemen. Well, distrust wasn't perhaps the right word. It was just that he was uncomfortable with the idea of these men with university degrees, products of the Grandes Écoles, men who wore expensive three-piece suits and smelled of eau de cologne. He was a working-class boy, a widow's son, reared in poverty by a mother who went out cleaning for the sort of ladies who had never done their own marketing and who might indeed be the mothers of men like the instructing judge. But Lannes had asked him to do this, and naturally he was ready to obey. So he sent through a note, saying that the superintendent had asked him to speak to the judge. He got a reply asking him to call at once if it was convenient. It surprised him to find his own convenience being considered, and he was happy that Moncerre was out of the office; he would have been first curious, and then offended if René had had to explain that the superintendent had asked him, rather than the bull-terrier, to approach the judge. But he was still unsure of himself when he was shown into Bracal's office, and since Bracal accorded exactly with his impression of these gentlemen, he felt out-of-place and tongue-tied.

To his surprise, however, the judge got up from behind his desk and came forward to shake his hand.

'I've had good reports of you,' he said. 'From Superintendent Lannes. He speaks highly of you. Do please sit down.'

And he returned to his own chair behind the desk.

'So?' he said. 'The superintendent has been unfortunate. But things won't long remain as they are now. I suppose you understand that?'

'Do you mean . . . ?'

'We don't need to spell it out. There are things better understood without words than spoken. But you say he has asked you to see me.'

'Yes, he asked me to give you these letters. They're copies of the originals which he has retained.'

Bracal glanced at them.

'Unpleasant.'

His well-manicured fingers tapped out a little tattoo on his desk. Lannes could have told René this was the judge's habit when thinking.

'Unpleasant,' he said again. 'To whom were they sent? Do you know that?'

'The first, the one about the girl, was sent to Madame Lannes. The second . . . ' he hesitated.

'Yes?'

René felt himself blushing.

'Yes?'

'It was addressed to Commissaire Schnyder. He wasn't in the office. It came to me that the writing – printing really – resembled the first letter which the superintendent had shown me. So . . . ' he paused and swallowed. 'I intercepted it.'

'Remarkable.'

René waited, nervously expecting a reprimand.

'So the commissaire hasn't seen it?'

'No.'

Bracal smiled.

'Good. The fewer who see such things the better, don't you think? But the superintendent asked you to give them to me?'

'Yes.'

'I'm honoured.'

He resumed his finger-tapping, then he got up, crossed to a cabinet, took out a bottle and two glasses, filled them and passed one to René.

'Schnapps,' he said. 'A present from one of our German friends. Not bad, actually. Your health or *prosit* as they would say on the other side of the Rhine. So, what next? Do you happen to know who the people referred to in these letters are? I'm assuming – not that it greatly matters – that there is, shall we say, no substance in the accusations, but that the two people nevertheless exist. I should tell you I have a considerable respect for the superintendent, as I'm sure you have yourself.'

'The girl, yes. She was a witness in a case, the murder of a retired professor. We never solved it, I'm afraid. Then she was assaulted by one of the suspects.'

'An attractive girl?'

René to his embarrassment blushed again.

'And indeed a tart?'

'I suppose so.'

'And the boy, this rent-boy? What do you know of him?'

'Only what Superintendent Lannes has told me, that he was involved in the case of that German officer, liaison officer, who shot himself, and also with a certain spook who went by the name of Félix and who mysteriously disappeared. The superintendent thought it better that you should be informed.'

Bracal smiled again.

'That means that things really are bad. Normally you in the PJ like to keep people like me at a distance. It's called the "need to know" policy, which means of course that we shouldn't be told anything but what it is absolutely necessary that we are made aware of. So the mysterious disappearance of this Félix was never brought to my notice, not officially, you understand. Drink your schnapps, inspector,' he said, picking up his own glass and draining it. 'Why didn't the superintendent come to give me these letters himself?'

'I suppose because he's suspended, sir.'

'Oh I don't think so, do you? It would really be much better if you were frank with me. I know that, since the Occupation, we've all got out of the habit of speaking the truth or saying what we really think. But there are times nevertheless when honesty is still the right policy. If I am to help the superintendent in the difficult position he finds himself in . . . '

Lannes had said, 'Tell him all you know.' So . . .

'He's in hiding, gone under cover,' and René recounted the incident with the lieutenant in the Milice, and how a captain in that force had come looking for Lannes, ignorant of his suspension . . . '

'Our friends in the Milice,' Bracal said. 'A tiresome bunch, and stupid, very stupid. They don't realise it's almost all up with them. What did the superintendent hope I might do for him?'

'He told me to ask you if you might be so kind as to get in touch with what he called a senior spook, name of Fabien . . . '

'That's flying high,' the judge said. 'Tell him I will if I can. One other thing, inspector. The author of these letters?'

'The superintendent is sure they come from the advocate Labiche.'

'Labiche? A man of influence, even power, but for how much longer? Tell the superintendent I'll do what I can. And be sure to tell him he has my respect. Sometimes I think that respect for individuals is all that's left to us. It has been a pleasure making your acquaintance, inspector.'

XXIII

Lannes, an only child, had always been happy on his own, happiest indeed, he sometimes thought. He was devoted to his family, and, being without religion, had no doubt that family was the most important thing in his life, his anchor indeed, without which he would drift he couldn't think where. Work also mattered; without it these years of the Occupation would have been even more grim, intolerable really. And yet he found any day, or worse a sequence of days, in which he didn't have some hours to himself, oppressive. It wasn't necessary to do anything with that time alone.

Yet now this retreat had him on edge. Anxiety kept him awake when he went to bed, and when he at last fell asleep, his dreams were disturbing. Their content had fled in the morning and couldn't be recaptured. But he woke feeling guilty.

René had come again yesterday, to report his meeting with Bracal; and it should have re-assured him to know that the judge was on his side, as it were. If it could be believed, of course, but what could be believed now? Who could be trusted? It was a foolish thought, but he couldn't set it aside. They were all waiting, day by day, for the Allied invasion that was promised but didn't arrive. And suppose it was defeated, as his brother-in-law Albert had so confidently asserted it would be, what would his position be then? He had never been a gambler, but everything he had done – or chosen not to do – in the last weeks had been based on the supposition, assumption really, that the invasion would be successful, the German forces withdrawn from Bordeaux to re-inforce the retreating Wehrmacht, and Vichy crumble. This was why he had taken refuge in the Pension Smitt.

He dipped a hunk of yesterday's hard bread in the bad coffee the old woman had brought him. Sunlight streaked through the dirty window-pane, suggesting, promising, a day to be enjoyed. Church bells rang. Would Marguerite be attending Mass where she would pray for her mother, for the children certainly, and perhaps for him too? He had asked young René to call on her and see that all was well. A stupid phrase; how could things be well?

Did he still love her? Another stupidity, that question. How do you define love? They were bound together, and must remain so unless she chose to snap the bond. He could never do that himself, but what he felt – tenderness, affection, pity, duty or obligation – did that amount to love? And did it matter in any case?

He lit a cigarette with a wax match. They were all in a maze. Perhaps they had reached the centre and now couldn't find their way out. And yet the sun was shining brightly and when he forced open the dusty window, there wasn't a cloud visible in the sky.

Marguerite on her knees praying, Miriam with whom, years

ago now, he had been tempted to betray her, dying, with Henri watching helplessly over her, Alain Lord knows where and in what condition, Clothilde dreaming of Michel, Dominique also probably in church, Fernand with his new girl and strangely evasive, up to something in his son Jacques' opinion, Yvette and that wretched boy Karim – why did he feel responsible for them all, even while he lurked powerless in this miserable pension? Had he made a mistake coming here, going into hiding?

Aurélien came through, rubbing sleep from his eyes. His sister brought him coffee and bread and left them without a word. Lannes found himself envying her utter indifference to everything except her bottle of white wine in the kitchen. Aurélien drank his coffee and dealt out his cards.

'Don't you get tired of that game?'

'I'm tired of everything. It keeps me from thinking.'

'What about?'

'Everything. Anything.'

'The mess you've made of your life?'

'If you like. I don't care what you think of me, superintendent. But I'll say this. Your own life seems a mess too. If it wasn't, you wouldn't be here.'

Lannes lit another cigarette and pushed the packet across the table.

'Take one,' he said. 'I can't argue with you there.'

'Besides,' Aurélien said, 'I've abandoned hope of anything better. There's some consolation in that.'

'Did the girl, Marie-Adelaide, represent some sort of hope?'

'Hope? I don't know. This game's not coming out.'

He collected the cards, shuffled them and began to deal again.

'Does it matter if it does?'

'Of course not. Nothing matters.'

Lannes got up, took the bottle of Armagnac from the sideboard and poured them each a glass.

'Tell me about her father. Tell me about Monsieur d'Herblay.'

'Another failure. What of him? I'm not a complete fool, you know. Being a failure helps me to see some things more clearly. The advocate Labiche, for instance. Yes, I'm afraid of him, you were right there, but have you ever seen a rat caught in a cage? It darts around, chews at the wire and believes it can find a way out. The more desperate it gets, the more it fights. That's the advocate and, like you said, it's frightening.'

'And Monsieur d'Herblay?'

'Another rat but one who doesn't know he's caught in a trap. I could see that. Therefore a fool. Who do you think will win this war, superintendent?'

'The Allies.'

'Exactly. I'm an idiot, a drunk and, as you told me, a queer that most people despise, but even I know that, even I can see that. Monsieur d'Herblay can't. So he's an even bigger idiot.'

'How do you know that?'

'Because he signed up for the Milice, that horror-comic body of losers. They gave him a uniform and told him he was an officer, saving France, and he believed them. What an idiot.'

He picked up his glass.

'Good brandy.'

'What does he look like?'

'D'Herblay? Tall, fair-haired, thin, handsome once, not now. His daughter, the little fool, is still crazy about him. That was why she came away with me when I pretended I was in love with her. Because I promised I'd take her to him. I suppose Labiche has done so. He may have kept his word for once.'

'Yes, I think he may have done. So you were always only pretending.'

'I don't know, do I? Maybe I hoped when I realised she was attracted to me. And she was, really. Then I understood that she was desperate to escape from that mausoleum her grandmother kept her in. So it was easy. Yes, I was acting under instructions, but I may have hoped. So once again I'm an idiot. Do you know the truth about life, superintendent? None of it matters. Doesn't matter a damn. I think this game's going to come out.'

He was wrong of course. Lannes sipped his brandy and drew on his cigarette. Utterly wrong. Things matter, they matter terribly, because if they don't, if you come to believe they don't, then there's nothing left. That was the choice, the ultimate real one, between nihilism and commitment. You had to hold to the belief that things could be better than they are. Deep down even Aurélien held to that, whatever he said. Why else play these endless game of Patience, one of which had at last come good?

XXIV

Jérôme trembled with excitement. Thirty years later, when he wrote his memoirs, he struggled to find the words that might recapture his mood of mingled exultation and fear. Exultation because this was the moment they had been waiting for, fear, not only because things might yet go wrong, there might be a disaster, but also fear that his voice would desert him, that he wouldn't be able to speak the words of hope, encouragement and exhortation that he had written and had approved by his superiors; fear too, selfish but not only selfish fear, he would think so many years on, for Freddie, somewhere between England and France, helping to land the troops on the beach, playing his brave part in the Liberation. Sitting before his typewriter in his study in the rue Monsieur-le-Prince in 1974 he found himself for the moment unable to find the words. Fortunately, he remembered , his talk on that June day had been recorded, not delivered live. If the landings had failed, it wouldn't have been broadcast.

*   *   *

Alain's head was thrust under the water again while at the other end of the bath a German sergeant pulled up his feet. His lungs filled with water. This time he was drowning. But no, absurdly, it came to him that a drowning man sees his life pass before him, and he didn't. A hand was thrust into the water, seized him by the hair and pulled him half-upright, while his feet were allowed to drop. He gulped and gasped for breath and bath water was spewed out of his mouth. He was hauled out of the bath and banged up against the stone wall of the cellar. It was icy cold, colder even than the water. A punch landed on his belly and he fell to his knees spluttering. Someone picked him up and threw him on to a wooden chair.

'Had enough? Are you ready to speak? Where is he?'

He felt a hand on his neck, and heard a gentler voice. It was the Boche officer, the man who had first interrogated him.

'You little fool, don't you want to live? Don't you want to see your girl again? Hold her in your arms, kiss her, fuck her? All I want is a word, one word, the name of the place where he's to be found. Give me that, and this will stop. It'll be over. The kind sergeant here will put you to bed, a nice warm bed where you can dream of your girl. Think of that. No?'

'He thinks he's tough, this one.'

'So many of them do and they're always wrong. Very well, you've asked for it.'

He felt them fix the electrodes to his genitals.

'Switch on.'

At the first flow of the current he began to scream.

*　　*　　*

Baron Jean, corporal in what was now called the Charlemagne Legion, was drunk, talkative drunk, cheerful drunk, singing drunk.

Michel held him upright, his arm under his corporal's, Jean's around his shoulders, and staggered as he tried to march him back to barracks.

'The secret of life, dear boy, never be sober, never be sober again. The Ivans know. Have you ever seen a sober Ivan? Never. Full of vodka, that's what they are, fighting mad on vodka. Tell you a secret, dear boy, I'm not drunk enough and you, why you're disgust . . . disgustingly sober.'

He freed an arm, dug a half-bottle of schnapps from his pocket, and thrust it into Michel's mouth.

'Do you know why we're losing the war? Tell you why? It's 'cos Stalin's drunk and Hitler's teetotal. Uncle Joe's pissed as a newt and the Führer's drinking tea. No good being a tea-drinker in war. No good. Silly little man, Adolf.'

'Oh do shut up,' Michel said, 'or we'll both end up in clink.'

*　　*　　*

The foyer of the Hotel des Ambassadeurs was busy, almost all the tables occupied. It might have been peace time when the rich and idle flocked to Vichy to take the waters. There were flowers in pots, roses, hydrangeas, carnations, and waiters in tail-coats moved between the tables, trays held high. Elegant women spoke in carrying voices and at the back of the room four elderly gentlemen were playing bridge, the baldest of them dealing cards with arthritic deliberation. Between each deal of four he paused to draw on his cigar, lay it in the ashtray or pick it up and draw again.

Maurice said, 'Father told me we should wait in the bar and order a bottle of champagne on his account.'

The barman came out from behind the bar to shake hands.

'We'll be crowded before long,' he said. 'It's only to be expected.'

'Why so, Pierre?'

'You mean you haven't heard the news?'

'What news?'

'It's begun. The invasion.' He lowered his voice. 'The Liberation perhaps. They've landed in Normandy. Or so they say. Of course it may be only a rumour. There's a new one every day.'

'Well, you're usually first with the news,' Maurice said. 'My father told me to order a bottle of Mumm.'

'I wouldn't advise it, sir. It might be taken amiss. There are eyes everywhere, you know. Champagne – it might be interpreted as celebration.'

*   *   *

'But they can't.'

Chardy was indignant, but also, Léon thought, close to tears.

'They can't,' he said again. 'The contract is ready to be signed.'

'These days, my dear,' his friend, the film director Marcel Pougier said, with the sort of smile which in actors is called rueful, 'you will find that anything is possible. The authorities are capricious. And your story, let's say it's just a little too 1940, a year we are all soon going to be happy to pretend was one in which we all behaved differently. It's not the German censorship this time, you know. It's simply that your producer is changing tack, and your novel – the sort of delicious thing you write so well, so unlike almost everyone else, even Cocteau – simply won't do, my dear. Jean-Paul, for instance, can sniff the changing wind. And what does his nose tell him? That there's a new mood, a stern morality. A story like yours would offend the Communists, and they're going to be in the ascendancy. They'll be the censors once the Boches have gone. Believe me. I have my little ear to the ground.'

'It's not fair,' Chardy said.

'Of course it isn't, ducky, it's how life is.'

'But you were able to make your *David*.'

'That's because I'm a clever clogs.'

And you're not was the unspoken part of the sentence, Léon thought. It was true of course. There was something pathetic about Chardy. He had reason to be grateful to him. He'd sheltered him, provided him with that room in the Place Contrescarpe and paid the rent, because he couldn't have him in the apartment in the rue Vanneau where he lived with his disapproving and possessive mother; and Léon knew that he might not have survived these last perilous months without his help, help that went with attentions which weren't, certainly, always agreeable. Nevertheless on this day of wonderful news to make a fuss about the film of a novel being abandoned – it was absurd.

That's how he put it later in the afternoon to the blonde Priscilla in the nursing home where she lived.

'Oh no,' she said, 'it's always the personal that matters most. You've a lot to learn, my sweet.'

XXV

'There was nothing in the market,' Madame Smitt said, 'no bread, not even an egg. Half the stalls had their shutters closed. I don't know what it's about and my feet are sore. So if you want anything to eat you'll have to find it for yourself.'

'Did anyone say why? Was there any news?'

'News? What do I care for news?'

And she shuffled off, muttering about her bunions, to give herself a tumbler of white wine.

Lannes had again slept badly. The atmosphere of the pension

was oppressive, intolerable. He thought of Aurélien's image of Labiche as a rat in a cage gnawing at the wire. Wasn't that what he was doing himself?

Without a word to Madame Smitt, he drew back the bolt which she had slid into place shutting the world out, and stepped into the street. The morning was fresh as a milkmaid's kiss, absurd phrase that came into his mind and wouldn't go away, though he had never kissed a milkmaid, not that he could remember. But someone had used it in his hearing – Fernand perhaps? – and it had stuck in his mind and now rang there insistently. No matter, it suited the morning. He swung his stick. Even his hip wasn't hurting.

He walked without intention, glad only to be free of the hole in which he had shut himself up. It had been a mistake, he had been behaving like that wretched Aurélien with his endless game of Patience. But one of them had at last come out. Was it this that had given him the incentive to return to the world? Later he would go home, see how Marguerite and Clothilde were, dare to see how Marguerite received him, whether she had accepted his denials.

Jacques Maso, a journalist on the *Sud-Ouest*, was in his familiar place in the Rugby Bar, under the photograph of the Bordeaux XV that had been champions of France in 1914. He raised his hand in greeting and Lannes joined him, calling to the barman to bring them beer.

'So,' Jacques said, 'it's begun.'

'What?'

'You haven't heard? Where have you been?'

'I've heard nothing.'

'The invasion. The Allies have landed, in Normandy it seems.'

Lannes felt a surge of relief.

'That's wonderful news. At last.'

'That's why I'm here,' Jacques said. 'I could hardly take it in myself, and I couldn't stay in the office. We're all at sixes and sevens there. Nobody knows what to write. Nobody knows what we may be allowed to write, what indeed we might dare to write. So I buggered off to think. On my own. And now you're here.' He picked up his glass, clinked it against Lannes', and said, 'To success! Victory! Liberation!'

'But how's it going?'

'Nobody knows. You can't believe the first reports that come in. But there's hard fighting, that's surely certain. And, while Vichy may be finished, there's still the shreds of a government, the Milice and the French Gestapo haven't gone away, far from it.'

'And the Germans are still here.'

'Very much so. They shot six members of a Resistance group yesterday, and put up posters listing the names and proclaiming that anyone suspected of Resistance would be shot on sight. And now the Director wants me to write our editorial for tomorrow. I came here to think. It's an impossible task, and if I strike the wrong note . . . what the hell can I say?'

Lannes had no answer. His hand was shaking. He couldn't even pick up his glass: Liberation. Resisters to be shot on sight. Alain . . .

'The paper's been loyal to the Marshal. We've had no choice.'

'Of course you haven't.'

The portrait of the Marshal above the bar looked down at them: benign, fatherly, reassuring. 'I have consecrated my person to the French people in their time of hardship.' Everyone knew the words. Many had believed the old man. Many had been comforted by his promise to share their sufferings, Marguerite who hated politics and refused to listen to the war news among them. The Marshal was all they had; she wouldn't hear a word against him.

'You'll have no news of Alain?' Jacques said.

'None.'

'No news is better than bad news. When it's over – and I pray that won't be long now – I look forward to seeing him play again. His change of pace and outside break, a happy memory. He'll play for France, Jean. Everyone at the club thinks so and looks forward to his return.'

'Don't,' Lannes said, 'don't speak like that. It's tempting the Fates, tempting that one with the scissors.'

'You're right of course, but often, these last years, it's been only the thought that things might be again as they used to be that has enabled me to keep going in my dismal trade. If only I'd been a sports writer . . . for four years now I've written little but lies.'

'They'll never be as they were,' Lannes said. 'However we come out of this it will be like stepping into a different world, utterly different. It couldn't be otherwise. Too much has happened, too much that has been dreadful and divisive. It will be years before we can look each other in the eye without a question: so how did you behave, what did you do, in the years of the Occupation? And that's only if the Allies win in Normandy. And if they don't . . . then it will be only the Soviets who have defeated the Nazis. And what would that mean for France, for French men and women?'

'Maybe you should write my editorial, Jean.'

'Not my job. Yours.'

'But what would you say?'

'Lord knows. All I know is that we'll have to live together whatever the outcome and that Frenchmen should stop killing Frenchmen.'

'I can't write that, but I'll drink to it.'

Lannes picked up his glass and drank his beer.

*   *   *

Nevertheless it must be good news. Would the Allies have launched an invasion if they weren't confident of success? They had the whole might of America behind them, and on the Eastern Front the Boches were being driven back, so far as he understood, by the Red Army with its inexhaustible supply of conscripts. Wouldn't the Boches recognise that they'd had it? The screaming maniac might not, but there were surely still men of sense in Germany. He thought of Schuerle, the *Junker* from East Prussia. Wounded on that Eastern Front, losing an eye and his left arm, he had been sent to Bordeaux as a liaison officer. They had become friends, as far anyway as friendship was possible for them, and he had spoken of his contempt for the Nazis, and of senior officers who shared his views; at the right moment they would remove Hitler. Hadn't that moment arrived?

Yes, it was a beautiful day. No wonder the sun was shining so brightly.

*   *   *

Even so he couldn't climb the stairs to their apartment without a fluttering of nerves. Marguerite had had several days to brood over that wretched letter, to decide if she believed his denial. Since she had said that her trust in him was broken. Well, he had to face it . . .

To his surprise the door was opened by René.

'So you've heard the news, chief?'

'Yes, it's wonderful.'

'What do you mean?'

'The Allied invasion of course.'

'Yes of course,' René said, 'but . . . '

Clothilde appeared behind him, her face white and drawn.

'Papa,' she said.

He took her in his arms and held her tight as she sobbed.

'What's happened?'

'It is sheer chance that I'm here,' René said, 'just at this moment, I mean.'

'Maman,' Clothilde said, 'they've taken her away.'

'Who? What do you mean?' he said again. 'Come, sit down, and tell me.'

'These men. They came looking for you, and when you weren't here, they took Maman away. Under arrest, they said.'

'Who? Which men?'

'I don't know. There were three of them.'

René coughed.

'There's a paper here, chief. Left for you.'

He handed it to Lannes. *Superintendent Lannes, suspended. You are charged with interference with an officer of the Milice in the exercise of his duty. In your absence, your wife has been taken into custody. She will be released if you present yourself at our headquarters. Otherwise she will be charged with Resistance. You know the penalty for that. Jean-Pierre Fracasse, Captain*

He stroked Clothilde's hair.

'Don't worry, darling, it will be all right.'

It was a lie of course, but what else could he say? He handed the letter back to René.

'I've no choice,' he said. 'Will you please stay here till Madame

Lannes returns. Then go to Bracal. Tell him what's happened. Say it's more urgent than ever that he speaks to Fabien.'

'And if she doesn't return? If they break their promise and don"t release her?'

'Then take Clothilde to her grandmother. She's out of hospital now. Say nothing about your mother, darling, just let the old lady think you've been sent to care for her, she'll like that. But I think it will be all right. I think they'll keep their word.'

I have to believe that, he thought. What have I brought on my family?

PART TWO

I

The cell stank; it was two days since he had been allowed to empty the bucket. But this morning the guard had winked at him, without, admittedly, otherwise altering his stony expression. Perhaps it was only a nervous tic. Lannes spent half an hour, more or less he couldn't tell, considering whether it was significant. Why not? He had nothing else to occupy his mind, not even a pack of cards like that wretched Aurélien. But the strange thing was that he had been ignored, since the day after he had presented himself for arrest, asking only that Marguerite be released and escorted home. He had been told that would be done. 'The captain's orders, sir.' Sir? So, even in prison, there was respect for the republican hierarchy. Remarkable. Would it be a case of 'we request you to wear this blindfold, sir', when they put him up against a wall to be shot? But here he was still, alive, twenty-three nights later – he had kept count of the coming and going of darkness.

It was on the second day that an officer in the uniform of the Milice had entered the cell and introduced himself as Captain Fracasse.

'That name irritates me,' Lannes said. 'I can't remember if it was Gautier or Alfred de Musset who wrote the book. Not that it matters because it's irrelevant, Monsieur d'Herblay.'

The officer straddled the only chair in the cell as if it was a horse he was riding, and said, 'So you know my real name. No matter. I'm Captain Fracasse now. It was Gautier by the way, they made me read it in school, very boring, but the name appealed to me, I don't know why. No matter. You were a fool to interfere with my lieutenant in the course of his duty – and to protect such a miserable object. Why did you do it?'

'I didn't like his uniform. I'm a policeman. I've no time for irregulars. Besides they'd have taken the boy away to be beaten up and shot. That sort of thing offends me too.'

'That's foolishness. A boy like that, scum. You're insolent, super-intendent, to speak to me in this fashion, and stupid. You're in my power. I could call my men, have you taken into the courtyard and shot. Just like that.' He snapped his fingers.

'It wouldn't trouble me at all,' he said.

'I don't suppose it would,' Lannes said. 'All the same, since you're here and I'm still alive, you might satisfy my curiosity. What have you done with your daughter?'

D'Herblay raised his chin.

'What are you talking about?'

'Marie-Adelaide, the daughter who, I'm told, adores you, despite everything. Where is she?'

'I don't understand you.'

It was strange. The roles were reversed. It was as if they were engaged in a dance in which they had shifted positions so that Lannes was now, as it were, behind his desk in the bureau, examining a suspect. D'Herblay's confusion was evident.

'Where should she be,' he said. 'She lives with my mother, her grandmother. I haven't see her in years, not since . . . what's it got to do with you?'

'Give me a cigarette, will you?' Lannes said, 'and I'll explain. Thanks. And a light? They took mine away. That's better. I'll tell you a story. Let's see what you make of it. I got a call from your mother's cousin, the Comte de St-Hilaire. That surprises you? A highly respected gentleman, as you know. He doesn't think much of you, I'm afraid, but he could be wrong. Then I went to see your mother.'

He recounted his investigation in detail – including the explanation of why he had been in Jules' Bar when the lieutenant arrived to arrest the wretched boy, Miki.

He omitted only any mention of Dr Solomons. He told him about Aurélien and Labiche's visit to the Pension Smitt.

'And then your Cagoulard friend, the man you stood beside when he forced that Arab boy to sign a paper setting out lying accusations about me – yes, I know about that too – went off with your daughter, the girl who, it seems, adores you, despite what you and Labiche did to her when she was only a little girl.'

*   *   *

He lay back on his bunk now, remembering, seeing again the way in which d'Herblay's face had crumpled, and hearing his voice, scarcely more than a whisper as he said, 'She was so sweet and my life was such a mess and she loved me and then all at once we were lovers, and it was wonderful and I hated myself for finding it so. Labiche was my mother's lawyer then . . . '

Lannes thought, that's something St-Hilaire didn't tell me. He must have known, he couldn't have forgotten, perhaps for some reason he was ashamed.

'He said he must question her, and then . . . my mother dismissed him and made me sign a document relinquishing all rights over Marie-Adelaide. Yes, she paid me off too, and insisted the matter must be closed, never spoken of again. Of course I submitted because I was ashamed. As for my mother, she has a horror of publicity. I can't believe she told her cousin.'

'Nevertheless she did,' Lannes said. 'Why I don't know. Perhaps because it was intolerable to keep the knowledge to herself. Secrets are corrupting. So she shared it with the only person she could trust. But now Labiche has your daughter – somewhere – and I find it hard to believe you didn't know. Why would he keep this knowledge from you? What does he want with her? Or from you?'

D'Herblay got to his feet. He turned his back on Lannes and pressed his face against the wall.

'Why does he do anything? What does he want of anyone?'

He swung round to face Lannes.

'And why should I believe you? You'd say anything to get out of here.'

'Not anything,' Lannes said, 'and if you think I'm lying to you, you can still have me shot. But you do believe me. I can see you do. It's in your face, and the questions you've just asked about Labiche, well you know the answer to them, don't you? Why did you join the Milice, Jean-Pierre?'

For the first time d'Herblay smiled. It wasn't much of a smile.

'That's easy,' he said, 'because I hate myself and what I've made of my life. So why not join an organisation that gives me licence to take out my hatred on others, that lets me have people like you shot. Yes, I know that decent people, respectable people like the Comte de St-Hilaire, despise the Milice. They think we're murderous hooligans, out of control. So we are. That's why the force appeals to me.'

'Yes,' Lannes said, 'that makes sense. But ask Labiche about Marie-Adelaide. You've a right to know – especially since she still adores you despite everything. And ask yourself what he wants of you.'

'I don't need to do that. I've got connections, connections that will get him out of France, into Spain, when it becomes necessary.'

'That makes sense too, and it may be that Marie-Adelaide is a means to keep you loyal. That makes sense, certainly. You're in a fix, Jean-Pierre. It might be better for you not to have me shot. But that's up to you of course. Meanwhile, I'd be grateful if you would leave me with that packet of cigarettes. You can get more. I can't, not while I'm here.'

And since then, he thought, nothing, nothing until that guard's wink – if it was a wink.

II

'It's your lucky day, sir,' the guard said. 'There's not many as have occupied this cell have been so fortunate, and I hope you'll bear in mind that I've treated you well. Haven't touched a hair of your head, let alone putting my boot in. Haven't even spat in your soup. All this though I've no cause to care for the likes of you. I've been on your side of the cell door myself. But you're being released, the Lord knows why, and there are two gentlemen waiting in what they call reception for you. So get moving . . . sir.'

Lannes eased himself off the narrow bunk. He was stiff and his hip ached.

'They took my stick away,' he said. 'See if you can find it.'

'No need. I have it here. We look after our guests, you see. When we don't shoot them, that is. It's a fine stick. I'd have kept it for myself if you'd had no further use for it, as you wouldn't if . . . well, no need to dwell on that. Just remember, sir, I've only been doing my duty. So let's go. You don't surely want to hang about. You never know when they might change their mind. These days, things change so fast that you don't know if you're coming or going. One day an enemy of the French State, the next a hero of the Resistance. Makes me laugh, that's what it does. It's a topsy-turvy world, no question.'

Bracal was there, spruce and well turned out as ever in a dove-grey, double-breasted suit, cream-coloured shirt, white-spotted blue bow-tie and polished black shoes, and with him the lean tawny-skinned spook who called himself Fabien.

'I'm sorry it's taken so long to extricate you,' Bracal said, 'but my own position has become precarious. The fact is, nobody knows what's what now, divergent orders come from all sides. Everything's at sixes and sevens and all the chains of authority have broken links. You've this gentleman to thank for your release rather than me. He has things to discuss with you and I accompanied him only to make sure that there was no hitch, no cock-up as you might say. So I'll be off. Meanwhile, I'm as sure as one can be of anything now that your suspension will be lifted in a day or two. Welcome back, Jean.'

'You'll be in need of these,' he said, handing Lannes a packet of Gauloises, and left them to a silence both seemed momentarily reluctant to break. Lannes looked at Fabien who was leaning back in his chair and smoking one of his long Italian cigars.

'So I've you to thank,' he said at last.

'Thanks? I don't know about that. Anyway I'm not looking for gratitude. I'm not disinterested.'

'I wouldn't have supposed you were. Nevertheless.'

'Nevertheless I seem to be making a habit of it, don't I? First, closing down the investigation into the killing of that ass Félix – and don't pretend, superintendent, that you didn't have a hand in that – and now getting you out of this hellhole. You look a mess, much in need of a bath and the chance to get rid of that beard. But that'll have to wait. I don't have long and we need to talk. So I think we should go for a drink.

*   *   *

When they were settled at a table in the back of the Café Régent, Fabien said, 'Only mineral water for me, I'm afraid. My liver's in a poor state, has been, as I believe I told you, since I served in Indo-China. But something stronger for you? Armagnac?'

He cut another Toscano in two, put one half in the top pocket of his jacket, and lit the other.

'When that fellow, the judge, told me you were looking for help – almost a month ago, I suppose – I thought it's no concern of mine. Besides I'd enough on my plate, and you can imagine that my own position is delicate. Whose isn't, the way things are?'

Lannes lit a cigarette and said, 'You forget, I've no idea how they are. I don't even know how the war is going in Normandy.'

'Oh, as to that, there's been stiff fighting, but, as far as we can tell, the Allies are advancing, slowly. The Germans are retreating, slowly. But they are still here in Bordeaux and, of course, Paris. Vichy as it was is finished, but the Marshal visited Paris and had a great reception, cheering crowds, much enthusiasm. Yet when the Allies arrive, half of those who cheered the old boy will be ready to shoot him. Scum, a wretched rabble, that's what most of our countrymen are, scum and bastards. And Laval has fallen out of favour with the Boches – they never trusted him far, now they don't trust him at all – but he still believes he has a part to play. That's more or less how things stand, though, as you'll realise, what stands today doesn't stand long.'

And you're Vichy, Lannes thought, you were at the heart of Vichy, I'm sure of that; so where are you now? I wonder if you too were a Cagoulard, it's quite likely, it would fit with everything I've learned of you. Fabien smiled, and, as if he had read Lannes' thoughts, said, 'So it's coat-turning time. Coats are being turned all over France, by anyone who can read the signs and isn't too thoroughly compromised. The Resistance is swelling by the day as people hurry to get in on the act. Even your old friend Fernand has, according to my information, set up as a Resistance leader. Good luck to him of course. Another drink?'

So that's what was disturbing young Jacques, Lannes thought.

Fabien put a match to his cigar which had gone out the way Toscani do.

'So if it wasn't Bracal, who was it?'

'It's like a country dance,' Fabien said, 'with people changing places, changing partners. They get cold feet, you see. Jean-Pierre d'Herblay's were suddenly as cold as ice, as cold as can be. He's not much of a man and he has always been afraid of responsibility which is why he amounts to nothing. So he asked for my help – and here we are. Does that surprise you?'

'I sometimes think I'm past being surprised by anything.'

Fabien looked at his watch.

'I've a train in a couple of hours,' he said. 'But I've asked two people to meet us here. You'll know them both. I hope they're not going to be late. They're connected to the advocate Labiche too.'

'Labiche?'

'Yes, this is all about Labiche. Don't pretend you don't know that. Don't insult me, superintendent, by feigning ignorance. By the way, what became of the rent-boy?'

'Who?'

'You're at it again. The rent-boy who shot Félix, a killing which we agreed should be ascribed to the Resistance. What became of him?'

'It was his mother who fired the gun that killed Félix, not the boy. And she's dead. As for him, it's you that's playing games now, for I've no doubt that you've learned of the anonymous letter accusing me of having had sex with the boy which, by the way, I haven't. I can't believe Jean-Pierre didn't mention it, and even that the letter was dictated by Labiche. Why, may I ask, are you so interested in the advocate?'

'*Pazienza*,' Fabien said. 'I must go and pee. A weak bladder is another distressing, even shameful, consequence of my medical condition. You'll recognise my guests if they arrive in my absence.'

Lannes watched him limp away, lit a cigarette and felt a wave of relief flow over him. It was like Aurélien's game of Patience when he turned up the card that unlocked an impasse. He picked up his glass. Georges, the old waiter whom he had known since he and the Chambolley brothers first frequented the Café Régent as students, came over.

'I've just come on duty and for a moment I didn't recognise you with that beard. If I may say so, it doesn't suit you, Jean.'

'I haven't been able to shave where I was.'

'I won't ask you where that was.' Georges said. 'There are questions better not put these days. But how is Monsieur Henri? It's a long time since he's been in.'

'He doesn't go out much these days, hasn't indeed since his brother's death.'

'Ah, that was a sad business. Poor Monsieur Gaston. Always ready with a laugh or a good story. And always champagne when he was in funds and often when he wasn't. You never found the bastard who murdered him?'

'We never brought him to trial.'

'Like that, was it? Like so much these days. If you want my opinion, Jean, we've never recovered from our war. Even our victory was a sham. A sort of delusion. That's the way I see it anyway. Another brandy? I'll put it on your companion's tab. He looks as if he can afford it. Which is more than most people can today. I don't know what the world's coming to, I really don't. You know I used to pity the boys who were killed in the trenches. But now, well, I don't know, they've been spared a lot. Armagnac as usual, is it?'

Georges shuffled away on his waiter's flat feet. Fabien returned.

'It's humiliating,' he said. 'You're in urgent need and only a dribble comes out, and you stand there waiting and know you can never empty your bladder though you need to do so. Sorry to burden you with this, but it gets me down. Ah here they are.'

Lannes looked up to see Edmond de Grimaud and Father Paul enter the café.

III

'No, really,' she said. 'You mustn't be upset or embarrassed. I enjoyed it. You were gentle. Some men come at you like a stallion, which isn't my cup of tea really, even though of course one usually has to drink it.'

She ran her finger along his lower lip.

'And they treat you like a tart, some of them, often, which isn't surprising, or no longer surprising. My husband, Robert, was like you, very gentle, because he didn't really want it either. That was why I fell in love with him, and then out too. Though I'm still fond of him. It's an odd world. You mustn't feel bad. I quite enjoyed it, and of course it was my idea, not yours. You're sweet and for a first time you weren't bad. Oh dear, that sounds patronising, it wasn't meant to. You're not in love with that man Chardy though, are you?'

Léon smiled. The pink roses in a vase on the little table by the bed smelled delicious.

'Not at all. But I've reason to be grateful to him, nothing more.'

'Oh gratitude,' she said. 'I know that all too well. But it's exhausting. What will you do after the war, the Liberation everyone's waiting for? You won't stay with him, will you?'

The Liberation? They all dreamed of the day, didn't, even now, dare to imagine what it might be like. The Germans, surely, wouldn't give up Paris without a battle.

'I shouldn't think so,' he said. 'What about you?'

'Oh me, I'll go back home to England, soon as I can. I'll have to.'

'I didn't realise you were English,' he said, so surprised by the admission that the strangeness of her last words for the moment escaped him.

'Oh yes,' she said, and smiled. 'It's made for a difficult war.'

She stroked his cheek and leaned over to kiss him on the lips.

'You are sweet,' she said again, 'and I'm glad we've done this, though I don't suppose we'll repeat it because I quite understand it's not what you really want. Or I'm not.'

Alain, he thought. They'd agreed they would meet under the Arc de Triomphe and Alain had said that of course they would both come through. They would talk and laugh and drink, but that would be all. He would never share a bed with him as he did now with Priscilla. Hadn't Jérôme once said 'you're crying for the moon, my dear'?

'What do you mean, you'll have to? Don't you want to go home?'

'I don't know,' she said. 'I don't even know what home is now, or where it might be, but as to your first question . . . ' She picked up the photograph of the smiling man in the sports car, her racing driver. 'Some of my friends have done well out of the war and the Occupation. That's why we've been able to drink champagne, you and I, his champagne. But they're tainted, they're collaborators, and I suppose I count as a collaborator too, though all I've done has been merely finding ways to survive. Still, it's better I get out, back to England, I won't be very popular with the French, especially once they've decided they've almost all been in the Resistance, and have never so much as given the time of day to a German.'

*   *   *

Maurice was in the library of the house in the rue d'Aviau where he had spent so much of his childhood. He was trying to read Proust, but it was impossible. His attention strayed in the middle of a sentence. Vichy was finished, the Marshal had been taken away from the Hôtel du Parc. His own work with the Chantiers de Jeunesse likewise. Dominique had vanished on mysterious business for François or whatever he was calling himself this week. So his father had brought him back to Bordeaux, and he didn't know why. Old Marthe, the maid/housekeeper who had been his grandfather's mistress, had greeted him with a sniff which was almost a mark of affection. His uncle Jean-Christophe was sitting in what had been his father's chair drinking port, stupefying himself. Upstairs his aunt, Madame Thibault de Polmont, had taken to her bed declaring she was dying, though Marthe said all that was wrong with her was a bad cold and a foul temper. 'She's missing her German friends, the old fool,' Marthe said. Dominique had told him to be sure to call on his mother and tell her all was well with him. 'Make sure you call when Clothilde's at home,' he said.

*   *   *

It was beastly hot in the wagon which still smelled of cattle and their dung. Alain ached all over his body, though the fiery pain in his genitals had eased a bit. He'd held out as long as he could, screaming and then longing for death to deliver him from the pain. But he'd talked. Of course he'd talked. As the Boche officer said, 'Everyone does in the end. It's so stupid to make me do this to you.' Relief had flooded over him, then came tears, then shame, shame of betrayal, shame that he was less of a man than he had thought himself. Everyone talks – the words rang in his head like the same note being struck again and again and again till the end of time.

There were more than thirty of them, all sweaty and stinking and some of them spewing in this cattle truck which stank of shit. And no water. They couldn't look each other in the eye. A thin boy, who might have been no more than fifteen, began to pray, Hail Marys, over and over again. It got on your nerves. On and on he went till the man next to him, a burly bald-headed fellow in a cheap and filthy blue suit, got to his feet and kicked the boy sharply in the ribs. 'The bloody Virgin's not going to answer you, Holy Mother of God she ain't. So fucking well shut up.' The boy rolled over and lay on his face, his shoulders heaving.

Alain said, 'There was no call for that. The kid's terrified. It's his own mother he's crying for. There's no need to behave like the bloody Boches.'

The train juddered to a halt. Someone peered through a crack between the slats.

'Middle of fucking nowhere,' he said.

'Could be worse,' someone replied. 'We might have arrived wherever the hell they're taking us.'

'Hell – that's the right word for sure . . . '

Even the priests no longer preach about hell-fire, Alain thought. So the Nazis have made hell reality here on earth.

*　　*　　*

The tea was the colour of mahogany. Mrs Spinks spooned in three sugars, stirred, and handed Jérôme the mug.

'Nothing like a good cup of tea,' she said

'You shouldn't be giving me your sugar ration,' he said.

She smoothed her hands over her apron. A gold wedding-ring bit into an arthritic finger.

'Plenty more where that came from, Froggie, if you know where to get it. And my brother-in-law does, the old devil. You'll be off home soon I expect now that Jerry's on the run. That Foorer of theirs won't be half so cocky these days, will he? No more screaming about *Deutschland über alles*. I mind when one of them Blackshirts came here trying to sign up young Fred, my old man sent him off with a flea in the ear. No silly bugger with a Charlie Chaplin mouser's going to win a war, he said. Pity he isn't here to see he was right. I miss the old bastard, I really do. Young Fred will have told you his dad caught it when they bombed the docks in the first raids of the Blitz. I told him to stay put that day, having what they call a premonition, but would he listen? Not him, never. Now drink your tea and tell me about Gay Paree to cheer me up. And don't fret yourself about young Fred, he'll sail in some day, merry as can be, saying, "Told you I'd be fine, Ma, it's only the good die young." '

*   *   *

Michel, naked to the waist, lay on the grass, the sun hot on his back. Somewhere, not so distant now in the East, the battle was being fought, tanks massed against tanks, infantrymen like him crouching in fox-holes, their hands over their ears to block out as much as they could of the rocket fire. 'Stalin organs,' they called them, Baron Jean had told him; and told him too that at last it wouldn't be long till they were in action. 'They're even calling up grandfathers and kids of fourteen and fifteen,' he laughed. 'Michel, my friend, we've signed up for Armageddon. If our girls could see us now!'

*   *   *

'Tell me,' François said, 'your father is a policeman, yes? A superintendent in the PJ. Is he a man of the Right or the Left?'

'He calls himself an old Radical,' Dominique said.

'An old Radical? That means nothing now. It's a description that belongs to the Third Republic. Whatever Vichy's faults, and it's been a mess, a proper mess, even if we may all someday come to experience a tender nostalgia for the time of the Marshal because it has been the time of our adventurous youth, there's this to be said for the regime: it got rid of all that, of the absurd and corrupt republic of mates. In the new world of the after-war, things will be very different. I'm afraid your poor father's out of date. But you have done well, Dominique. I'm pleased with you. Attach yourself to me, be loyal, and there's a bright future ahead of you. And abandon this notion of becoming a priest. I've been an altar-boy myself, but the fact is that the Church has had its day. The problem now is how do we prevent the other Church, the Church of Moscow, from taking over. And I have to tell you that de Gaulle has no answer to that question. In my opinion, the *cocos* will run rings round him.'

IV

'Your wife will recognise you now, you look respectable again,' the barber said. 'I didn't recognise you myself when you came in, superintendent. With that beard you looked like one of these Resistance thugs come to demand money in return for their protection at the Liberation.'

'Is that what they do?'

'It's what they try to do.'

The barber picked up a towel to wipe his razor.

'When do you think the Boches will march out?' he said.

'I've no more idea than you have.'

'It can't be too soon. Not that what follows will be a picnic, not at all, in my opinion. There's too much water has flowed under the Pont de Pierre, and it's been stained with blood. My intention is to shut up shop, pull the shutters down, for as long as it takes for some sort of normality to be restored.'

'That might take some time.'

It might indeed, he thought. He had been surprised to see Edmond de Grimaud looking as spruce and debonair as ever. He played over the encounter in his mind.

'You all know each other,' Fabien said. 'So there's no call for introductions. Good. I don't have long. I've a train to catch. But explanations, that's another matter. De Grimaud here,' he turned to Lannes, 'has been a loyal and efficient minister. But that's over.'

Edmond smiled.

'As usual,' he said, 'our friend here comes straight to the point. You're in my debt, superintendent, you'll admit that. Now I'm calling it in.'

'I've been in the Milice's prison for three weeks,' Lannes said. 'I'm out of touch with events. So I've no idea what you want of me. If it's only assurance that I'm not going to pursue any investigation that might compromise you – such as that shooting outside the Hotel Splendide in 1940 – that's fine. I'd say we're quits. In any case I'm still officially suspended. So I don't know what purpose this meeting serves. As for you, Father, I certainly have information which compromises you, but it's none of my business and I'm not interested in your bedroom activities. Is that what you want to hear? What does puzzle me is why you're here. You're Labiche's man, aren't you?'

The priest, who had been chewing his fingernails, shook his head, but made no other reply.

Lannes turned to Fabien.

'Perhaps you can explain why these gentlemen are here.'

'You're being obtuse, superintendent. I'd thought better of you. I told you this meeting was all about our friend the advocate. We have a common interest in him. You say Father Paul here is Labiche's man. Correct, but what does that mean? As for Monsieur de Grimaud, he blocked Labiche when he was trying to destroy you, didn't he? That's not been forgotten, I assure you.'

De Grimaud smiled and fitted a cigarette into a long amber holder.

'Labiche collects information,' he said. 'Information is power, now more than ever. Father Paul here admits, Fabien says, that he has been one of his informants, certainly. But ask yourself why? As for me, I won't pretend to you that my own record is unblemished. Years ago we talked about the Spanish girl, Pilar, who was briefly my mistress and the wife of your friend Henri Chambolley. Then she returned to Spain, was arrested and shot by the Reds, her own side. She was betrayed of course, and had herself been playing a double game. But who betrayed her? Who found the means to lay information against her? Believe me, my friend, I would like to know the answer to that question. I rather liked her, you know. And Father Paul here, I dare say he has his own reasons to fear the advocate.'

The priest examined his fingernails, but remained silent.

'You're Madame d'Herblay's parish priest,' Lannes said. 'I was commissioned to find her granddaughter. Marie-Adelaide. I thought her father knew where she is, but it seems he doesn't? Finding her is my only immediate concern, at least till I'm officially reinstated. Do you know the answer?'

'I can't help you,' the priest said. 'I can't even help myself.'

* * *

A strange, inconclusive meeting, Lannes thought. Yet Fabien, hurrying for his train, had seemed satisfied. He had set things in motion, even if Lannes had little idea what they were. Nevertheless, it was clear that something was expected of him, and that all three of them had reason to fear Labiche who held damaging information on them, even on Fabien despite his air of self-assurance. There had been a moment as he left when, drawing Lannes aside, he said, 'The gun that killed Félix? I suppose you disposed of it? A pity. Not that obtaining a gun that's hard to trace is any sort of problem, is it?' Was he hinting that Lannes should rid them of the advocate? Ridiculous notion. And Edmond de Grimaud's remarks about Pilar. What did they signify? None of it made sense, and yet Lannes knew that something was expected of him. Why else had Fabien responded to Jean-Pierre d'Herblay's appeal when he had shrugged his shoulders ignoring Bracal's?

* * *

When he entered the apartment, it was a relief to find that Marguerite wasn't alone, but was sitting there with her mother. She looked up as he entered, said 'Jean' as if he had just returned from a normal day at the office, and added, 'You see, Maman is much better.'

He kissed her, again like a dutiful husband who comes home at the same time every evening, and she didn't quite turn her head away to avoid his kiss. He turned to Madame Panard and said he was happy to see her on the way to recovery.

'I wouldn't say I'm that,' she replied, 'far from it, I have to be very careful, but, by the mercy of God and the Holy Virgin, I'm still alive. You've been away yourself, Marguerite says, you should remember it's your duty to look after her, especially in the absence of our dear Dominique. I worry about the boy, you know, whether he takes care of himself and gets enough to eat. Not that any one of us can claim to get that, and Albert says it will be worse still if these hooligans of the Resistance take over. Thieves and scoundrels, he calls them.'

'Where's Clothilde?'

'That nice boy, Maurice, Dominique's friend, called and they've gone out for an ice-cream.'

'Has he word of Dominique?'

'Only that he is well, which is one worry less.'

'He should be at home,' Madame Panard said. 'A boy like that, heaven knows where in these troubled times. I'm not surprised that my heart started racing nineteen to the dozen. It's worry and anxiety sets it off, the doctors say.'

'Well, we're happy to see you out of the hospital and at home.'

It was almost as if he had never been where he was for these weeks.

V

He left early the following morning. Marguerite had said she was glad he was back safe, but little more. Perhaps she blamed him for her own brief arrest, with reason of course. They moved politely around each other, warily as if any word spoken would be the wrong word, and he knew she was pleased to have her mother there, as intermediary and excuse for saying nothing that mattered. Clothilde had received him ecstatically, leaping into his arms and hugging him, but when he asked Maurice about Dominique, the boy flushed, stammered and said he was well as far as he knew but the Chantiers de Jeunesse were finished, which was why his father had brought him back to Bordeaux. Then he left, saying he was sure they would want to be alone as a family.

It was a beautifully fresh morning and yet the streets were almost deserted. Everyone would be waiting to see how things turned out; only then could they know what it was safe to do or say. It was like the last weeks of the school year when all the work has been done, exams taken, and it's a question of how to get through empty and meaningless days before the release of the vacation. Only now the days weren't that; the truth, he sensed, was that there were too many meanings and they clashed with each other. Moreover, a pall of shame hung heavy as river mist over the city. There couldn't be anyone who didn't have cause for shame.

He turned into the rue Belle Étoile, to the house where poor Gaston had had his secret apartment where he taught his students and received his boyfriends, where he had also been so horribly tortured and killed. There had been an old lady, he remembered, in the apartment on the other side of the staircase who had heard nothing and spoke of him with admiration, first of all because her cat had taken to him. Gaston had entrusted her with a paper relating to his sister-in-law Pilar, a paper with the information his murderers had been seeking. He wondered if the old lady whose name he had forgotten was still alive; she had been fragile in 1940. No matter; it wasn't her he had come to see, though he thought he might look in on her later.

The concierge recognised him.

'If it's Mam'zelle Haget you've come to see again, you'll find her in, though she goes out more often than she used to. I'm pleased to say she's taken a grip on herself, fewer empty bottles since her friend moved in with her. I wasn't sure about that because the apartment was let to her as a single tenant, but as she said, it's wartime and things are difficult for so many people. Which I couldn't deny. In any case, you can see now that she is really a well-brought-up young lady, which I assure you wasn't apparent before, what with the bottles and that Boche officer calling on her. But that's all in the past, I've no complaints now, it's all respectable and we've really become quite good friends. So I hope she's not in trouble with you lot, that would really disappoint me, to think I'd got her wrong again.'

'No trouble. I'm only seeking information about something that may have happened a long time ago.'

'Very well then, it's the third floor left, as I expect you remember.'

But it was a plump blonde girl, not Catherine Haget, who opened the door to him. She was wearing only a dressing gown, tied round the middle but revealing her breasts. When he told her who he was and asked for Catherine, she gave him a cheeky smile, called out, 'Kiki, it's the police,' and turned away to lead him into the apartment. Her hips swayed as she walked.

The room was more fully furnished than when he had been there two years ago. There were soft coverings on the couch and the two mock-Directoire chairs, and several vases of flowers.

'Yes,' the girl said, 'when you're short of food it's nice to have flowers to smell,' and giggled. 'You really are a policeman? What has Kiki done? I'm sure she can't be in trouble and you've come to the wrong place, barking up the wrong tree, as they say. She's really sweet, you know.'

'I don't do much barking,' he said.

'Well, that's nice.'

Catherine came through from the bedroom. Like the other girl she too had pulled on only a dressing-gown. Her curly hair was tangled, she was rubbing sleep from her eyes, and smelled of bed. Without a word she flopped down on the couch and smiled.

'You look happy,' he said, surprising himself.

'Strange, isn't it? I was in such a state before, wasn't I.' She stretched out, took hold of the other girl's hand, squeezed it, and said, 'Make us some tea, will you, sweetie.'

'And leave you alone with the handsome policeman? Can I trust you? Can you trust him? All right, all right, dogsbody will do it.'

And, giving Lannes another ravishing smile, she left them, pretending to flounce out.

'Yes,' Catherine said, 'I'm happier than I've ever been. It's all thanks to Lucille. I fell over in the street, drunk. She picked me up, brought me home, put me to bed, joined me there and we just clicked. It hasn't worn off and it still feels to me like a fairy-story. I adore her, and when I'm in one of my down moods, she gives me a hug and a kiss and tells me not to be an ass, life's good. Sometimes I almost believe her. Give me a cigarette, would you please?'

Lannes produced the packet of Gauloises he had bought at the tabac on the corner, passed one to her, lit it and then one for himself.

'I'm sorry to disturb the idyll.'

'You're laughing at me.'

'Not at all. I'm delighted to see you happy, and sorry only that I'm going to ask you to turn your mind back to a time when you weren't.'

She looked away. Did her lips quiver, or was that only his imagination?

'Gabrielle?' she said, and it was little more than a whisper. 'But you found the man who murdered her, didn't you?'

'Oh yes, he's been dealt with.'

'I'm glad. She really was a bitch and I came to hate her, not only for the reasons you know, but also because I had once loved her to distraction. You understand?'

She drew deeply on her cigarette.

'All the same, nobody should die like that, so brutally and without any dignity.'

'Nobody,' he said, thinking of the countless brutal and undignified deaths and suffering all over France, all over Europe, thinking too of Gaston's murder, tied to a chair and tortured one floor down from this apartment occupied by these two delicious girls.

'It's not about Gabrielle,' he said, 'but I'm afraid it's going to be painful for you.'

'So can we wait till Luci comes back? To give me moral support. Anyway I'm dying for a cup of tea. That's good, isn't it, that it's tea I want, not that rough red vin ordinaire I used to swig. I scarcely drink any wine now, thanks to her. Remarkable, isn't it?'

Lucille returned carrying a tray with three cups and saucers on it.

'I don't know if policemen drink tea, but I made you a cup all the same. If, that is, you really are a policeman. Has he shown you his badge or whatever,' she finished by giggling again.

'He hasn't needed to. I know who he is.'

Lucille settled herself on the floor, leaning against Catherine's legs.

'Do you disapprove of us?' she said. 'I bet you do. Men always think it's a waste of girls like us, being as we are.'

'Not at all,' he said, as Catherine stubbed out her cigarette, took a sip of tea and began to stroke Lucille's blonde hair which lay abundantly on her shoulders.

'Not at all,' he said. 'Why should I?'

'Well, that's all right,' she said, 'because if you did disapprove, I'd happily show you the door, tell you to bugger off.'

She smiled again. A Renoir girl, Lannes thought. It didn't embarrass her at all that she was giving him a good view of her breasts. Perhaps indeed it amused her.

'I'm sorry but I have to ask Catherine painful questions,' he explained.

'It's about my sister, isn't it?'

'Yes, I'm afraid it is. Did she look like you?'

She shook her head.

'We had different fathers, she took after hers, a blond, a Belgian I think, though he didn't last long and I don't really remember him. Then our mother died and she was placed in the orphanage, and you know what happened. It's horrible.'

She began to cry. Lucille uncoiled herself and sat beside her on the couch cradling her in her arms.

'Is this necessary?'

'It is. Catherine, I know the man for whom Gabrielle procured your little sister. I've seen a photograph of him with a naked girl of about twelve. She was wearing a black mask over her eyes, but she had dark hair. So it was another girl, not your sister. That's the first thing cleared up. But now I need to find her. Urgently. Might you have any idea who she might have been?'

No answer, only sobs.

'I think she probably came from the orphanage too. You don't happen to have a photograph of your sister and the other girls?'

'What do you want it for?' Lucille said.

'To destroy the man who bought them.'

'Do you mean that?'

'Yes.'

'In that case . . . '

She untwined herself and got to her feet.

'It's all right, darling, I know where you keep that photograph. He has to have it. He may be a policeman but he's on the right side. I won't be a minute. Just leave her alone now, will you?'

Lannes lit a cigarette, got up and crossed to the window. The sun was high now, but the street below was deserted. A woman was hanging out washing on a metal frame attached to the window of the top-floor apartment opposite. Two small boys with cropped hair came running round the corner, passing a rugby ball to each other.

'Here . . . ' Lucille thrust the photograph into his hands. It was ragged at the edges and blurred in the middle but the half-dozen girls were clearly identifiable. There was one blonde, Catherine's sister. One of the others had dark curls cut short; that fitted his memory of the photograph of Labiche, but he would have to check.

'Do you know any of the other girls? This one for instance?'

She shook her head.

Lucille said, 'Stop it. She doesn't know and she doesn't want to know. Take this away with you and ask them at the orphanage. You probably won't get an answer. If the nuns suspected something nasty was going on, you certainly won't. But you can try and it's your best hope. Now leave us alone, please. You've upset Kiki, done enough harm for one day stirring up bad memories I've tried to get her to wipe out.'

She looks strawberries and cream, this girl, Lannes thought.

'You're quite tough, aren't you?' he said.

'I've had to be. As you'll have gathered I don't care for men and have good reason not to.'

'No exceptions?'

'Don't fish for compliments, Mr Policeman. But if you nail that bastard, I'll think well of you.'

'I will if I can. Now you look after Catherine.'

'I don't need you to tell me to do that.'

It was only when he was half an hour away from the house that he remembered he had intended to ask the concierge about the old lady with the cat. No matter; his fingers stroked the photograph in his pocket. It was good that Lucille had been there.

VI

Old Joseph, the office messenger and doorkeeper, greeted him with a handshake.

'What times we live in,' he said. 'Suspending you, I never heard the like of it. You'll be surprised to know that your boss is in, and that's a rare event, I don't mind telling you.'

The Alsatian was indeed there, leaning back in his chair with his feet on the desk, which was bare of papers or any evidence of work.

Lannes said, 'Judge Bracal told me that my suspension was about to be lifted. I haven't heard anything. So I thought I'd call in to ask you if you have.'

'Nothing, Jean. Not a word.' He didn't remove his feet and added, 'Not that anything matters now. After all, it was the Boches who insisted you should be stood down and there was nothing I could do about it. But they're not going to be about much longer, and then . . . who knows? So if you want to resume work, it's fine by me. Everything's in a state of confusion and I haven't seen Inspector Moncerre for more than a week. Not that it matters. Nobody's been murdering anybody, except as what they will call war-work. For the moment the PJ is utterly superfluous. What do you think the reckoning will be? For my part I'm happy that we have served France to the best of our ability in difficult times. I expect you agree with me.'

His voice was slurred and it occurred to Lannes that this was the first time he had seen the Alsatian drunk.

'Young René handed on the cigars,' Schnyder said. 'Thank you.'

'That's all right,' Lannes said, and left him for his own office.

But there was nothing for him to do there. Of course there wasn't. He was as idle as the Alsatian, every bit as much at a loose end. In limbo – the words came to him. In limbo and also confused – he wasn't even sure why he had come in. His presence had disturbed a butterfly which had been snoozing in the sunshine that lay on the corner of his desk. It fluttered against the window pane.

How long did butterflies live? He sighed. There was indeed no point in being here.

But it was no better outside. He wandered the streets aimlessly. It was as if his weeks in detention had sapped his will, and he was amazed to think that only a few hours ago, in Catherine's apartment in the rue Belle Etoile, he had felt full of energy and purpose. Now he was as empty as that wretched Aurélien or his broken sister. When he was young and the priests spoke of the Seven Deadly Sins he had never understood why Sloth was included among them. Surely his own reluctance to get out of bed on a cold morning wasn't a sin of any magnitude? Of course it had been explained to him that Sloth meant more than that: that its real meaning was *accidia*, a weariness of the world, of God's Creation, He had nodded obediently, scarcely interested. It wasn't a sin to which he supposed then that he would ever be drawn.

His wandering had taken him to the Place de la Cathédrale, and he saw Father Paul crossing the square. Their eyes met, each looked away, but then, to his surprise, the priest approached him.

'You don't think much of me, superintendent,' he said, 'and I can understand that. Nevertheless I should like to talk with you.'

They walked in silence for some minutes till they came to the Bar Météo to which Lannes had first been summoned by the spook who called himself Félix. It would do as well as anywhere. The patron greeted him with a nod in which he might have detected wariness – but who wasn't entitled to be wary? They took a table in the back corner of the bar which was in any case deserted, and Lannes ordered an Armagnac, the priest a bottle of Vichy water. Lannes lit a cigarette and waited. The priest took a gulp of water.

'You were surprised that I approached you. I was surprised myself, and then I thought, even if he despises me, we're on the same side now, on account of our conversation in the Café Régent.'

'Why should you think I despise you?'

'Because you're entitled to.'

'You think so?'

'Naturally. Since I despise myself, I can't look for respect from you. I'm not a bad man, at least I don't believe I am, only a bad because inadequate priest. I took the cloth because I believed doing so would enable me to resist temptation, even to banish it from my thoughts. But of course it didn't, quite the reverse indeed. The more I suppressed my desires the more fiercely they burned until it seemed that they were consuming me. I came to know that there is no difference, no essential difference between sinning in your imagination and in the flesh. And so I yielded, and you who may never have felt the urgency of such desires presume to judge me.'

Lannes said, 'I don't judge you. It's not my job and I'm content to leave you to your own conscience. We have all done things since 1940 of which we should be ashamed. That's undeniable, before too as likely as not. Certainly there will be many who will soon assume the right to judge others, if only to escape judgement themselves. It doesn't greatly interest me. My concern is with the girl Marie-Adelaide, and with what Labiche has done with her. That's all that interests me. Her grandmother – your parishioner, Father – commissioned me to find her. If you can help me, fine. If you can't, I see no point in this conversation. Are you Labiche's confessor by the way?'

'If I was there's nothing I could tell you. You must know that, superintendent. But since I'm not, and not in his confidence, then there's nothing I know. But ask yourself this: is there any reason to suppose the girl wants to be found? From what I have gathered, she has not been subject to any coercion. But, please answer my question: what did the boy Karim tell you about me?'

Lannes lit a cigarette from the stub of his first one.

'Why should we have spoken about you? What do you think he might have said? You handed him over to Labiche, didn't you?'

'Please.'

'As you like. It was quite simple. He didn't care for whatever it was you did or wanted him to do. I didn't ask him what that was.'

'I spoke to him of sin and the need for sin to be punished, my sin and his sin. The Devil has to be whipped out. Surely you can see that? I'm not a bad man, you know, only a bad because inadequate priest. And then he has such beautiful eyes. You must have remarked them, superintendent, because, whatever you say . . . I won't say more except that he spoke of you as his policeman friend in a manner which suggested it was more than friendship.'

'And that's what you told Labiche?'

The priest took another sip of his mineral water.

'Yes,' he said. 'Perhaps, superintendent, you have never been subjected to blackmail. I've no reason to suppose you have. Well, let me say this. Eventually you tell your blackmailer, who is also your torturer, whatever you think he wants to hear. I've thought long about these matters. I've been compelled to do so. And this is the conclusion I've come to: that a bond is formed between the tortured and the torturer, and in the end, what the tortured man comes to feel is something like love. Because the torturer knows the worst of him. Isn't this how we approach God, how we come to love Him? Because there is nothing hidden from Him, nothing that can be hidden?'

'I'm not interested in that,' Lannes said. 'Metaphysics are beyond me.'

'Really? Why do you think I guided you to this bar? Because it was where my brother used to come when he was in Bordeaux, my brother whom you knew as Félix, and for whose death I believe you were responsible.'

The priest's voice trembled as he spoke and in his agitation he knocked over his glass.

Lannes said, 'It's hard to know where responsibility for a death lies. I might say you were responsible for that one yourself, since I take it that you directed your brother to the boy Karim when he was in search of an instrument. I know what he did to Karim and to another boy before him, a young Jew, and the consequence of that was that a man – a German officer certainly, but a good enough fellow with some sense of decency and of honour – shot himself. No doubt your brother believed he was acting in the interests of France. Did he bring his death on himself? Were you responsible, Father? Karim didn't kill him by the way. Nor did I. Your brother, Félix or whatever his name was, was mired in death. Perhaps you loved him, I don't know. But I tell you this: even those he worked for, even our friend Fabien who belongs to the same organisation as he did, found his death convenient. He had become an embarrassment, you see. As for Karim, he'll have troubles enough, I'm afraid, in the months ahead. But leave him alone. You've done him enough harm, more than enough. And if you want to make amends, help me bring down Labiche.'

VII

Clothilde sat on the couch with Alain's cat, No Neck, on her knee. She scratched him behind his ear, making him purr happily. She stroked him and wished it was Michel's hair she was stroking.

'Poor No Neck,' she whispered, 'will you recognise Alain when he comes back. If he comes. Three years, it's a long time for a cat.'

She had kissed Michel on this couch and said 'no' when he sought to go further – 'no, please' – and he had obeyed and now she wished he hadn't. He was her first true love and perhaps they never would. The news of the failed attempt to assassinate Hitler meant that there would be no early peace, no armistice, and Germany would fight to the last man, even the last Frenchman. She remembered the day he left, kissing her tears away, as he promised he loved her and said that he couldn't love her, couldn't be worthy of her love, would be ashamed if he didn't engage in the struggle against Bolshevism. She couldn't recall what she had said herself. Perhaps she had said nothing, only wept. And did she believe him? She had to, but really she didn't know. He chose war, not me; it was a thought she couldn't rid herself of, no matter how she tried to silence the doubting voice.

The doorbell rang. No Neck jumped off her lap.

'Maurice.'

'You don't mind that I come to see you?'

'Of course not. You're Dominique's best friend.'

'Only that?'

'Don't be silly. You're my friend too. Of course you are. And I'm glad to see you. I've been feeling low. No Neck likewise, we're both pining.'

*   *   *

Léon wasn't sure he should have come. In fact, he was sure he should have said no. A party – a last party? – at the offices of the

German Cultural Mission to France, no, he shouldn't be there. But Chardy had been insistent. 'It's an occasion,' he said, 'a historic occasion. The Paris wake of the Third Reich, the Thousand Year Reich that has been here in Paris for only a little more than a Thousand Days. It will be something to write about. And you know, my dear, it's been a remarkable relationship, the best of Germany and the best of France. As Robert said to me the other day, 'Whatever anyone denies, the truth is we've all slept with Germany for four years and for the most part we've enjoyed it. It's enriched our life.' And he's right, of course. I could never have written *La Maison d'un Reveur* otherwise, and it's not only my best book, but the only one published in Paris since 1939 which tells the bitter-sweet truth about our times.'

So there they were, and a German private soldier, acting as a waiter, was inviting Léon to take a glass of champagne from the tray he was carrying. Good champagne. That was one thing Chardy had taught him; how to tell good wine from bad.

And Heller, the German cultural chief, was indeed charming. He had said how pleased he was to see him – of course he didn't know who he was or that he was Jewish. But perhaps he wouldn't have cared. He was a civilised man after all, as Chardy had insisted. And now he was talking and laughing with Robert Brasillach, the most violent of anti-Semites, who wrote disgusting stuff in *Je Suis Partout*, but whom Léon had met several times with Chardy and found gentle and friendly in conversation, likeable and sympathetic indeed. He had even suggested Léon write something for his rag. 'We don't have enough contributors of the younger generation, and Chardy has told me you are very intelligent. I'm sure you could give me something good.' And the terrible thing was, he had been flattered.

Now he stood with his back to the wall, surveying the scene, listening to the buzz of talk around him. They were all people dancing on the thinnest of ice. Even though such news as he had was slanted, there could be no doubt that the Allies would be in Paris in weeks, if not days, and yet Heller's guests, most of whom had engaged in whole-hearted collaboration, were still capable of laughter. He recognised many of them, friends, or at least acquaintances, of Chardy's, and he had eaten at the same restaurant tables with several.

Then he became aware that a man on the other side of the room was staring at him: a stocky figure with his light-brown hair cut *en brosse*. The steady gaze unnerved him. For a moment he couldn't think why. But then it came to him: La Chope aux Capucines in the Cours du Marne, eating there with Gaston with whom he had spent the evening and who had an hour to wait before his train back to Bergerac; how Gaston had become agitated, even fearful, disturbed by this man at a table on the other side of the room. He had insisted they change places so that he was no longer facing the man who was wearing a heavy overcoat even though it was hot in the café on account of the stove for which there was still fuel in the days of the phoney war. Gaston had asked him more than once if the man was looking at him, and it was clear that he would rather miss his train than risk showing himself to him as he got up to leave. But in fact the man and his companion had left first, and when Léon described the man to Alain's father, and said that Gaston had seemed frightened by his appearance there and had fobbed off his questions saying he had had an embarrassing encounter with him some years ago, that was all, which he didn't believe, the superintendent had told him to be careful, not to approach the man if he saw him again, because – Léon remembered his exact words – 'I rather think you are one of the few people who can identify your friend's killer.'

And now the man was here, in Paris, staring as if the sight of him had stirred his memory too.

*   *   *

When the explosion threw the train off the rails, crashing down an embankment, and the rotting wood of the wagon splintered and it broke up, Alain had found himself tumbling down the slope until his fall was checked by the undergrowth on the fringes of the forest. A moment later, another body had landed on top of him, and when they shook themselves free of each other, he found that it was the young boy who had been muttering Hail Marys in his fear and who was indeed starting to do so again. Alain told him to be quiet, and, to make sure, placed his hand over the boy's mouth. Then, after listening hard and hearing only shouts of confusion and a couple of shots, followed by a silence broken only by the whispers of the wind in the trees, he took the boy by the hand, and telling him to make as little noise as possible, led him into the forest.

That had been three weeks ago now. They had lain hidden for a day and a night by which time the boy who said he was called Vincent and was indeed only fifteen had begun to recover his nerve. By sheer chance they had stumbled on the group of the Maquis who had effected the derailment, and so they enlisted with them. They were Communists and when one of them said that after the Liberation the first problem would be how to get rid of de Gaulle, Alain forced himself to smile and made no other reply. Vincent said, proudly, that his father was a Communist and it had been in trying to carry a message from him that he had been arrested. Nevertheless Alain knew that they were both viewed with some suspicion, which is why he kept the boy by his side.

Now he was lying watching the movement of a German contingent retreating North.

'Shouldn't we fire on them?'

'They're going fast enough,' the man who called himself Colonel Fermier said. 'We'll conserve our ammunition for the real enemy.'

*   *   *

Jérôme to his dismay found that he had become superfluous. The broadcasts from the Free French station were now full of instructions, no longer of exhortation. And his voice wasn't deemed right for them. It lacked authority. Whatever qualities he had – one of his superiors had called his tone 'lyrical' – weren't needed now. He had encouraged the youth of France to hope, in talks which he had often been allowed to write himself, though they were of course subject to editing. But now hope had been overtaken by reality. The Germans were retreating, even if by all reports fighting their losing battles grimly, and soon Paris itself would be liberated. Plans were being made for de Gaulle to be there as soon as it was possible in order to set up the Provisional Government and prevent, as everyone in London knew, the Communists from taking over. The question was how quickly the internal Resistance could either be disbanded or incorporated into the regular army and subjected to military discipline. There was much excited argument about this, but it all left Jérôme feeling like a wallflower at the dance. Freddie had been home on a short leave, with stories about the horrors of the Normandy landings, which in his telling weren't horrors at all – though the look in his eyes contradicted the words he spoke. His mother gave a party to welcome her boy safely back. Jérôme spent the night there with him in his bed, and when Freddie left the next morning to go back to his ship, his mother said, 'He didn't tell me the half of it, Froggie, you'd think it was water off a duck's back to listen to him, and I don't suppose he told you either what it was really like.' 'No, he didn't,' Jérôme said, thinking it better not to say how he had woken to find Freddie sitting upright in the bed moaning and shivering. So, instead he just reminded Mrs Spinks that Freddie and he were still planning a time in Paris when it was all over. 'Gay Paree,' she said, 'the pair of you. The larks you'll get up to, I shouldn't wonder, not fit for a mother's ear.'

But now he was at a loose end, spending hours in the Soho pubs, usually alone even when engaged as he often was in conversation. So when Sir Edwin Pringle invited him to his place in the country for the weekend, he was happy to accept.

*   *   *

François said, 'You know, Dominique, despite everything the Marshal is a great man. That's something that those of us who were in Vichy shouldn't forget. Without him – and indeed without Laval – things would have gone much worse for the French. Of course it's going to be impossible for years to say this publicly. He's going to be humiliated – they're both going to be humiliated – and it wouldn't be a surprise if they were put on trial and even sentenced to death. The French have a passion for revenge and in making the Marshal a scapegoat, they'll excuse themselves for their collaboration and will be able to pretend that they were always engaged in resistance. It will be a necessary lie – that's one point on which I agree with de Gaulle. But those of us who experienced the sweetness of Vichy shouldn't reject the memory, even though it will be wise to say nothing about it. You enjoyed your work with the Chantiers, didn't you?'

'Yes,' Dominique said. 'We loved it, and so did many of the boys in our charge.'

'Who will, many of them, now be flocking to the Resistance – except for those misguided enough to sign up for the Milice. What a mess it all is, what a glorious mess! And how much repair work there will soon be to be done.'

*   *   *

'If this thing will stop a tank, I'm a Dutchman,' Corporal Jean said. 'Remember when they told us the German tanks were made of cardboard. No you're too young, but we soon found they weren't in 1940 when, I don't mind admitting to you, my son, I ran as fast as anyone. But when we go into action this time, there'll be nowhere to run to.'

'You think we're really going to be in real action again soon?'

'I know we are, with the Ivans in front of us and the Gestapo behind. What are you smiling about, young Michel?'

'It's just that I'm happy.'

'Or mad. If your girl that you're keeping yourself for, most nights anyway, could see you now . . . '

'Yes,' Michel said. 'But I was also thinking of Count Pierre, the old White Russian who taught me to box, and how he used to speak about Holy Russia.'

'Holy Russia be damned. There's nothing holy about the Ivans, my son. Unholy devils, that's what they are, and don't you forget it.'

VIII

The Mother Superior was tall, thin, with a beaky nose and beautiful hands. She had kept him waiting in a barely furnished room that was chill as a cellar even though the sun was shining brightly in the city, and now she sat with her hands folded in her lap, and said, 'I cannot believe I can be of any assistance to you.'

Lannes apologised again for intruding on her. He hesitated, unsure how to begin. He had never felt easy with nuns, couldn't forget that his father, the free-thinking Radical, had credited them with what even as a boy Lannes could see were improbable powers. All the same his father had had a point. People who shut themselves up in convents or monasteries saw the world in a different way. That was true of priests also, even that wretched Father Paul. He took out the photograph Lucille had given him and handed it to the Mother Superior.

'It's some years ago I know,' he said, 'but I'm interested in tracing this girl.'

He put his finger on the one who resembled the little girl in that other dreadful photograph sitting naked alongside Labiche.

The nun looked at it, briefly, without evident interest.

'You must understand, monsieur, all these girls, they came from unfortunate homes, dreadful backgrounds, many the products of sin. Some of them stayed with us for years, till they were almost grown-up indeed. Others were with us for only a short time, till perhaps their family situation had resolved itself. We cared for them to the best of our poor ability, but, though it is a terrible thing to say, a few were beyond help. They were already corrupt. You find that horrifying perhaps? That I should speak of young girls as corrupt? And yet you shouldn't, superintendent. As a policeman you must know that there are some for whom nothing can be done. No doubt you would express it differently, but there are those who refuse God's Grace.'

'And this girl, was she one of those.'

'Why are you looking for her, superintendent?'

'As a witness. To help with our inquiries. Nothing more. As it happens, I don't even know her name. Doubtless you have records?'

'Oh records, certainly, but I doubt if they will help you. She was called Amélie, Amélie Hire. Her mother was a fallen woman, a prostitute. She disappeared and the child was brought to us. We were pleased to receive her as an act of charity which is of course our work. She seemed a bright pretty child, I thought we might make something of her. But, as I say, she was already corrupt, and then she absconded.'

'Is that easy, to run away?'

'Our girls are not prisoners.'

'Did you report her disappearance?'

'Naturally. But she was fifteen. Your colleagues in the police weren't interested. They shrugged their shoulders. So you see why I say we can be of no help. Your colleagues in that branch of the police which concerns itself with morality, or rather acts of immorality, are more likely to have information about her. We live in a sinful world, superintendent.'

She spoke with self-assurance, but also, it seemed, indifference.

'If a person refuses God's Grace . . . ' she said and held up her long-fingered hands towards, he supposed, her idea of heaven.

'So you have no idea where she might be, what may have become of her?'

'It's impossible that I should have. We live withdrawn from the world.'

'And yet,' Lannes said, 'didn't some priest say that no man is an island? There's another girl in that photograph, the one with fair hair. I believe she hanged herself while she was in your care.'

The Mother Superior glanced again at the photograph and then laid it on the table between them. Neither spoke. The door opened and a young nun entered with a tray on which there was a carafe of yellowish wine, two very small glasses and a plate of biscuits. She poured the wine, set a glass before each of them and, passing the plate to Lannes, said, 'The biscuits are of our own baking.' It was sweet wine which Lannes disliked. He replaced his glass.

'You can't have forgotten.'

The Mother Superior made no reply, but sipped her wine.

At last she said, 'It is inexpressibly painful to discover that a child in our charge is guilty of a mortal sin.'

'What do you mean?'

'Life is a sacred trust, superintendent. To take your life is to deny God. I pray for that poor child's soul every day.'

'And you have nothing to reproach yourself with? A failure of care, perhaps?'

'You have no right to presume so. We cared for the poor child devotedly, as for all those entrusted to us, but the Devil entered into her, and she surrendered to him. Do you know the greatest of his temptations? It is not, as some believe, wealth or power; it is despair. That is the ultimate sin, and the poor child was guilty of it.'

Something in what she said hit home. Lannes had never sought wealth and distrusted rather than envying the rich. He was wary of power as he believed any good policeman should be, for he had known some corrupted by it. But he knew the temptation of despair. The difference was that he didn't believe in any Devil. The temptation for him was innate, temperamental. But for the 'poor child', Kiki's sister, it was self-disgust, horror at the abuse inflicted on her, that drove her to put a noose round her neck. He was sure of that. It was madness to think that the Devil entered into it, even if you thought of what had been done to her as devilish. It was doubtless futile to argue the question here. Nevertheless, he said, 'As a policeman I deal with crime, not sin, which isn't indeed a word in our vocabulary. The poor child you speak of was the victim of a crime, abused by an adult man. And I suspect that the girl I am seeking – the girl of whom you say you know nothing – was another victim of the same crime, committed in both cases while they were in the care of this orphanage.'

'That is a terrible allegation. It is slander. I think I must ask you to leave, superintendent.'

Lannes looked the Mother Superior in the eye. Her gaze was steady, unwavering.

'Unpleasant facts may often seem slanderous,' he said. 'Truth is unwelcome. I understand that you live out of the world, Mother, but the world may invade even the most closed of convents. Seclusion can't shut out the law, and isn't entitled to do so. Moreover the police don't leave merely because they are asked to do so.' He took the other photograph, of the advocate Labiche sitting with the little girl naked but for the mask concealing her face, and said, 'This is the girl you say "absconded", the girl I am searching for. Do you recognise the man?'

The photograph fell from her long shapely fingers and fluttered to the floor.

'Yes?' Lannes said.

'There must be some mistake.'

'There's no mistake.'

'There must be.'

'You recognise him?'

'It looks like the advocate, Monsieur Labiche, which is why I say there must be some mistake, or deception. As you say we live out of the world, but I believe it is possible to do remarkable things with photography, perhaps to superimpose one face on another or to splice two unrelated photographs together. Monsieur Labiche is one of our benefactors, I know him for a man of deep religious feeling, scrupulous in his observances. Which is why I cannot believe what you have shown me and why I say there is deception and trickery here.'

'It is indeed the advocate,' Lannes said, 'and the photograph does not lie. Monsieur Labiche is a hypocrite and a pervert. Now will you help me find the girl?'

'It is impossible,' she said.

Her voice was firm but her hands were trembling.

'It is evidence,' Lannes said.

'I cannot believe it. I will not believe it. Monsieur Labiche is a distinguished citizen, a patriotic Frenchmen and a devout Christian. This is some plot, a conspiracy, concocted by the enemies of the Church, the Jews or the Communists I suppose.'

'It is no plot, no conspiracy, the Jews have been deported by order of the Germans and with the collaboration of the agency of which Monsieur Labiche is the head here in Bordeaux; and I am not a Communist.'

'Then perhaps it is you who are deceived. Yes, that is quite probable. I assure you, superintendent, I know Monsieur Labiche to be a man of honour.'

'And I know him, Mother, to be a scoundrel, and I intend to destroy him.'

IX

It had been easy to say that, satisfying also to think that his words might have pricked her self-assurance, but he had achieved nothing. He heard the door of the convent close behind him with a note of finality which suggested he would be refused admission if he ever called there again without a warrant; and there was no reason to ask for one. It was probable that the Mother Superior had been telling the truth; that she did indeed know nothing about the girl in the photographs beyond what she had said. The girl had gone out into the world, years ago; and who could guess what had become of her? It was probable that she had left Bordeaux – he could imagine her eager to do so, to shake, as the saying went, the city's dust from her feet. Why wouldn't she have done so? What could there have been to keep her there in the place where she had been so monstrously abused? But, without her testimony he had no case against Labiche. As the advocate himself had said when shown that first photograph, it was evidence of nothing. The Mother Superior had been right in saying that photographs could be falsified. And even if this wasn't the case and it was proved genuine as he had no doubt it was, no examining magistrate, not even one as well disposed as Bracal, would order the arrest of a distinguished citizen on such flimsy evidence. Not in ordinary times anyway, but then the times today weren't that. Even so he hesitated to approach Bracal, who would surely hesitate to commit himself.

He had allies of course. The spook Fabien, for whatever undivulged reason he might have, had directed him against Labiche – but given no hint as to how he should proceed. And Fabien too might soon find himself in trouble, an object of suspicion to whatever regime succeeded Vichy, while the same was true of Edmond de Grimaud and that wretched priest.

Moreover time was short. If d'Herblay – Captain Fracasse, ridiculous *nom de guerre* – was to be believed, Labiche was already preparing to head for Spain. It was quite likely; he was no fool, could read the writing on the wall, must know that Vichy was finished and that his own role in the deportation of the Jews would at the very least compromise him; he was after all an arch-collaborator. The moment the Boches moved out, he was finished, no matter how many fellow Cagoulards might be willing to offer him protection. And once beyond the Pyrenees he would again be untouchable. No doubt fat-arsed Franco would offer him sanctuary.

Lannes banged his stick against a lamp-post. It wasn't, he recognised, only a zeal for justice that drove him on. He was engaged in a personal vendetta. Labiche had tried to destroy him with his malicious accusations. He might have destroyed what was left of his marriage; it was unlikely that Marguerite would ever trust him again, for he sensed that she didn't believe him when he denied having had an affair with Yvette. He couldn't blame her for that. He had indeed destroyed her trust when he omitted to tell her of Alain's plans, and she had said, roundly and more than once, that for this reason she could never trust him again. Moreover, wasn't it likely that there had been something in his voice when he spoke of Yvette that had betrayed him? He had committed adultery so often in his imagination that he might as well, he thought now as before, have yielded to temptation, acted on his desire for the girl. If he went to her now in the Pension Bernadotte, wouldn't he say 'yes' and eagerly accept what she so willingly offered? Perhaps he was going mad. But at least his steps weren't leading him to Mériadeck . . .

Labiche? There were two possible courses of action.

The shutters of the house in the rue d'Aviau were closed; there would be many, especially perhaps in the city's 'upper crust', who would be anxious and eager to shut the world out now. He pulled the bell-rope and lifted the door-knocker and banged it hard, remembering how he had been kept waiting there on his first visit more than four years ago when it was still the *drôle de guerre*, the phoney war which so many of the French – and not only those on the Right – hoped would never come to action but would be resolved by men of good sense. Who wanted, as the question had been, to die for Danzig, or to defend the integrity of Poland? So many deaths since; so many, he feared, still to come. The old count, who had requested the visit of a senior policeman on a confidential matter, was one of the dead, murdered, Lannes believed, by his illegitimate son, the Fascist and criminal Sigi. How long ago it seemed! The Count had been a wicked old man. Lannes had rather liked him. He banged the knocker again, and waited, the sun hot and high in a cloudless sky.

At last he heard bolts being withdrawn and old Marthe stood before him.

'So it's you again,' she said, 'like the bad penny.'

'How are you, Marthe?'

'How should I be? Is it the Count you want to see, or Monsieur Edmond? You'll get no sense from the one and no truth from the other.'

'I've come to speak with the Count, but I'll happily see Monsieur Edmond too.'

She sniffed loudly and turned away, moving slowly on account of her arthritis, and showed him into the salon.

'It's that policeman again,' she said. 'Tell him whatever he wants to know, and don't be daft. Then he'll maybe stop disturbing the house.'

Jean-Christophe, the present Comte de Grimaud, was sitting where Lannes had last seen him, in his father's chair, with the canaries flitting about in the cage which stood on a pedestal behind it. He wore a silk dressing-gown over an unbuttoned shirt, and, though the room was cool, even chilly, behind the closed shutters, sweat stood out on his forehead. There was a decanter of wine on the occasional table to the right of the chair, as there had been every time Lannes had seen him sitting there, and he was holding a glass which he emptied and then refilled, knocking the decanter against the rim and spilling a little, as soon as he recognised the superintendent.

'I've done nothing. You've no reason to be here,' he said.

Lannes sat down and lit a cigarette.

'I don't suppose you've done anything,' he said, 'nothing, that is, that might concern me. You've got a record of course, of interfering – to put it mildly – with little girls. We've talked about that before, when the woman who used to procure them for you was murdered, and you assured me then that all that was behind you. I believed what you said, and I still do. So you have no cause to be alarmed.'

Jean-Christophe mopped his brow with a handkerchief which he then replaced inside the sleeve of his dressing-gown.

'You despise me,' he said. 'I know that, so it's natural that I should be disturbed to see you.'

'Despise you?' Lannes said. 'People are always telling me I despise them, and they're always wrong. I deplore, even detest, what you have done in the past, that's true, but to my mind you are weak, not wicked, which is why you can't live with yourself without the support of alcohol, and why I feel sympathy for you, and not contempt. However . . . '

He took the photograph of Labiche and the naked girl from his pocket and handed it to the Count.

'I showed you this photograph two years ago and you told me you knew nothing of the girl.'

'And I didn't, I don't.'

'But you know the man of course. The advocate Labiche was your lawyer, he defended you, and perhaps you are grateful to him. But you are also afraid of him, aren't you? And that's natural enough. A lot of people are afraid of Labiche, and with good reason. He collects information, he's a blackmailer, though it's power, power over others, that he desires, cherishes indeed, rather than money, isn't it? I can guess the hold he has over you, but what I've come to say is that Labiche is on the way out. His time's up. He's backed the losing side and is preparing to escape, to flee France and get to Spain. I want to stop him. So, again, I ask: do you recognise the little girl?'

Jean-Christophe glanced at the photograph and looked quickly away. He handed it back to Lannes and poured himself another glass of wine.

'I know nothing,' he said. 'I've never seen the girl or, if I have, which I won't say is impossible, I don't recognise her and certainly couldn't put a name to her. It was all years ago. In any case it would be better if Labiche gets to Spain and has to live with himself there. That's my opinion.'

'It's not mine,' Lannes said. 'I want him to have to live with himself in prison, with other men who have no time for someone with his proclivities which are, after all, yours too . . . '

'I can't help you.'

'Can't or won't?'

'Can't . . . won't . . . what does it matter?'

The door opened. Edmond de Grimaud entered.

159

'Marthe told me you were here. Bullying my poor brother, super-intendent? You won't get anything from him. But we should talk. So leave him alone and come with me.'

He turned away and led Lannes to the little salon with the case of stuffed birds where they had talked several times before.

'This is the only room in the house,' Edmond said, 'where I feel comfortable and at ease. I think of it as my den, even my sanctuary.'

'And you are in need of a sanctuary?'

'Aren't we all? Aren't we all, Jean? You don't mind that I call you Jean now. We have – haven't we – much in common.'

'Do we?'

'Oh yes, undoubtedly.'

'If you are referring to your half-brother Sigi's suggestion that I too am one of your father's bastards, let me say it means nothing to me.'

'But it should, Jean, it should. Blood, as they say, is thicker than water.'

'That didn't count for much when you arranged to have me shot outside the Hotel Splendide. Even if I am what you say I am.'

'Yes,' Edmond said. 'Like the shooting of the Duc d'Enghien, that was worse than a crime, it was a blunder. You remember Talleyrand's judgement? Or was it Fouché's? I was, quite soon, very glad you survived. Now sit down, please, and have a cigar. We have much to talk about.'

'I prefer cigarettes.'

Edmond clipped the end off a Havana and rotated the other end in the flame of a match, before putting the cigar in his mouth and drawing on it.

'And besides,' he said, 'our sons have become great friends, "bosom pals", as the English say. It has pleased me greatly, helped Maurice to grow up. And their work was much praised in Vichy, which may not, I fear, stand to their credit now. Of course I'm in the same position myself as you are well aware. You were surprised, weren't you, when Monsieur Fabien, as he chooses to call himself, brought me to see you, in the company of that deplorable priest.'

'Surprised?' Lannes said. 'I don't know. Curious certainly. But then I know very little about him. It has occurred to me that he may be an old friend of yours.'

'Friend is putting it too strongly, but we have done business together.'

'In Vichy, I assume.'

'In Vichy, and before Vichy. Why do you suppose he directed your attention to the advocate Labiche.'

'There was no need to do so. He was already in my sights.'

'Good, good.'

Edmond got up, crossed the room, opened the door, then shut it again.

'Fabien and Labiche,' he said. 'They're two of a kind, you know.'

'What do you mean by that?'

'Two of a kind and now they've fallen out. I don't know why, and when I don't know something like that, I feel a shiver on the back of my neck. Why did you come to question my wretched brother?'

'Police business.'

Lannes thought: we're like fencers, each looking for an opening, hesitating to lunge, wary of the riposte if our stroke is parried. Well, to change the metaphor, why not put a card on the table?

'My business is crime,' he said, and passed the photograph of the advocate with the little girl to Edmond. 'I hoped the count might identify the girl.'

'And of course he didn't?'

'Of course he didn't. Whether he could have is another matter.'

Edmond took a bottle of Armagnac from a cupboard, poured two glasses and passed one to Lannes.

'Crime, as you say, is your business. I understand that, but hasn't it occurred to you, Jean, that just at present, the sort of crime this photograph represents is – how shall I put it? – irrelevant, pre-war? We are engaged, caught up in, something much bigger and more dangerous. I repeat my question: why do you suppose Fabien directed your attention to Labiche? Not on account of his doings with little girls, however sordid, disgusting, criminal such behaviour may be. Fabien would care nothing about these matters. You can be sure of that. You hope, I assume, that if you can find this girl and she is willing to testify against the advocate, you can take your case to an examining magistrate – you may even have a sympathetic one in mind – and obtain a warrant for Labiche's arrest. Well, it's a long shot, I would say, and I am by no means certain it is what our friend Fabien would wish. It's politics and political manoeuvring that concern him. You may have heard of the Liste Cortin?'

'Yes,' Lannes said. 'I've heard of it . . . the list of members of the Cagoule discovered by the Sûreté in Paris, or handed over to them, wasn't it?'

'Just so. But what is less generally known is that the Liste Cortin was incomplete, and not only because it was restricted to members based in Paris and the Ile-de-France. There were other lists, nobody doubts that, one of members here in Bordeaux and the Gironde and parts of the Midi. Or so it's said.'

And are you on it, Lannes thought.

'Such a list would mean trouble for a good many people, including some close to de Gaulle perhaps, certainly some who hope to play a role in whatever regime emerges from the Liberation. And of course others too. It's my belief that Fabien thinks Labiche has it.'

'And Fabien wants it?'

'Undoubtedly.'

'And hopes that I can find it for him?'

'It seems likely. That list represents power. Better, don't you think that a friend has it rather than Labiche?'

'If he is indeed a friend.'

'That, Jean – my brother whether you like it or not – is something we have to take on trust. Not a word I often employ, but, with things as they are, you have to put your stake on red or black, odd or even.'

'It's an interesting suggestion,' Lannes said. 'This is very good Armagnac.'

'I'm pleased that you approve of it. One other thing, Jean: Labiche is a clever man, and can read the weather as well as anyone. No doubt he has, as you say, made arrangements to seek a refuge in Spain. But only as a last resort. He's the kind of man, I suspect, who will always back a horse each way. So I would be surprised if he hadn't built bridges with the Resistance too. If you have any friends there, that's something else you might look into.'

X

Friends in the Resistance? Lannes sat smoking on a bench in the Public Garden, the very one where he had sat with Schuerle, the German liaison officer who had so improbably become his friend, and who was now, he feared, dead or in prison as one of the conspirators who had failed to kill Hitler. They had talked, he remembered, of the roots of evil, of the moment in a life when beliefs, emotions, desires become pathological. Is anyone born a criminal, born evil, Schuerle had wondered. Even Hitler was once a little boy, perhaps cherished by his mother, and – he had laughed – there's no evidence he was the kind of small boy who tears the wings off flies or tortures animals; indeed even now he's devoted to his dog. And likewise Lannes had no reason to believe that Labiche had been born malignant. Perhaps he didn't even hate the Jews, and his anti-Semitism was adopted to further his career. If so, then Edmond's suggestion that Labiche might already have forged links with some elements of the Resistance made sense. There would be many who were changing sides or seeking the means to do so, many also who would have seen the wisdom of backing, to use Edmond's illustration, both red and black, odd and even. And wouldn't there be those who would judge that as a policeman he was himself a faithful servant of the regime, doing his duty as Vichy commanded?

The sun beat down but the garden was almost deserted. It was a summer which nobody yet dared to enjoy. He closed his eyes, and thought, I'm so tired of it all, so tired of dishonesty, hatred and death. Clothilde pined for Michel who, if he ever returned which was unlikely, would not be the boy who marched with such blithe and gay stupidity to war, a boy with a radiant smile who had chosen the dark side. And if Alain came back to them, wouldn't he too have learned what a boy of his age shouldn't know? There was a chatter of bird song. Not fifty metres from where he sat, a boy of Alain's age in the first weeks of the Occupation had shot a German soldier, off-duty and perhaps simply taking pleasure in the garden which may have reminded him of some public garden in his home town in the Rhineland or Bavaria.

He remembered how years before the war Laval had said that France would always have a frontier with Germany and that consequently the two nations must either fight a war every generation or come to an accommodation, even, he implied, some form of union. He himself had survived the trenches, had survived Verdun and been wounded there; he had fought blindly because that was what he had been required to do. It had been terrible, came back to him horribly at nights even now, but this war was worse, more corrupting because it had been all but impossible when you came to the crossroads to be certain which path to follow. And those who had taken what proved to be the wrong path – like Edmond de Grimaud, he supposed – while believing they were serving France, would be charged with a crime which had not been a crime when they followed the arm of the signpost pointing towards Vichy. Of course Edmond still hoped – it was clear he hoped – that somehow he might work his passage back. And was such a hope dishonourable? Was it vain, absurd? He had looked his idea of reality in the face, and now that face was turned against him. He had, as he admitted, tried to have him shot, and now extended the hand of friendship which Lannes could not refuse.

*   *   *

The brasserie was almost empty, only a couple of tables occupied. An elderly couple sat at one of them. The man, who wore the ribbon of the Légion d'Honneur, had tucked his napkin into his collar; the woman wore gloves. They ate in silence. Perhaps they lived in silence, either because over years of marriage they had exhausted conversation or because anything either might have to say was better left unsaid.

Jacques however approached Lannes with a smile.

'The old man's himself again. Whatever you said to him seems to have done the trick. I'm grateful.'

'I don't recall saying anything of value. Is he in?'

'He'll be back soon. Are you eating?'

164

'I've no appetite. Some bread and cheese perhaps, if you have cheese, and a glass of beer.'

'Fine.'

He sat down to wait. The elderly man had picked up a chicken leg and was gnawing it. Drops of juice fell on his napkin. His face was flushed.

'I'd a visit from young Karim,' Jacques said. 'He was asking if I'd seen you.'

Lannes sighed.

'He's not a bad lad, you know,' Jacques said, not for the first time. 'He gave me a message to pass on if you came in. Said he could help you, which sounds unlikely, I know, because in the past it's been your help he's needed, hasn't it. Anyway he said you could get in touch with him at Chez Jules. I wouldn't like to venture in there myself. Ah, here's the old man.'

Fernand raised his hand in greeting, went behind the bar, and picked up a bottle of Armagnac and two glasses.

'Jean,' he said, handing him a glass, 'here's to Liberation.'

'A bold toast, even now. How's the new girl? Still with you?'

'A perfect peach, old boy.'

Lannes fingered his glass.

'I've been hearing things about you.'

'Nothing bad?'

'That you've become active.'

Fernand laughed, downed his brandy and poured himself another.

'Cautious as ever, aren't you, Jean? And not even drinking. It seemed about time, that's all. The Boches are pulling out. I've done well out of them, as many others have. So it's a good idea to get myself on to the winning side. I don't give a damn about politics, you know that. Vichy were idiots. You know that too. And the new lot may be bastards. All the same I've joined the Party, better to be with them than against them. You should do the same. You've heard what they are calling themselves – the party of twenty thousand martyrs. They're taking all the credit for the Resistance and indeed they've done most of the fighting, most of the sabotage, or so I'm told. And they're going to come out on top, not that comic general from London. So I'd rather be with them than against them. Besides the peach has been a party member for years.'

'You surprise me.'

'Surprised me too, but she was born into it, seems her father's a big shot, big enough to have spent the war years in Moscow, wise man. So when she suggested I sign up, I thought, "Why not?" Like I say, you should do the same. Besides my lot are all right, good kids most of them, eager to line up collaborators against a wall. I'd rather be on the side of the firing-squad. What about it, Jean?'

Lannes smiled.

'Good luck to you, but it's not for me. But I heard a strange thing the other day.'

'What was that?'

'That our friend the advocate Labiche has taken the same route.'

'Labiche? Don't make me laugh. He's one of the first my boys would string up.'

'Really?'

'No doubt about it.'

'Not if I get him first, they won't. But if you hear anything to the contrary of what you're saying, you'll let me know, won't you?'

'Naturally. But someone's pulling your leg, Jean. Believe me, the boys wouldn't accept the likes of Labiche if he approached them waving the hammer and sickle and swearing blind that Stalin is his cousin or boyhood friend. The comrades have their faults but they can recognise a stink when it's near them, and our friend the advocate stinks to high heaven.'

XI

You never saw Germans in the streets now. They had been pulled back into barracks, and the word was that they were preparing to retreat, fight their way North. But the Milice were still active, and for the moment ruled the streets, reason enough for careful people to stay at home. They had shot up a café yesterday, killing three men believed to be in the Resistance and a couple of others, pensioners who had merely dropped in for their usual glass of wine.

Jules hadn't taken Lannes' advice to shut his bar for the time being. He was there behind the counter, fingering the wart on his cheek.

'I'm still waiting for the Americans,' he said. 'Or the English. You said they would be better customers, even though the Americans have more money.'

'Did I? But what do I know about the Americans except from the films? And I don't recall seeing a bar like yours in any Hollywood movie.'

'Well, we'll see. Armagnac, I suppose, and I suppose you'll expect it on the house. Why not? I'm always happy to help the police as you know. But actually, superintendent, I've had no reason to close up. I've got protection. To my surprise, the Doc over there has turned up trumps.'

'What do you mean?'

'Ask him yourself.'

Lannes turned and saw Dr Solomons sitting at a table in the corner with the curly-headed boy – what was his name? Miki? – whom the Milice lieutenant had tried to arrest.

He put a note on the counter, and said, 'I'll pay for my own drink, thank you, and bring the Doc and the boy whatever they're drinking.'

'My dear superintendent, what a pleasant surprise. No longer suspended, I trust? I wondered what had become of you – your friend Monsieur Chambolley said only yesterday when I took the good lady another supply of morphine that he hadn't seen you for weeks. We were both anxious. When people disappear these days, they seldom emerge again.'

'No? I've been fortunate then.'

But he felt guilty. The shameful truth was that since he was released from prison he hadn't dared to visit the bookshop in the rue des Remparts for fear that he would find that Miriam had died.

'How is she?'

'Stronger, astonishingly, I believe she may survive, and, soon, we should be able to get her treatment in hospital. I'm not convinced it is cancer, though I can't be sure.'

'That's a relief. I'm grateful to you.' When Jules had placed their drinks on the table, a Cassis for the doctor and orangeade for the boy, and returned behind the bar to finger his wart and gaze into the distance, Lannes said, 'Jules tells me you've arranged protection for him. I'm puzzled.'

'He puts it too strongly. You wouldn't think it to look at him, but the man must be an optimist.'

'Really?'

'Do you have such a thing as a cigarette, superintendent? Thank you. I really shouldn't, but at my age I ask myself what possible harm can it do. It's an amusing story. This pretty boy here,' he leaned across and tweaked his ear, Napoleon-style, 'proved not to be the innocent I supposed – you supposed? – when you intervened to save him from being beaten up, and perhaps worse, by those thugs in the Milice. Quite the contrary. They had good reason, hadn't they, my dear?'

Lannes looked at the boy who smiled, sipped his orangeade and then flicked out his tongue to lick his upper lip.

'I thought I'd had it,' he said. 'I was so scared I wet myself. I couldn't believe my luck when you stepped in and lied about me. Thanks. I reckon you did us a good turn. I knew what they're capable of and I was afraid I would talk before they killed me. I can't say I wouldn't have. Actually, afterwards, I wondered if you were in the Resistance yourself, but the boss said you weren't, to his knowledge anyway.'

'You surprise me,' Lannes said.

'Tell you the truth, I surprised myself. My father used to say I was soft, and I believed him. But I'm not really. I fancy girls too – sorry, Doc – but that's not the point. You maybe think a boy like me can't be a patriot and, to be honest, it's not a word I like. Seems to me everyone calls himself that. The Marshal said he spoke for France and my mum and dad believed him. Maybe they still do, I don't know. But I couldn't stand seeing the Germans swanning about here in Bordeaux as if they owned the city and all of us, and as for these fuckers in the Milice, I'd be happy to string them up. Anyway I joined the party a couple of years back when it was still deep underground because my dad said they were scoundrels and low-lifes, which is how he thought of me. And I was right because it's the Red Army that's winning the war, isn't it? I'm quite tough really, you know, I've discovered that, even if I did wet myself that day when they took me by surprise. Sorry, I don't usually talk this much, do I, Doc? But I reckon I've you to thank for being alive still, so I wanted to explain myself. You go on, Doc.'

'There's not much to add. May I take another cigarette? Thanks. It's quite simple. After that little incident, Miki confessed to me – I won't say where – that he was indeed active in the Resistance. I was astonished and then excited. And then the chief of his Resistance group was wounded, shot, when an attempt to lay a bomb on the railway went wrong. He needed a doctor, and Miki had the good sense to call me in. I extricated the bullet and patched him up, and that's that. It helped that I'm an old Party man myself recruited years ago by the old tailor we spoke of, Ephraim Kurz, long before he lost the faith which I have never done, quite, and have now found it, I have to say, revived by the Occupation, not to speak of young Miki here. So when Jules got nervous about what might happen here when the Boches pull out, I was able to arrange that the Comrades would keep an eye on the place, which is what those two gentlemen across the room are doing. No, superintendent, don't look at them, it would really embarrass them. Like most of the comrades, they're stern moralists, and think people like me decadent bourgeois perverts, even when we are loyal Party members. They would normally disapprove of Miki too, even despise him, but actually he's their blue-eyed boy. You wouldn't believe the risks the child has run.'

'Don't listen to him,' the boy said. 'He exaggerates. It's because he's a romantic. A Jew, a queer and a romantic, some combination.'

'You talk nonsense yourself,' Solomons said. 'There's not an ounce of romance in my body. But tell me, superintendent, did you find my poor Aurélien? And how deep is he in trouble?'

'I found him, and the only trouble he is now in is being himself. Thank you for an interesting story, and thank you for what you have done for Miriam. As for you, young man, you've evidently done what you needed to do, and proved yourself. But just remember this. When the Germans have gone we are going to have to live with ourselves and with each other, Frenchmen with

Frenchmen, in something like concord and normality. We don't need more deaths, and, if you forget this, then remind yourself what would have happened to you if I hadn't chanced to be here. And do you know what prompted me to speak up and tell a lie on your behalf? Pity, simply pity for one in misfortune. It's not an ignoble emotion, pity, though there are many who think themselves strong who despise it. And now I must have a word with Jules. I wish you both well.' At the bar, lowering his voice, he said, 'I'd a message that Karim wanted to see me. Tell him to come to the bar he knows of behind the station tomorrow afternoon at three o'clock.'

'And if I don't see him.'

'I've no doubt you'll manage to get word to him.'

Outside, in the street, he felt for a moment curiously light-hearted. For a moment.

XII

Lannes knew that he really didn't want to see Karim again. He had had enough of the trouble he associated with the boy, and, though this time Jacques had said that Karim claimed he could help him, Lannes found it hard to believe. If he kept the appointment it was only because being in the office or at home were equally disagreeable options, and he could think of little except Labiche. This worried him; the man had become an obsession. He hadn't spoken to him for more than two years and yet his face, with its expression of sour arrogance, was always before him. He was also uneasy, Fabien had got him out of the hands of the Milice, but he couldn't escape the suspicion that he was himself a pawn in whatever game the spook was playing. Nothing in his conversation with Edmond de Grimaud had dispelled that thought.

To his surprise Karim was already in the bar, leaning back in a chair with a cigarette dangling from the corner of his mouth.

The bar was almost deserted, as so many were in these days, but when Gustave said, 'I reckon you'll want the back room again,' Lannes agreed and, having asked about the family and heard that the grandchild was pure delight, nodded to Karim and made his way through. Karim sauntered after him, the cigarette still held dangling in the manner of a gangster in a film.

'You're looking very pleased with yourself,' Lannes said. 'Sit down.'

Karim did so, took the cigarette between his thumb and third finger, and smiled.

'Maybe yes, maybe no. You remember that priest, well of course you do. It's odd. I knew just what I intended to say, and now find it difficult. You ever feel like that? I suppose you don't, being a cop and all that.'

'Get on with it. I don't have all day to waste.'

Which, he thought, was a lie, because his afternoon was as empty as a deserted house.

'He came to me again,' Karim said.

'I'm not surprised. He told me you had such beautiful eyes. Go on.'

'Did he now? Well then . . . '

He broke off as Gustave came in with an Armagnac for Lannes and a lemonade for him.

'Everything all right?'

'Fine, thank you.'

Karim waited till the door had closed behind Gustave.

'Well then,' he said again. 'I told him nothing doing, bugger off, because, like I said, what he wants isn't my sort of thing. Then he began to cry. It was disgusting. I mean, have you ever seen a priest weeping?'

'There's a line in the Bible which says, "Jesus wept." Is this story going anywhere?'

'Oh yes, but I don't much like where it's going. That Félix my old woman shot, it seems he's the priest's brother. He said, "I know you didn't kill him, but I believe your policeman friend did." "Why should you think that?" I said. "Information," he said, "from those Félix was working for, higher-up ones. He's not going to get away with it." I told him it wasn't like that. I even told him the old woman did it, and that she's now dead. "Convenient," he said, "but I don't believe you. So your policeman friend's a marked man." What do you make of it? It sounds crazy to me.'

'It's a crazy world,' Lannes said. 'It makes no sense. But you were right to tell me. And if I was you, Karim, I'd make myself scarce. Things may be different in a few weeks, but if there's anywhere you can go, anyone you can safely hole up with, do that. If they try to pin Félix's death on me, there's a fair chance you'll be tagged as an accessory to the crime. But what puzzles me is why you looked happy when I came into the bar.'

'You don't understand, do you,' Karim said. 'Give me a cigarette, will you? Thanks. You really don't understand and I suppose that because of what I am and what I do, you think I'm . . . never mind what I think you think I am. The point is, I've got human feelings. You've been good to me, got me out of trouble a couple of times, and passing on this warning's the first thing I've been able to do in return – even if the warning frightens me, it's better you should know what that slimy priest said than you shouldn't. So, if I looked happy, that's why.'

'I'm sorry. I owe you an apology.'

'What'll you do?'

'I don't know,' Lannes said. 'I'd hoped we'd heard the last of Félix, but it seems he's almost as big a nuisance dead as he was alive. I'll think of something. But, as I say, you should keep out of sight well away from Father Paul and whoever is behind him, whether that's the spooks or the advocate Labiche. It could be either, though I favour the latter. And thank you. As Jacques says you're not such a bad kid.'

'Jacques said that? Really?'

'Yes, but don't tell him I told you. And don't get your hopes up. Remember he goes for girls and indeed is engaged to be married.'

'And so?'

Karim smiled broadly.

'And so?' he said again.

*   *   *

It didn't make sense. Even if the priest was playing a double game – Fabien too perhaps – why should he have approached Karim? Did he expect him to pass the message on? 'Your policeman friend's a marked man.' Marked by whom and for what purpose? Any legal action – if he was thinking of legality – could surely be taken only after the Liberation. Which meant . . . what did it mean? He had no idea.

Heavy clouds had gathered while he was in the bar, but it was still hot, oppressively hot, scarcely a breath of air, not even when his steps took him to the river and he leaned on the parapet watching the water slide away below him. Whatever game was being played, he had lost control of its development. Was he a pawn or a hunted animal? There came a crackle of thunder, immediately overhead, and a flash of lightning, then a burst of rain. He didn't move, continued to gaze at the river, till the rain penetrated the jacket of his suit and he felt his shirt stick to his body. The thunder rolled, the lightning lay for a moment yellow on the water, and when he turned his head to the left, westward, the fringe of the sky was pale blue lit up by gold.

XIII

For a moment Léon didn't recognise the girl sitting diagonally across from him in the Metro. It was only when their eyes met and she gave a small, scarcely perceptible, shake of the head that he realised it was Anne who had been his liaison with the group, who passed on the messages and information he was trusted to relay to London. Then she had failed to keep an appointment, three days in succession, first by the statue of *Le Marchand de Masques* in the Luxembourg Gardens, then at the brasserie in the Rue de Buci which was the first back-up rendezvous and finally on that bench in the Tuileries Gardens, and he had known that the Group had been betrayed or somehow broken, and that Anne which wasn't of course her real name was either dead or in prison. That was when and why, alone and afraid, he had accepted the refuge and protection offered him by Chardy who had first approached him as a likely pick-up in a bookshop in the rue de Tournon. And now here was Anne, sitting demurely in the Metro, and again giving that small shake of the head.

She got up as the train pulled into St-Michel. He followed her out of the station, at a distance he thought discreet, watched her cross the Boulevard, followed her along the rue St André-des-Arts and round the corner into the rue Mazarin where she entered a little bar. He waited for five minutes, smoking a cigarette, and leaning against a wall at the junction of the streets. When he was sure nobody had followed her in, he eased himself off the wall, and, assuming a casual air, strolled into the bar. She was alone, standing at the counter. For a moment he hesitated – had she indeed intended him to join her? But then she turned towards him, and held out her cheek to be kissed. 'Late as usual,' she said, for the benefit of the barman. 'It's meant to be the woman's prerogative, isn't it? Coffee? Two coffees then,' and led him over to a table in the window.

'I couldn't believe it.'

'Neither could I.'

They didn't speak more till they were brought their coffees and had drunk them.

Then Anne said, loudly, 'We'd better go, or we'll be late.' In the street she said, 'Have you a room?'

'Yes, in the Place Contrescarpe.'

'We'll go there, then, shall we?'

In the room she took off her skirt and lay on the bed. He sat beside her. They kissed.

Later she said, 'I always fancied you, but I was sure you didn't like girls. You've changed haven't you.'

'Or grown up,' he said, thinking of Priscilla. 'Now tell . . . '

'No,' she said, 'I can't. It was too horrible. Have you been in Paris all the time?'

'Yes, I didn't have anywhere to go, didn't know what to do.'

'But you've survived.'

'Yes, I've survived.'

Shamefully, he thought.

'Clever of you to have found this room. It's safe, isn't it?'

'I think so. I didn't find it. It belongs to a friend.'

'Oh . . . that sort of friend?'

'If you like. He lives with his mother and he's had this room for years. I don't have to tell you why, do I.'

'He won't come in, will he?'

'No, he left Paris yesterday, for their place in a village near Versailles. He's afraid of what's going to happen.'

'Oh,' she said again. 'And you didn't go with him. You weren't tempted?'

'No. I wouldn't miss it for worlds. Besides his mother went with him.'

'That's good, because tomorrow we sign up with the FFI. You know about them, don't you, even though the circles I guess you've been moving in stink, don't they?'

'I suppose so, but I've learned one thing, that nothing is as simple or straightforward as I used to believe. For instance, you guessed I was queer. Did you also guess I was Jewish?'

'It doesn't matter,' she said. 'You've told me your secret. I'll tell you mine. Before the war my father used to say, "That fellow Hitler may be a disaster but he has the right idea about the Jews." And my mother agreed. So there: if your friend was a collaborator as you imply, my dreadful parents were fierce anti-Semites and supporters of Doriot's Fascists. So we both have reason for shame. Didn't your friend mind that you are Jewish?'

'It's on my mother's side only. My father wouldn't let me be circumcised. So he never suspected.'

'Lucky you, in the circumstances, I mean. What's your real name?'

'Léon.'

'Nice name.'

'And yours?'

'Berthe. Not such a nice name. I prefer Anne. I'm going to stick with Anne, if we come through.'

She stretched out her hand and stroked his cheek.

'I want you to make love to me, Léon. Make love as if there was no tomorrow. We may both be dead soon.'

'No,' he said, 'we're survivors. I don't know what you've gone through, since we last met – one day you'll tell me – but you've survived. That's the great thing. Me too. We're going to be all right. We'll cheer General de Gaulle outside the Hôtel de Ville. I was presented to him once in London, you know.'

'Did he speak to you?'

'Yes. He looked down his big nose at me and said, "Stand up straight, young man." '

He leaned over, kissed her lips lightly, and unbuttoned her blouse.

*　　*　　*

Michel crouched in the fox-hole. Sweat ran down his face and the back of his neck. There was an itch in his groin and another in his toes – he hadn't had his boots off for three days now.

'These fucking guns are no good,' Corporal Jean said, for the third time that morning. 'If this is German engineering at its best, no wonder the war is being lost.'

They had been issued with Jagdpanthers which stood under their camouflage netting. They would fire well enough so long as you aimed them at a target straight ahead of you, but they had no revolving turrets, so that you had to heave the whole gun round if the attack came from the flank, either flank.

'Fucking useless,' Jean said again.

'At least they're light.'

'Which means we can take them with us again when the order comes for the next retreat. Great way of delaying our flight.'

'They're what we have,' Michel said.

When they were pulled back five kilometres the day before, they had travelled along a road lined with half-shattered lime trees. Bodies hung from the branches, bodies in the uniforms of a Wehrmacht reserve battalion. Cardboard notices were pinned to their chests, branding the dead as cowards and subversives. One of them was a boy who looked younger than Michel, blond like him.

In the distance, astonishingly, they had seen peasants harvesting. Poles, Michael supposed.

'Yes, Poles,' Jean said, 'the buggers France went to war to defend. Crazy.'

*　　*　　*

Jérôme hauled himself out of the lake and lay on his towel on the grass, letting the hot sun dry him. Only the sound of an aeroplane was a reminder of war. Wood-pigeons cooed from the trees across the lake and if he raised his head and looked beyond the trees, he could see cattle grazing, red cattle with white faces, 'my prize Herefords', Sir Pringle had said. He knew now this wasn't the correct form, and he had come to address him as 'Edwin', though he still thought of him as 'Sir Pringle'. Lines from the book Sir Pringle had given him – 'so that you can understand the real England, dear boy, the essence of England' – ran in his head: 'Into my heart, an air that kills/ From yon far country blows;/ What are those blue remembered hills?/ What spires, what towers are those?' Beautiful lines which he had tried to render into French, but it hadn't worked. They sounded dead in his version, in his language.

He shouldn't be here. He should be in France. But he was happy to be here. He turned his face and felt the sun hot on his cheek, and drifted into a half-sleep.

A shadow fell over him. He looked up to see Sir Pringle with a glass in his hand and his face wet with tears.

'I got through to the Air Ministry,' he said. 'There's no doubt, I'm afraid. Max's plane didn't return, they've written it off.'

*   *   *

Dominique was in a sub-prefect's office in a small town in the Ile-de-France. He had delivered François' message, a message of reassurance that the sub-prefect, despite his record of loyalty to Vichy, was well regarded by the Resistance on account of his role in enabling so many young men to evade the draft for compulsory labour service in Germany.

The sub-prefect had smiled.

'For years patriotism has worn a double-face,' he said. 'I've done my duty to France as I conceived it, nothing more than that. But I confess your friend's message comes as a relief, one I didn't expect in these savage times. I had even warned my wife to prepare for the worst. Well, let us open a bottle of wine. You served in Vichy yourself, I think.'

'Yes,' Dominique said, 'with responsibility for the boys of the Chantiers de Jeunesse.'

'And now you've changed sides – like my friend François himself.'

'That's not what it feels like,' Dominique said. 'I was taken prisoner in 1940. I've always detested the Nazis, but it seemed to me that the Marshal was France. I still think so really, that's what he was, then anyway.'

'Yes,' the sub-prefect said. 'That's what he was.'

They drank, smoked, and talked in a mood of harmony achieved. Then, towards midnight, they heard footsteps on the stairs, and the door opened and a young man, a boy really, stumbled over the threshold and into the room. His face was streaked with mud and blood, and he was trembling, his whole body shaking.

'Thomas,' the sub-prefect said, putting his arm round the boy and settling him in a chair. 'Thomas, who has attacked you? Who has done this to you?'

'You know him then?'

'Yes, his father's secretary-general of the local Mairie.'

The boy retched and began to sob.

'He's only sixteen,' the sub-prefect said. 'Only sixteen.'

It as a long time before the boy was able to speak, and then he said only 'my father' before he broke down again.

They sat, waiting in silence. The night was hot and the scent of honeysuckle wafted in through the open window.

'I'm afraid,' the sub-prefect said, 'afraid of what he'll eventually tell us. I know his father, a good man, but . . . '

'But what?'

'He used to be a Communist, an ardent one. Then in '39, disgusted by the Nazi-Soviet Pact, he tore up his Party card, and after the debacle he became an enthusiastic supporter of the Marshal and the National Revolution. You see why I'm afraid.'

'He's bleeding again,' Dominique said, 'we must bandage his throat and get him to hospital.'

'Certainly, but . . . '

'What?'

'We have to hear what he has to tell.'

It took more than an hour for the boy to do so. He spoke haltingly, his voice now almost inaudible, now rapid, his words tumbling over themselves in his confusion, his body still twitching, as he relived the horror of the last hours. Dominique had difficulty in following the narrative, but this was its gist, as far as he understood.

The boy had been at home with his father. They were playing chess – he repeated time and again that he had moved his queen to put his father in check, as if it mattered. Maybe it did because he recognised one of the armed men who broke into the house, an old comrade, Joseph the *garagiste* – 'They used to play chess when I was a little boy,' he said again and again. They forced them at gunpoint into a lorry and drove them out into the forest. He tried to break away, but was hauled back and hit on the face with a rifle-butt. Then they were both tied to trees. One man slashed his father's face with a knife and Joseph said, 'We're going to kill your boy before your eyes, traitor.' They kept calling him traitor and my father said, 'Let the boy go, kill me if you must, but let him go, he was never in the Party.' 'They slashed him again,' the boy said, 'and then something worse, I can't repeat it, and my father screamed. My father screamed, like when you cut a pig's throat.'

He had blacked out then, mercifully, Dominique thought, and when he came to, his ropes had been cut, he was lying face down on the ground, and his father was dead. 'I couldn't touch him,' he said, 'I couldn't even touch him . . . '

He fell off the chair and lay curled up on the floor. Once he lifted his head and howled.

'Hospital,' Dominique said. 'We must take him to hospital now.'

'Yes,' the sub-prefect said, 'and then organise a search for his father's body. I don't look forward to finding it.'

'And for the assassins . . . '

'You think so?'

'Surely.'

'I'm not persuaded that would be sensible. Not now, not today, not for a long time, if ever. *Oh la belle France.*'

When they had left the boy in the hospital, Dominique said, 'Why do you think they let him go? After all he's a witness, he recognised the man he called Joseph and can testify against him.'

'You think a trial's likely, young man? And in any case the boy's already half-demented. He may never recover. I'll be surprised if he does.'

*   *   *

Alain lay, not sleeping, in the open air, under a big moon, his rifle by his side like a lover. Tomorrow, he thought, tomorrow belongs to us. Paris would rise, to free itself by its own efforts – and theirs. The boy Vincent lay next to him, not sleeping either. 'I'm trembling with excitement,' he said, but Alain heard anxiety, even fear, in his voice. 'Don't worry,' he said, 'it's going to be marvellous. These are days we'll never forget.'

XIV

'Can one trust Fabien?' Lannes said.

Bracal raised his left eyebrow. His fingers, still carefully manicured, despite everything, beat their reflective tattoo on his desk. The shutters were closed against the day and the street. It was cool in the judge's office. The electricity was working again and a fan scythed the air. Outside the heat was still oppressive. Last night's thunderstorm had failed to clear the atmosphere. There wasn't even a breath of wind and the sun was hidden behind deep purple clouds.

'That's not a question I can answer,' he said. 'You've been reinstated, Jean. You're a servant of the Republic, as Fabien is too.'

'So we're talking about the Republic again?'

'It has never ceased to exist. We have served Vichy, but knowing always, or at least since November '42 and the North African landings, that it was only – how shall I put it? – an expedient? Yes, that will do: an expedient. That's been my position. Yours too, I believe.'

'And Fabien's?'

'Why not? He extricated you from the hands of the Milice. Without his intervention, you would probably have been shot. You are in his debt. And yet you seem to distrust him. Why?'

Because, Lannes might have said, of a conversation with a disreputable rent-boy.

'I don't know,' he said instead. 'Perhaps because I find it so hard to trust anyone now, so hard to believe in any simple explanation. That's what we have learned, isn't it, in the last four years: that almost nothing is what it seems to be.'

'We have to live with uncertainty,' Bracal said. 'We'll have to do so for a long time to come, eyeing so many with suspicion. As for the other matter you have brought to me, unless you find that girl and can persuade her to testify, you have no evidence to justify the issuing of a warrant for the arrest of the advocate Labiche. Why not leave him to the Resistance?'

'Because I don't want him dead, I want him in the dock. You spoke of the Republic, which implies republican values. One of these is legality.'

'It will be a long time, I fear, before legality is restored. Whether we like it or not, for months to come, it will be a question of revenge, not legality, and I suppose revenge is a form of savage justice.'

'You can't believe that, you're a judge. You can't wash your hands of legality.'

Bracal smiled, and held up his hands which smelled, even across the desk, of expensive soap – and where had he got that, Lannes thought.

'I've never been an idealist,' the judge said. 'I take the world as I find it. For four years the prevailing wind has come from Vichy. Now the wind has shifted. It blows with the Resistance, and, believe me, Jean, for weeks and perhaps months to come, the Law will be whatever the Resistance says it is. Again, believe me, I don't like that either, but if we are to survive we bend before the wind. Which is why I say: leave Labiche to them.'

'One suggestion is that he has made plans to escape to Spain.'

'And so?'

'He will never stand trial. I have the impression you think I'm obsessed with him. Perhaps I am. If so it's with reason. Before the war, in '38, he raped a young girl of eleven or twelve. A few weeks later she hanged herself. The advocate was morally responsible for her death. I want him to pay for it.'

'Jean, Jean, morally responsible is not legally responsible. If what you say is true – and I don't doubt it even though I say "if" – Labiche was guilty of abuse of a minor, perhaps of rape, not of her death. And since she is, you say, dead, she cannot testify against him, and I assume you have no witness, merely hearsay, that is, what you have been told. Is that correct? Yes? So you have no case, no case at all. And, by your own admission, your chance of finding the other girl you speak of – the one in the photograph you carry around with you – is slim. Leave Labiche to the Resistance.'

'To mob law?'

'To mob law, yes. To the horrors of mob law, even. Heaven knows there will be enough of its horrors.'

*   *   *

Lannes couldn't say just what he had hoped for from Bracal, but more than he had got, certainly more. Encouragement at least, he had supposed. He had come to respect the judge, and now he felt his respect diminished. He was unfair perhaps; he recognised that. What Bracal had said was reasonable; he had no case against Labiche. The suggestion that he should leave him to the Resistance made sense. And yet it rankled. The world might be a cleaner place if Fernand and his friends put him up against a wall and shot him. He understood why Bracal thought that would be the simplest and neatest solution. There was no case. So close the book, no matter how.

But it wasn't right.

It was intolerable to stay in the office, and in any case there was nothing for him to do there, except to brood. Remembering his conversation with Dr Solomons, he picked up his stick and headed for the rue des Remparts. At least he wouldn't be met with the news that Miriam was dead. She might even agree to see him. But it was Henri he wanted to speak to.

He walked slowly. The heat was still oppressive and he was sweating heavily. Another thunderstorm was on the way and as he turned into the rue des Remparts, the first drops of rain began to fall and a flash of lightning stabbed through the gloom. The street was deserted. He imagined people all over Bordeaux closing their shutters against the world. All day he had been aware of a mood of expectation in the city, expectation shot through with anxiety. A black cat crossed his path and jumped on to a window ledge from which it eyed him warily.

Music sounded as Henri opened the door.

'Wagner again?'

'*Tristan und Isolde*, with Flagstadt. Somehow,' Henri said, 'it's Wagner that suits my mood now.'

'I saw Dr Solomons the day before yesterday. He gave me good news.'

'Yes, indeed. Miriam's asleep now, but if you can stay till she wakes, I know that this time she'll be happy to see you. And I have news too, but that can wait.'

'You look happy, Henri.'

'Is that so strange? But you, Jean, look wretched.'

Upstairs Toto came and sniffed at Lannes' trouser-legs, declared himself satisfied, and returned to curl up in his basket.

'It's almost over, isn't it?' Henri said. 'Any day now, they'll be gone, and, do you know, I believe I'll have the heart to open the bookshop again. I never thought I would.'

He pulled the cork from a bottle, and poured a glass which he handed to Lannes.

'A dry Graves,' he said. 'You remember Gaston's English joke: only sextons drink Graves.'

'He had to explain it to me, that a sexton was a grave-digger. Was it a line of Shakespeare?'

'No, Byron.'

He lifted the arm of the gramophone and stopped the whirring of the record.

'So, Jean, what is it? What ails you?'

'Yes, you're right. You know me too well. I've come to unburden myself.'

'As you always used to do. In the old days.'

It took Lannes a long time, beginning with the search for Marie-Adelaide, speaking then of the anonymous letters, of his going into hiding, of his imprisonment, of Fabien, Edmond de Grimaud, the wretched priest, and Labiche. Labiche most of all. Henri listened without interruption, smoking his pipe and not touching the glass of wine which sat on the occasional table by his armchair.

'My poor Jean,' he said at last. 'You're obsessed.'

'Yes, that's what I am. Obsessed and confused.'

'And unhappy, I think.'

'Aren't we all?'

Henri occupied himself scraping out the dottles from his pipe, re-filling it, pressing the tobacco down with his thumb, applying a match, and getting it going with short rapid puffs.

'You take too much on yourself, Jean. You always have, ever since we met as students. Does it matter what becomes of the man Labiche? Whether he is shot or escapes to Spain? His day is over, done with. He's a failure. You don't really need to concern yourself with him. I'm a failure myself, Jean, I've known that for years, at least since Pilar found me an unsatisfactory husband and our life here in Bordeaux insufficient for her. But I've come to terms with my condition. You take too much on yourself, I say again. You should have said all this to Marguerite, not to me. But you're too proud to do so, too proud to share your anxieties with her. It's as if you wanted to watch your marriage disintegrate before your eyes, and seek consolation in work, in the consciousness that you are doing your duty. There: you may think I shouldn't be saying this, but we're old friends, you're my only true friend and have been that since Gaston was killed, and I don't like to see you destroying yourself by your insistence on taking the weight of the world on your shoulders. These girls you speak of. Well, first, this Marie-Adelaide seems to me from what you say to have acted as a free agent. So let her be. Then this other girl, the one in the photograph, you don't believe you are ever going to find her; yet you gnaw at it like a dog with a bone. She may be dead. She may be married. You don't know. You merely assume that she wants to be revenged on Labiche, because you think she should want that. But perhaps she doesn't. Perhaps she has put it all behind her and got on with her life. And then there's the other girl, Yvette. You feel in some way responsible for her. Yet from what you say, she seems quite capable of looking after herself. If you were in love with her, it might be different. But you're not, are you? Desire, yes, no doubt you feel that. It's natural that you should, but you won't allow yourself to act on it – and quite right too. Yet you allow that desire to corrupt your relationship with Marguerite. It doesn't make sense. And then you speak of what you call the sin of *accidia* – though you don't recognise the concept of sin any more than I do. Jean, my old friend, you're in grave danger – forgive my blunt speaking – of drowning in a sea of self-pity. I can say this because I recognise the same temptation in myself. We're too conscious of responsibility, pride ourselves on it, and resent the consequences. We're not like Gaston who went through life taking what he wanted, even if it damaged him. You know, I used to talk with Léon about Gaston, not at first of course, but as I came to know him and like him, and one day, he surprised me by saying, "But you forget, Monsieur Chambolley, or don't perhaps realise, that Gaston was happy, he had a zest for life. He was a natural teacher, you know, I learned a lot from him and am grateful." And I realised he was right. I'm a greater failure than Gaston was, because I have preferred to shut myself away, deny myself new experiences. And perhaps you have done so also, Jean, though in a different style. There: I've probably said too much, but if friends can't speak frankly to each other, what is friendship for?'

Lannes fingered his glass, set it aside and lit a cigarette. He sat in silence while he smoked half of it. Henri bent down and scratched Toto behind the ear.

'I'm sorry, I've said too much.'

'No,' Lannes said. 'No, you haven't. I don't dispute any of it. But there's more to it still. More and worse. I'm being eaten up with hatred, not only of Labiche. Indeed it's quite possible that he is no more than a symbol of everything I detest. But what I feel is hatred of this war, hatred which has grown more intense even as the war seems to be coming to what we must think of as a happy end. We've lived through defeat and humiliation, and it appears that we are going to be included among the victors, even though we don't deserve to be – we have lived with defeat and accustomed ourselves to its consequences. But that's not it. It's not even only the pervasive dishonesty that has been forced on us. It's the damage it has done to the ordinary – the ordinary decencies of life. Clothilde is breaking her heart over a boy who chose the wrong side, chose it with a wild gallantry – and the man who influenced him will probably come through unscathed even though he is a criminal as well as a scoundrel. Dominique, your godson, did good work in Vichy. Will he be forgiven for that? And Alain went as you know with Léon and little Jérôme to join de Gaulle. We have heard nothing from him or of him for more than two years. He may be dead. If he isn't, what will whatever he has experienced have done to him, two years, I repeat, in which he should have been studying, playing rugby and flirting with girls. All of them – and indeed all the youth of France – will have learned what they shouldn't know at their age. And now we are going to be required to engage in a new round of dishonesty, in which we will be required to pretend that these last years haven't been what they have been, but that instead all of us except a few guilty men and women have engaged in Resistance. For a generation at least France will live a new lie. Do you wonder I hate them all?'

'Jean, Jean, the world is as it is, and everyone must find a means of accommodating themselves to its reality.'

Lannes drank his wine.

'You're right. I suppose you're right, and I'm a mess of, as you say, self-pity, resentment and hatred. Enough of that. You said you have some good news.'

'Yes,' Henri said, 'Miriam and I are going to get married, whether she recovers her health or not, and I am now ready to believe that she will indeed do so.'

Lannes got to his feet, embraced Henri and said, 'That's wonderful. It's more than wonderful. It's an expression of faith in the future.'

He could only wish that he shared that faith.

XV

As news came of the Allied advance in the North, and rumours of the imminent Liberation of Paris circulated, there was no in-surrection in Bordeaux. Someday soon, it was clear, the Germans must leave if they weren't to be trapped in a city they had occupied and pillaged for four years, but which their garrison, considerably reduced in numbers, could not reasonably be expected to hold much longer. The choice for the German command was between withdrawal and surrender. This was clear. Lannes suspected that many of the rank-and-file would have opted happily for the latter. Better surely to be prisoners-of-war, safe in captivity, than to continue fighting a war that was evidently being lost; he couldn't believe that the private soldiers had any stomach for battle now. It might be different, probably was different, on the Eastern Front where nobody would choose to be transported to a Russian camp, and where in any case they would soon be defending their homeland against an enemy whose revenge for their own atrocities they must fear. But here in Bordeaux the troops of the Wehrmacht were no longer the swaggering self-confident blond warriors of 1940, but reservists, many of them middle-aged and veterans of the First War, or beardless boys, to all of whom surrender surely made good sense. Nevertheless he feared that the commanders were still in thrall to their Führer, and that they would obey any order, no matter how demented, to hold their ground here in Bordeaux, or – worse still perhaps – to destroy public buildings and block the river to prevent the much-needed import of provisions to the miserably malnourished citizens. If only, he thought, the Allies hadn't demanded unconditional surrender . . .

Meanwhile he found himself in limbo. In these days in which anxiety mingled with exultation, the PJ was for the moment redundant. As Moncerre put it, downing a glass of wine, 'Even the criminals are on holiday or posing as Heroes of the Resistance; it makes me sick.' But the truth was that ordinary crime itself was indeed taking a holiday; murders were being committed only in the name of France.

Nevertheless Lannes went to the office every day where he sat for hours at an empty desk; it was an escape from home if nothing else, an escape from Marguerite's cold silence and Clothilde's anxiety, her longing for news from Michel which might never come. Maurice visited twice, was asked if he had had word from Dominique, shook his head, and tried to divert Clothilde. Lannes wished he could do so; he was so evidently attracted to her and so much more suitable than Michel.

Old Joseph, the office messenger, knocked at his door, and said, 'There's a young lady wishes to speak to you.'

For a moment he hoped it would be Yvette.

'Has she been here before? Did she give a name?'

'The answer's "no" to both questions,' Joseph said. 'Unless my memory's failing with regard to the first, I've never seen her before, and even at my age I've a good eye for young ladies, and as to the second, she declined to say who she was but insists it's important.'

'Show her in then.'

The young lady was wearing a summer frock, cream-coloured and patterned with red and blue flowers, and a cardigan slung loosely across her shoulders. She wore court shoes and her brown hair had been given a permanent wave, as if, even in these days, she had found the time and inclination to visit a hairdresser. His first impression was that she appeared to be very self-assured.

'I believe you've been looking for me,' she said.

'I have?'

Could she be the girl in the photograph he carried?

'So I'm told,' she said. 'My name is Marie-Adelaide d'Herblay and it seems that my grandmother commissioned you to find me. So here I am. I understand that you also know my father.'

She settled herself in the chair across his desk, crossed her legs and smiled.

'You've caused a lot of trouble,' Lannes said, 'and distressed your grandmother. Have you returned home?'

'Certainly not.'

She smiled as if the idea of returning to her grandmother's apartment was preposterous.

'What has puzzled me,' he said, 'and puzzles me more now that I have met you, is why you should have gone off with a fellow like Aurélien Mabire.'

'I could say that I thought I was in love with him. Would you believe me if I said that?'

'Probably not, seeing what I know of him. Besides, he told me you were desperate to be re-united with your father.'

'You've met my father. Do you think that likely?'

'Daughters and fathers, you can't tell,' Lannes said.

'My father's a failure, a washout. Surely you realised that?'

She smiled again.

'Why are you persecuting Monsieur Labiche?'

'Am I?'

'So it appears.'

'And you can't guess why?'

'Of course I can. Because he likes little girls. I suppose you would say, he abuses them. Hasn't it occurred to you that the little girls, some of them, one anyway I can say with assurance, might like him equally?'

'And you do?'

'I dreamed of him for years. No, superintendent, happy dreams, or, if you prefer, dreams of desire, not nightmares. Do you find that impossible to believe? Or does it disgust you?'

Lannes sighed. The girl kept her gaze fixed on him and continued to smile. Her self-possession was as irritating as it was surprising. She wasn't in the least like the girl described to him by her grandmother and the Comte de St-Hilaire. Or indeed by that wretched Aurélien. He got up, crossed to the window and looked out on the street which was empty but for two priests walking side by side, heads bowed as if they might be reciting their office. He took the bottle of Armagnac from the cupboard, poured them each a glass and gave one to the girl. She accepted it without a word, took a sip, and waited till he had sat down again.

'That's nice,' she said, 'but you haven't answered my question.'

'It doesn't matter what I believe,' he said. 'That's irrelevant. So you ran away with Aurélien because he promised to take you to Labiche? And yet he told me that it was Labiche who introduced him to you.'

'That's right. But I couldn't go straight to Monsieur Labiche, could I? Not to a man in his position. But Aurélien, that was different. It was easy to make him believe I was attracted to him. It amused me to do so, and it was all the easier because I'm not pretty, which is why he could believe I welcomed his attentions. He really is such a fool, that man.'

'I see. So it was Labiche all the time, not Aurélien, not your father. And now?'

'Now I'm no longer twelve, and I find Monsieur Labiche rather sad, even pathetic. It's a disappointment of course.'

'So why are you here?'

'He's afraid,' she said. 'Everything's gone wrong for him, and now he wants to meet you.'

'Really? He tried to destroy me. Did you know that?'

'Of course. And now you're trying to destroy him. Well, as I say he's afraid. He wants to get away, but that's not going to be easy without help. So he wants to meet you. He said to tell you he has something you want and is willing to hand it over – for a consideration of course. Do you understand?'

'I think so,' Lannes said. 'Tell him to send me a note saying when and where. Tell him to make it an anonymous letter. He's got experience of such things. What about you? Do you intend to go off with him, assuming he gets away?'

'Oh I don't think so. I mean, what would be the point now?'

'So will you return home, to your grandmother?'

'And be cooped up in that mausoleum again? It's not an attractive prospect.'

'She loves you, she's anxious for you. To my mind the least you can do is to go home and put her mind at rest.'

She smiled and picked up her glass.

'I spoke of her house as a mausoleum,' she said. 'More exactly, it felt like a prison. I've no intention of living there again, but if she started to weep and clung to me, well, I don't know that I mightn't weaken. She has always used tears as a means of exerting control. So there it is. You say she commissioned you to find me, well, go and tell her you've done so and she needn't worry. It's not as if I've broken her heart, for I can't tell you how many times she has assured me it was shattered years ago. In any case, she's tougher than she seems and a terrible hypocrite. She threw out my father, you know, while protesting that he was the light in her life, and, though I've no time for him myself now, I can't respect her either.'

'At least go and speak to your godfather, Monsieur de St-Hilaire.'

'You do that, superintendent, if you like. I've certainly no intention of doing so.'

'Then tell me where you are living.'

'I don't think so, but I'll pass your message on to Monsieur Labiche.'

XVI

He had tried to telephone the Vichy number Fabien had given him, but there was no reply. That wasn't a surprise. He supposed that most of the offices in the hotels that the administration had commandeered as government offices in Vichy were now deserted. Why would anyone linger there? There were rumours that the Marshal, Laval and whatever survived of what was now only a shadow government had been carried off to Germany. He couldn't suppose the Marshal would have gone willingly; the man who had dedicated his person to the French people and who by all accounts had refused to fly to Algeria in November '42, at the time of the American landings, would surely have chosen to stay and if necessary die in France; he was a Man of Honour, the Hero of Verdun. Many would revile him now; Lannes felt only pity for him; no, more than pity, there was still respect and admiration for his old chief. As for Monsieur Laval, Lannes had never met him, but from what Edmond de Grimaud, who had served briefly in his private office, had said, he supposed he might have received this order to be one of the caravan of the defeated and disgraced with an ironical smile. He remembered how the barman in the Hotel des Ambassadeurs in Vichy had spoken of Laval as 'a deep one – you never know what he is really thinking, and the more frankly he seems to be speaking, the more you feel he is saying nothing that matters or he believes in'.

He telephoned Fabien's number again, futilely. It was extraordinary, he thought, that the system was still working, and that you could hear a bell ringing in an empty room halfway across France, extraordinary too that there were telephone operators still connecting distant cities as if times were normal, attempting to do so indeed politely in this case.

The office felt like an antechamber to the morgue. He picked up his stick.

The sky had cleared. There were only a few little clouds, fleecy as young lambs, dotted against its deep blue. The gutters still ran with rain-water, but the air was as fresh as a spring morning. Waiters were unstacking chairs outside cafés, wiping them dry, and a few people were sitting there as if they were early customers for the day when peace returned. In the Place de la Cathédrale, a one-legged man was juggling small Indian clubs watched by half a dozen small boys who broke out in jeers when he dropped one.

But the rue d'Aviau was as empty as ever, many of the houses shuttered, their owners having probably, he thought, judged it wise to leave the city for their place in the country, to wait there until they saw how things panned out and normality was restored. There were few people who could be confident that they would be cleared of collaboration. Even the Rich must be anxious. Nevertheless he didn't doubt that he would find Edmond at home; his pride wouldn't permit him to run away.

When old Marthe opened the door more quickly than usual, she said, 'For once, Mr Policeman, I'm pleased to see you. Sigi is home. The nerve of him to show his face. I trust you've come to arrest him for the murder of his father.'

'No, Marthe. In the first place I didn't know he was in Bordeaux, and in the second, as you are well aware, there's no evidence against him, whatever you may believe.'

'That's as may be, but you know as well as I do that he killed the Count.'

'Perhaps he did, but, if so, his punishment will have to be in the next world, if there is such a place.'

'You know there isn't. I wonder why I don't stick a knife in him myself. The Count was an old devil, but he loved life. The night before his murder he had his hand up my skirt and when I reproved him laughed and told me I used to welcome his attentions. "Stop being an old fool," I said, but he spoke the truth and it's four years now that I still miss him every day. So is it the poor sot in his chair or Monsieur Edmond that you're here to see?'

'Monsieur Edmond.'

She sniffed. 'At least you'll get some sense from him, whatever lies he tells you. You know where to find him.'

De Grimaud was reading, but laid his book aside when Lannes entered.

'Gide,' he said, 'how I responded to him when I was young, and what a canting old hypocrite he seems now. He'll be back soon, from his refuge in Algeria, if he's not already in Paris. So I thought I should renew my acquaintance. Strange how what used to excite me now seems like cold mutton. What do you think, Jean?'

'Nothing. I've never read him, nor been tempted to do so.'

'No, I suppose not. You're a Romantic at heart, aren't you. Your boy Dominique told me how you repeatedly return to the Musketeers. All for one and one for all – not a contemporary sentiment.'

'I don't know,' Lannes said. 'Some of the young men in the Resistance probably endorse it.'

Alain, he thought, remembering how Léon had confessed that when they first formed their own short-lived Resistance group here in Bordeaux, they had called each other by the names of the Musketeers, Alain of course being d'Artagnan.

'Do you know Madame d'Herblay?'

'By name and reputation only. She never goes anywhere. Why?'

'But you'll know her son.'

'Long ago. A useless fellow.'

'You may know then that he has a daughter, who lived with his mother, in her charge, very much in her charge. Then she disappeared, apparently running off with an art dealer called Aurélien Mabire, another useless fellow as you might say. Her godfather, the Comte de St-Hilaire whom you undoubtedly know, asked me to look for her. I found Aurélien but not the girl. Then when the Milice arrested me, I was interrogated by her father who called himself Captain Fracasse – ridiculous name, more literature as you see. Fabien arranged my release. You know that of course. Now this morning the girl, Marie-Adelaide, came to see me. She's living with Labiche, I think. Anyway she brought me a message from him. He wants to meet me, come to an agreement, says he has something he knows I want. Any idea what that might be? No? I've been trying to call Fabien, without success. What do you think?'

De Grimaud got to his feet. His left trouser-leg was rucked up, and he kicked out to free it.

'What do I think?' he said. 'More alcohol is perhaps best. Brandy for heroes, though I never felt less heroic. Fabien is dead. His body was found in the urinal of the railway station this morning. He had been shot in the back of the head, presumably while peeing, for his flies were undone. Or so I hear. The death hasn't been reported to you?'

'No.'

'It won't be, I'm sure of that.'

'How do you come to have heard of it?'

De Grimaud smiled and raised his glass.

'Your health, Jean. In a city of secrets there are always those ready to sell them.'

'The Resistance?'

'Perhaps. Our poor Fabien was responsible for the arrest and therefore indirectly the execution of a number of Communists, more than twenty to my knowledge, all now martyrs as you know. But then perhaps not. We spoke of the Liste Cortin. Fabien wanted it, for good reason; it represents power. And perhaps it is this that Labiche is now ready to trade. So who can tell? We may be sure that a man like Fabien had made many enemies.'

'Is your half-brother or nephew, as you prefer, Sigi, one of them? Marthe tells me he is back in Bordeaux? The Liste Cortin that Labiche may have, and that we suspect Fabien wanted . . . might Sigi's name appear on it? Was he a Cagoulard? And didn't Labiche defend him once, just as he defended your other brother Jean-Christophe?'

'Your half-brother too, Jean . . . don't forget.'

'I've no time for that nonsense,' Lannes said. 'Even if it was true, which I don't believe, it would mean nothing to me. The man who brought me up is the only father I'll ever acknowledge. Why has Sigi returned to Bordeaux? Tell me that.'

Edmond held up his hand and seemed to examine his fingernails.

'It's his home,' he said. 'This house is the only real home the poor chap has ever had. So naturally he returns to it as to a refuge.'

'A house where old Marthe would stick a knife in him without any compunction? Not much of a refuge.'

'Words, words, only words. Whatever she says now, she can't

forget that Sigi was a neglected child who used to run about her kitchen and hide under her skirts. She'll do him no harm.'

'Did he shoot Fabien?'

'I've no idea. It seems unlikely. Fabien was a man who moved in the shadows. He must have had many enemies. I should think it will be convenient to attribute his death to the Resistance. They're the people who are piling up corpses now. For my part I regard his departure as an inconvenience.'

Lannes lit a new cigarette from the stub of the previous one which he then crushed in the ashtray.

'Yes,' he said, 'it would doubtless be expedient to hold the Resistance guilty, and so there would be no investigation. But I'm puzzled by the role of that priest, Father Paul. He seems to be playing a double game. So why, I wonder, did Fabien bring him to that meeting?'

'That's a question I can't possible answer, Jean. Fabien rarely let his right hand know what his left was doing. As for me, I know nothing of the priest. I was as surprised by his presence there as you seem to be.'

'Might he have betrayed Fabien?'

'It's possible. We live in a time when anyone may betray anyone.'

'Is that a warning?'

'Not at all,' Edmond said. 'Merely a statement of how it is.'

XVII

It had been a profoundly unsatisfactory conversation. But that had been his experience with Edmond. Their dialogue was like one of these country dances where you step forward and back, come close to your partner but your hands never meet. And Fabien shot. Standing there trying to pee, on account of his bladder trouble. Doubtless he had been taken unawares; it was a humiliating way to go. No, 'humiliating' must be the wrong word – he wouldn't have known anything about it and you can suffer humiliation only if you are conscious of what has happened. So, not humiliating, but sordid. Edmond was probably right in asserting that nobody would want that death investigated. Like so many. But it went against the grain. Fabien had after all saved his life, almost certainly saved it, because without his intervention, he feared he would never have emerged from the Milice's prison. So he owed him a debt, or at least owed his memory one. And though he hadn't found Fabien sympathetic, he had felt respect for him.

No doubt Edmond was right. It would be convenient to hold the Resistance responsible. No questions were to be asked of the Resistance, not now, not for months as Bracal had implied, perhaps never. So any killings attributed to the Resistance could properly be shuffled out of sight.

But suppose it hadn't been the Resistance? Fabien had, for reasons he never divulged, been determined – seemed determined – to bring Labiche down. He'd made that clear in that meeting at which Edmond and the priest, Father Paul, were present. And Father Paul, as he'd said to Edmond, seemed to be playing a double game.

Then – Lannes' thoughts were like autumn leaves torn from the trees and swirling in a gale – there was Sigi back in Bordeaux. Was this a coincidence? He too, Lannes was certain, had moved in the Secret World. A man of no scruples and ineffable conceit. Marthe was sure he had murdered the Count, his father. She had, as he told her, no evidence – only her knowledge of his character. And he himself was equally certain that Sigi had murdered Gaston and also that he had tortured and killed the Catalan refugee Cortazar. Edmond had protected Sigi then; he had intervened to do Lannes a service with the result that the investigation had been abandoned. The shame of his agreement still lay on his conscience like a dark shadow.

In his confusion he might have been walking without intention, but his steps had taken him to the Gare St-Jean. That was how it happened sometimes. You arrived at a decision without conscious thought, just as so often it wasn't reasoning or the intellect that enabled you find your way to the solution of a case.

He went first to the tabac for a packet of Gauloises, and then to the bar for an Armagnac. He took it to the corner table where he had sat on his first meeting with Léon. The boy had arranged the meeting. He had looked up from the book he was reading – a

Balzac novel, he remembered – and spoken of Gaston with affection and without shame, despite what he had been to him, and then described the man he had seen Gaston afraid of in La Chope aux Capucines, and Lannes remembered how Maurice, leaving Gaston's apartment on the night he was murdered, had been embarrassed to hear one of them speak contemptuously of him as one of Chambolley's 'bum-boys'. Maurice had not been able to identify either of them as Léon did, and it was because Léon had impressed him that he had asked Henri to employ him in the bookshop which was where he had met Alain. More than four years ago, he thought, 'And I've failed in almost everything since.' Thinking of it now, he found he envied Alain and Léon – yes, and little Jérôme too – who had had the courage to break free and join de Gaulle, while he had remained tied to his duty, persuading himself he was not only acting honourably but was doing what was necessary to protect his family. Well, he wasn't alone in such self-persuasion, but where had it got him?

He drank his Armagnac, and, resisting the temptation to return to the bar, and have another and another and another, headed for the bureau of the railway police. The clerk, a middle-aged bald man, nodded when Lannes produced his badge and asked to speak to the senior officer on duty. Without removing the stub of the cigarette from the corner of his mouth he jerked his thumb at a door behind him.

'You'd a shooting here this morning,' Lannes said.

'I wasn't on duty then and know nothing about that. They may help you through here, and then again they may not. I wouldn't count on it if I was you.'

He lifted a shelf to enable Lannes to pass behind the desk and sighed deeply.

Lannes knocked at the door and, receiving no answer, opened it. A young police lieutenant was sitting with his feet up on the desk. He was smoking a pipe and reading a comic magazine.

Lannes identified himself and again said, 'You'd a shooting here this morning, I understand.'

'So I'm told, but I know nothing about it. I came on duty only at midday.'

'I see. Who found the body?'

'Couldn't rightly say.'

'Surely the information was logged in.'

'Suppose it might have been.'

'Then, look it up, will you, unless you want to be put on a charge for negligence, insolence and obstruction of an officer of the police judiciaire in the performance of his duty.'

'Case been handed to you, has it?'

'That's none of your business.'

'Expect it is, really. My superiors are inclined to get tetchy when there's interference from another branch of the police. Not that I give a damn, you understand.'

'Really?' Lannes said. 'You surprise me. Is there anything you do give a damn for? No, don't bother to answer that. Just give me the information I need.'

*   *   *

'Six-thirty in the morning. Not many people about, and not only because it's difficult to run trains these days, with half the lines blown up.'

The officer, to whom he had been reluctantly directed, a weary-looking middle-aged man, removed his cap and scratched his head.

'It's not the first murder we've had in recent months, you under-stand. But it's a surprising one.'

'What do you mean?'

'Well, it's unusual for people to arrive to remove the body even before a doctor has examined it. You'll grant me that?'

'Certainly, and who were these people?'

'The Milice. That's why nobody questioned them. Tell you the truth, superintendent, it surprised me to find they were still active, still capable of this sort of professionalism. Frankly, I rather thought the Resistance had more or less taken over, shut them out. But they were quick enough, make of that what you please.'

'Who identified the body then?'

'Nobody, far as I know. There wasn't time and in any case he had been stripped of any identification he was carrying. His wallet and papers had gone, you see.'

'Yes,' Lannes said. 'So there's little doubt it was an execution.'

'A bullet in the back of the head, sounds like that, don't it?'

And yet, though the railway police had no name for the victim – and were evidently happy to write the case off as being the kind of thing better not investigated – Edmond had heard of it within hours and knew – or believed? – that the dead man was Fabien.

'Who reported the crime? You must have a note of that.'

'Certainly. Even the boys who were on duty this morning aren't that slack. A Monsieur Pomathios. He'd arrived, by his account, on an early train from Biarritz. I've checked and there was such a train. Some of them, you know, are still running.'

'You'll have his address, I hope.'

'Here it is, 47 rue Xantrailles. Mériadeck, isn't it?'

Rue Xantrailles, where the Catalan Cortazar had been murdered in his apartment; coincidence surely.

'Yes, Mériadeck. You've been helpful. Thank you. And you should tell that young lieutenant at the desk to wake up.'

'That would be pointless. He's a washout. An uncle got him the job to prevent him for being conscripted for labour service in Germany. Pity, really. If they'd put him to work in a factory, he'd have mucked up their war effort.'

'Thank you. You've been helpful.'

*   *   *

There was no concierge in the building, but a card fixed in a metal holder on the wall to the left of the door directed him to an apartment on the second floor. He rang the bell and waited, lifted a knocker and banged it hard. He heard shuffling feet and the door was opened a few centimetres on a chain.

'Police judiciaire.'

'Oh Lord. Wait till I unhook this.'

Monsieur Pomathios was a small thickset man with a bald head and thick grey moustache, He was in shirt-sleeves and braces. When he turned away Lannes saw that his trousers sagged and he was wearing carpet slippers.

'You'd better come into the parlour,' he said.

It was a small stuffy room, over-furnished and Lannes had the impression that the window that looked on to the street hadn't been opened in a long time.

There was a half baguette on the table with a hunk of cheese beside it.

'I thought I'd eat but I'd no appetite. I've never known a day like it. I thought somebody might come to question me, but I have to say the police at the station seemed happy to be rid of me as quickly as possible. Which surprised me. Police judiciaire, I think you said you are.'

'Yes. It's my job to investigate cases like this. You'd come in on the early morning train from Biarritz, I'm told. What were you doing there?'

'What was I doing there? You may well ask. Yes indeed. I'm a commercial, see. My line's ladies' underwear, good quality, I've always dealt in good quality, but you'll understand, what with the Occupation and all, trade's been poor. There are some businesses, superintendent – it is superintendent, isn't it – that have done well out of the war and the Occupation, but ladies' underwear isn't one of them. And it's not just trade that's been slack. My employer, I have to tell you, well, he's no longer in Bordeaux. A Jew, you see. I don't need to say more, do I. As decent and straight a man as you could find anywhere, and a good Frenchman, we served in the same infantry regiment in our war. That's how I knew him. Well, I used to have a shop of my own, but when the wife died ten years ago, well, I ran into difficulties. She was the business brain, you see, and that's when Reuben Marks offered me a job and, what's more, invited me to come to share this apartment with him, he being a widower too and lonely himself, you understand, I didn't hesitate the time it would take me to cross the road. You couldn't have a better friend than Reuben was to me. So, when they started the *rafle* of the Jews – a right disgrace that was – he said to me "Pommi" – which is what he called me – "Pommi, I'm leaving everything in your care. Keep the business going and when I come back, we'll settle up." Well, I've done what I can, but trade's been poor, as I say. Still, things look brighter now, so the day before yesterday I said to myself, I'll just pop down to Biarritz, we used to do well there, and see if I can drum up some orders. Which I did, and with some success I'm glad to say, but whether poor Reuben will be back to profit from it, well, we won't go into that. It's a bad wicked business in my opinion.'

'So you stayed overnight in Biarritz,' Lannes said.

'Not of intention, but I got delayed, talking to an old customer, and then caught the first train I could. Feeling like death myself, if I say so. That's why I went to the buffet when I arrived, for a nip and a coffee and a piece of bread. And that's where I saw the dead man, not that he was dead then, you understand. It was the linen suit he was wearing caught my attention, it's not only ladies underwear I've an eye for. Good quality it was, and well cut. I notice such things.'

As he spoke, Monsieur Pomathios nodded his head up and down like a mechanical doll, as if he was numbering the points of his narrative.

'Was he alone?'

'At first he was, standing at the bar drinking his coffee. He looked at his watch a couple of times, so, if I'd thought about it then, I'd have assumed he was anxious not to miss his train. But I thought that only later, you understand.'

'You say, at first . . . '

'Yes, because he was joined by two others whom he was evidently expecting because they shook hands straight away.'

'Can you describe them?'

'Indeed, yes, because I've got what is called a noticing eye, as you have doubtless realised. One was a stocky fellow wearing a trilby hat and a buff-coloured or yellowish trench coat, even though it was a fine morning and good weather is forecast. But it was the other man I recognised and the sight of him . . . well, superintendent, I'm ashamed to say it, but for years I've had trouble with my bowels being loose – it's not a nice topic of conversation. And I wouldn't mention it but for the fact that the mere sight of him had me hurrying to the toilet with what I can only call considerable urgency.'

'To the public conveniences,' Lannes said, 'even though there's a toilet in the Buffet de la Gare?'

Monsieur Pomathios nodded again as if acknowledging that Lannes' question was reasonable.

'Indeed there is,' he said, 'but to reach it I'd have had to pass close to them, and even the sight of that bastard of a lawyer had me near soiling myself. You may know him, superintendent, indeed I expect you do, for he's what they call a prominent citizen, a member of the body set up to get rid of the Jews like my poor friend Reuben. And hadn't I myself gone to plead Reuben's cause to him and been dismissed with contempt and a warning that any more lip, as he said, and I'd find myself going the same way as the Jews?'

'Monsieur Labiche?'

'That's right. I'm not one to pass judgement on my fellow men, there's good buried somewhere in most of us, I like to think, but if anyone deserves to rot in hell it's that lawyer. To think of how he spoke to me of these poor Jews, it sickens me even to remember. So that's why I made for the public convenience, and I got into the cabinet to do my business just in the nick of time, which was a great relief. Then when I'd finished and had hooked up my braces and was getting my suit jacket on again, I heard this noise, a sort of squelch or phut, and the sound of a man falling. I thought someone had had an accident and stepped out to see if I could help. But there the poor gentleman was, lying with his face in the urinal and his beautiful linen suit filthy. I don't mind telling you I started to retch.'

'But did you see anything else.'

'Only, as I told the railway police, the back of that trench coat rounding the corner out of the toilets. It surprised me that they didn't seem much interested.'

Not sufficiently so to mention it to me, Lannes thought.

'Thank you, Monsieur Pomathios,' he said. 'You've been very helpful, a model witness.'

'I've always prided myself on my eye, never been one to miss much. You can't be a good salesman if you're not a noticing man.'

'I suppose not. Meanwhile I would be grateful if you would come to my office this afternoon to look at some photographs. It's possible that you may be able to identify the murderer. Shall we say five o'clock?'

XVIII

He felt elated as he descended the stairs and stepped into the street. The little commercial salesman was indeed what he had said, a model witness. And, though by his account it surely wasn't Labiche who had murdered Fabien, he was evidently involved, sufficiently involved at any rate to justify bringing him in for questioning. And indeed he might have fired the shot; Pomathios had seen only one man leaving, the fellow in the trench coat, but it was quite possible that Labiche had been a step or two ahead of him. He would put that possibility to Bracal anyway. But it was the trench coat and the description, however brief, of the man wearing it that interested him. Interested and disturbed, he had to admit. Sketchy as it was, it fitted Sigi who had returned, unexpectedly he thought, to Bordeaux, and who had long been, he believed, a gun for hire. And the fact that Edmond knew that the dead man was apparently Fabien, even though the railway police hadn't identified him – didn't that point to Sigi? Yet it was odd. Why should Edmond have mentioned it to him? Lannes hadn't been serious when he asked Edmond if Sigi had shot Fabien, or not wholly serious, had intended to do no more than rile him, but now it seemed likely that his question, plucked out of the air, had been a good one.

The sun was high in the sky and hot, a beautiful late summer day. He was near the Pension Bernadotte, and was tempted to call in on Yvette, only of course to reassure himself that she was well and safe. But, when he approached the building, he saw old Mangeot standing in the doorway, taking the sun in shirt-sleeves, and picking at his teeth with a matchstick.

'You're out of luck, superintendent,' he said. 'She's not at home. Out drumming up trade, I expect. She'll have to make do with the natives now that the Boches are on the run.'

'Enough of that,' Lannes said. He stepped forward and took hold of Mangeot by his shirt collar. 'Enough of that,' he said again. 'I've no doubt you've done well enough out of her, taken your cut, haven't you? There are difficult times ahead. I'll ask you to keep an eye on her and hold you responsible if anything happens to her.'

'I don't know what you're getting at, superintendent.'

'Don't you? Just remember you've a licence to lose. You're in my sights, Mangeot.'

It was worrying. He had no doubt Yvette would be in danger, for there would be people who knew of her dealings with German soldiers. He had warned her to steer clear of them, and perhaps she had done so recently, but there were others, besides Mangeot who would remember the young blond German she had called Wolfie, whom she had spoken of with affection so that he had suspected her interest in him had not been merely commercial. Horizontal collaboration wasn't something that would be overlooked. He had warned her, and she had smiled and said, 'What's a girl to do?' And Wolfie, she had said, was a sweet boy who missed his mother and had never wanted to go to war.

Back in the office he had old Joseph take a note through to Bracal asking for an appointment. He sat at his desk smoking and thinking of Fabien, taken by the urgent need to pee, taken by surprise as he stood at the urinal. Whatever the outcome of his meeting with Labiche and the other man – Sigi? – he had surely been taken by surprise, never suspecting that he was in danger. Did that suggest that his conversation with Labiche had been satisfactory? He had made an impression on Pomathios, or at least his beautiful linen suit had.

Joseph came back to say that the judge was not in his office, but he had left the message with his clerk.

'But, surprise, surprise,' he said, 'the Alsatian's at his desk and asked me to say he would like to see you if you came in. I didn't let on you were here already, in case you preferred to keep clear of him.'

'Thank you, Joseph, but you can tell him I'll be with him in ten minutes.'

The picture came to him of Fabien sitting opposite him, almost two years ago, here in his office, self-assured, sardonically dismissive of the Alsatian as one who preferred not to know what it might be uncomfortable to know, and smoking his long black Italian cigar. At their last meeting in the Café Régent Fabien had seemed confident he could effect the passage from Vichy to whatever New Order took its place, to Gaullism – surely he would manage that on account of old connections – but perhaps not to the Communists. He sighed and went through to the Alsatian's office.

Like everyone Schnyder was shabbier than he had been when he arrived in Bordeaux in 1940. The double-breasted grey suit was unpressed, there were flakes of dandruff on the collar, and the tie spotted with white horses was a little frayed at the knot. But he still had the air of a man confident of his own abilities, and the hand with which he waved Lannes towards a chair still clutched a fat cigar.

'Strange times,' he said. 'The word is the Germans will be gone in a couple of days. Do you know, as I walked through the city this morning, it felt like a theatre in which the audience is waiting for the curtain to go up, and is puzzled, even worried, by its delay in doing so. After all, Paris has already been liberated, but nobody here dares to make a move. It's as if the audience is wondering if something has gone wrong behind the scenes and is afraid the play will never start. Of course, I've been here long, enough, Jean, to have learned that you Bordelais like to keep your cards hidden, don't like to show your feelings till you're certain it's safe to do so. But it's going to be all right, you know. I have that on good authority. Plans have been made for an orderly transfer of power, to the FFI, but I can't see why this should affect us. All we have done over the years of the Occupation has been to perform our duty. I think we can congratulate ourselves on having managed to steer clear of politics. Yes, I rather pride myself on that. We've served the State, we'll continue to serve the Republic. A seamless transition, that's the thing.'

'Fabien has been shot,' Lannes said. 'Dead.'

'Fabien? I'm sorry, Jean, I don't know who you're talking about.'

'The spook, the senior spook I first met here, in your office, two years ago when that other spook who went by the name of Félix was killed.'

The Alsatian frowned. He drew on his cigar and turned the signet ring he wore on the little finger of his left hand.

'I remember,' he said. 'Lean fellow, served in Indo-China, didn't he? Friends at Court, as I recall. And you say he's been shot? I don't like that. Bound to be political, wheels within wheels. The Resistance, I suppose. Not for us, Jean. As I said, we steer well away from anything political.'

'You think so?'

'Indeed. Yes, certainly. We don't want to get involved in this sort of thing. That's why I asked you to come in, to tell you that for the coming months we must walk warily, like that king we spoke of in the Bible, Agag, wasn't it? There, I've remembered his name this time. So it's the Resistance, and there will be other Resistance killings, and they are no concern of ours. You understand? Things will settle in a few months, but meanwhile, we do nothing to attract attention till we see how things pan out.'

'I understand, sir, but I think I should say that the judge – Bracal – may have different ideas. I have the impression that Fabien was by way of being a friend of his.'

'No,' the Alsatian said, 'he's a careful man. He'll see the wisdom of turning a blind eye to Resistance activities. The trouble with you, Jean, is that you're a Romantic at heart. I'm a Realist.'

*   *   *

Lannes had long thought the Alsatian was a coward. That didn't mean he wasn't capable of good sense, following a prudent course. Cowards being alert to danger sometimes see things clearly, and if the Resistance had indeed been responsible for Fabien's murder, turning a blind eye would indeed have been sensible, and he would have obeyed reluctantly. But Pomathios' evidence couldn't – and shouldn't – be set aside.

Bracal sighed.

'So do I do as the commissaire has ordered, and let it go?'

'You didn't mention your little salesman to him?'

Lannes made no reply, kept his gaze fixed on the judge, and waited.

'You're obsessed with Labiche, Jean.'

'So was Fabien. And he does keep cropping up.'

'So what do you want?'

'Your authority to bring him in for questioning, and hold him pending further enquiries. That's all.'

'And the other man?'

'If he is who I think he is, he's a gun for hire, a hardened killer. There are two other deaths I would pin on him.'

'Very well, Jean. If you had come with this request even a week or ten days ago, I'd have told you to hold your fire. But, as it is, Labiche is finished, one way or another. And you said some time ago, as I recall, that you had reason to believe he had made plans to escape to Spain. I confess my first inclination would be to let him go, good riddance to bad rubbish, as they say. But I had some respect for Fabien. As you surmise we go back quite a long way. So you have my authority. Here, take this, it'll serve as a warrant. But be careful.'

*　　*　　*

At five o'clock, punctual as he had promised, Monsieur Pomathios presented himself at the desk. He was shown up to Lannes' office where a selection of photographs was spread before him on the desk. He examined them carefully, taking his time, then put his finger on one of Sigi, and said, 'That's the man in the trench coat, no doubt about it at all.'

'You're absolutely certain.'

'I'd swear to it on my mother's name. Like I told you, I'm a noticing man.'

'Thank you. You understand that if it comes to a trial you'll be summoned as a witness.'

'I'm prepared for that. You can trust me.'

When he had gone, Lannes went through to the inspectors' room.

'We've got permission to pick up Labiche. Moncerre, my old bull-terrier, I think that's a job for you. Better you do it than me. Take two men with you and bring him in. Don't rough him up, please. I don't want him to have any cause for complaint. He's being summoned only for questioning, not charged with anything. Not yet. Put him in a cell to cool his heels. René, you'll come with me to pick up Sigi. I don't think he'll try anything, but bring your revolver and be on your guard in case he does. But I think he'll come quietly – he's the most conceited man I know.'

XIX

'Paris liberated, liberated by its own people.' The General's words resoundingly pronounced as he stood on the balcony of the Hôtel de Ville, arms held aloft as if to embrace the crowd surging below him, echoed in Léon's mind as he woke in the room over the Place Contrescarpe. He had at last done his bit, presenting himself with Anne at a post manned by irregulars only tenuously attached to the FFI – like so many others. He had been given a rifle. He had fired at a German soldier and might have hit him, and he had heard a bullet strike the wall above his head. It had been a sort of battle and it expunged the shame of the months spent with Chardy.

Anne stirred, turned towards him, pressed her lips against his, searched for his tongue, then rolled back and pulled him over on top of her.

Later she said, 'I'm so happy, so happy we found each other again. At the right moment. Here, in Paris, liberated, isn't it wonderful? We're free. I do love you, Léon. Whatever happens we'll never forget these days.'

'I love you too.'

I really mean it, he thought, it's a miracle, and then, but for Priscilla, the Englishwoman, would I ever have?

'Kiss me again.'

Later she said, 'In a little we'll go out and join the crowd. Listen, they're singing the Marseillaise in the square. Aren't we lucky to be so happy?'

'Yes,' he said, 'we're among the lucky ones.'

He wondered where Alain was. Hadn't they promised to meet under the Arc de Triomphe?

*   *   *

'Of course your story's a horrible one,' François said. 'But I warned you, Dominique, the first days and weeks of Liberation weren't going to be a picnic. Too much has happened. Too many acts of betrayal have been committed. Too much blood has been spilled.

For many it's a time for revenge. And that's understandable. Vichy was always a mess. I knew that from the start, even though I served the regime diligently while it retained authority. Vichy was necessary. I'll never deny that – except in public. But now there's work to be done. De Gaulle has promised me a post even if he doesn't trust me. I don't deceive myself about that. "Oh, it's you again" – that's what he said when I presented myself at the War Ministry. You know that's where he went first, just to show he was in charge, and that it was Free France, Fighting France as he calls it, not the Resistance, that was, as he would put it, the true France. But he can't write off the Resistance, he can't sideline us altogether, and he knows that. Which is why there is a job for me – and for you, Dominique, on my staff. What do you say?'

Dominique hesitated. He thought of that ruined boy compelled to watch his father being tortured and murdered. By Communists, but Communists who would call themselves patriots. But here he was . . .

'Of course,' he said, 'I'm honoured. But if the telephones are still connected to Bordeaux, I must call my mother.'

*   *   *

'It's only a flesh wound. You'll be right as rain in a couple of weeks.'

'That's good,' Alain said. 'There's more fighting to be done.'

'Well, don't get yourself killed,' the doctor said. 'My own father was shot advancing on the ninth of November, 1918, two days before the Armistice. I don't believe my mother ever forgave him. Why couldn't he have stayed safe in a trench like a sensible man, she used to say.'

'The war's not won yet,' Alain said, 'and in any case if France is to be recognised as one of the victorious nations we have to take part in the invasion of Germany. I've already managed to get myself transferred to a Hussar regiment. So I'm glad to hear you say I'll be fine in a couple of weeks.'

*   *   *

'Paris liberated!' Corporal Jean de Flambard put his arm round

Michel's shoulder and hugged him. 'What do you say to that, kid? We've certainly backed the wrong horse.'

'Liberated? Or in the hands of the Bolsheviks? Or the American money power? Either way, with the Ivans advancing, it's only Germany that is defending European civilisation.'

'If you say so, kid. Meanwhile I'm thinking of those bodies we saw swinging from the trees.'

'Traitors, deserters . . . '

'Well, that's something we can't do – desert, I mean. We wouldn't get five miles. I've made a mess of my life, I've known that for years. But you had yours before you.'

'I still have.'

He ran his hand over his bristly chin and wondered if Clothilde would recognise him.

'I'd be fine if it wasn't for these fucking lice,' he said.

A shell howled overhead.

'Missed us again,' the Corporal said. 'I tell you, my luck's right out.'

'That's pathetic,' Michel said. 'But I know you don't mean it.'

*   *   *

'So you are off to Paris,' Sir Edwin said. 'I'll miss you, dear boy.'

'Duty calls,' Jérôme said. 'Not that I know exactly why they're sending me there, or what I'm supposed to do.'

'You're excited?'

'Of course. But I'll miss London.'

'London will miss you. I'll miss you.'

'You'll find another boy.'

'Undoubtedly. Though actually I'm thinking of getting married.'

'You?'

'Why not? It's a time of change, and anyway the war has taught us all the importance of camouflage. I'm not exactly popular with my party, you know. Now lift your glass, dear boy, and let's drink to happy days in Paris. I hope to have some there myself again before long. But now, alas, I must get back to the House to listen to Winston, boasting as usual I suppose . . . '

Left alone in the downstairs American Bar of the Ritz, Jérôme looked at his watch. Half an hour before he was due to meet Freddie. Goodbye or au revoir? Freddie too was speaking of marriage.

'The old woman's changed her tune,' he had said. 'She wants a grandchild, silly old thing. Help you to settle down, she said. Not till I'm out of the Navy, I said. And anyway, Froggie, you promised me Gay Paree, I'll hold you to that.'

He probably would. Fine. But Sir Pringle was right. It was a time of change.

He picked up the bottle. Still a glass left. One thing to be said for Sir Pringle, he always ordered the best champagne. Krug '28 . . .

XX

The Germans were still in Bordeaux, even if pulled back into barracks they were no longer seen in the streets. Yet you couldn't but be aware of their presence, and the thought that Paris was liberated while Bordeaux was still formally an occupied city was disturbing. You could be certain of nothing. Even the Resistance groups were on edge. And it was still August, holiday time, though as in every year since 1939 almost nobody had left the city, except, Lannes thought, for the rich who had withdrawn to their properties in the country. So schoolchildren roamed the streets, on the loose, nervous and excited, as the sun continued to beat down.

Moncerre had brought Labiche in, slipping cuffs on him when he protested, but when Lannes and René presented themselves at the house in the rue d'Aviau, old Marthe scowled and told them they were too late.

'Monsieur Edmond found petrol for the car, and the pair of them left in a hurry.'

'In which direction?'

'How should I know? They don't tell me the likes of that. If you'd done as I told you and arrested him for the murder of his father . . . the only people here besides me are the poor sot in his father's chair, and Madame in her bed saying she's dying, which she isn't, the stupid cow. I told you before, this house is a place of wickedness, but you didn't listen to me.'

'And young Maurice?'

'Lord knows. He left, after words with his father. Now be off with you.'

'They'll be heading for Spain,' René said, when the door was closed behind them.

'Probably. At all events, we'll alert the Border guards, though whose orders they'll follow is anyone's guess. Meanwhile, will you pick up that clerk of Labiche's and bring him in. He may be of some use.'

It was unlikely. The young man almost certainly knew nothing. But his arrest might puzzle Labiche.

*   *   *

He had passed a bad night. Marguerite was on edge. If Paris had been liberated, surely they should have heard from the boys. Weren't the telephones working? It wasn't like Dominique – he would know how anxious she was. And Alain might be dead for all they knew. Sometimes she was certain he was. It was hard to hold on to hope when they heard nothing. Surely there was something Lannes could do as a policeman to find out? There were days when she thought he didn't care, that he was concerned only with his beastly work and neglected his family. Then she dissolved into tears, cried that she had spoken harshly to him only because she was miserable and afraid. He tried to comfort her, without success. They both slept badly. Now arriving in the office in the morning, he passed his hand over his brow. He was sweating freely and there was a stabbing pain in his head. He felt terrible.

Moncerre was in the inspectors' room with his feet up on the desk.

'I enjoyed that,' he said. 'You should have seen his face when I put the cuffs on him. One of these "this can't be happening to me, I'm a distinguished member of the Bordeaux bar" moments. "Oh yes, it can and it is, matey," I said. It was as good as a play. Mind you, if you hadn't told me not to rough him up, I'd have been happy to have some fun with him. I can't stand these types as you know. Anyway, he's cooling his heels in the cells, just as you instructed. Did you get your chap?'

'No, it seems as if he's left town.'

'Pity.'

'Yes.'

The smile on the bull-terrier's face suggested he was more amused than displeased by Lannes' failure.

'Have him brought up to me in ten minutes,' he said. 'We'll have a go at him together.'

In his own room he took two aspirin, and followed them with a nip of Armagnac. He sat behind his desk, staring at the ceiling and listening to children's voices from the street below.

Labiche was unshaven after a night in the cells, but they had given him back his braces to prevent his trousers from falling down as he climbed the stairs to Lannes' office. He stood there thickset and glowering between the two policemen who were guarding him.

'You can take the cuffs off,' Lannes said, 'and return to your other duties. I'll send a messenger to fetch you when you're needed again. Sit down, Monsieur Labiche, and make yourself comfortable. We've a lot to talk about.'

'I've nothing to say, except to the judge who signed the warrant your man here produced.'

'Don't be silly. It's unworthy of you, as an intelligent man. Sit down. Besides, when Marie-Adelaide called on me – at your request, as I understood – she said you wanted to talk with me. So here we are, let's talk. Sit down.'

'Very well, but I do so under protest. I should like that recorded.'

'I'll remember that,' Lannes said, 'but we're not at the stage of recording anything, are we, Moncerre? I hope they gave you some breakfast, even if the coffee's terrible. You've had a busy war, Monsieur Labiche, but that doesn't concern me. It'll be for another sort of court some day to investigate your role in the deportation of Bordeaux's Jews. That's none of my business. And I'm not concerned with your attempt to destroy me – these anonymous letters, you know. Nor with your role in the assault on the boy Karim, to persuade him to sign a paper implicating me. That's all in the past, and, as far as criminality goes, it doesn't amount to much. It's small beer, as they say. It's true your clerk – Jacques

Bernard, isn't it – is being questioned now, but I doubt if we'll get much of interest from him. And then the last time you were brought here . . . '

'When I came of my own free will, on account of my respect for the police and the authority they derive from the State.'

'Quite so. I remember you saying that then. And I remember too that when I showed you that photograph of you sitting beside that naked young girl, you tore it up, and told me it signified nothing.'

'Which it didn't.'

'Which of course it doesn't unless I find the girl, and I admit I have failed to do so, though I'm still looking. And the other girl who hanged herself, well, there's no evidence that you were responsible for the degradation that drove her to that. Likewise, your niece, Mademoiselle Jauzion, is certainly not going to testify against you, not only on account of her career in the theatre, but because she is too proud to speak publicly of how you abused her as a child. So, although I personally find your behaviour repulsive as well as criminal, I have to say that as far as your abuse of young girls is concerned, there's no evidence that would allow me to charge you.'

He paused to light a cigarette.

'Nothing to say, Monsieur Labiche?'

The advocate made no reply, kept his gaze watchful as the squatting toad Madame Smitt had compared him to.

'Of course there's that wretched priest,' Lannes said. 'He's afraid of you, so he may tell us something when he knows you're under arrest, but that's not my concern. In any case it's the Vice Squad who will examine him, and I'm ready to admit that till things have settled down nobody will be much interested in the sort of crimes the Vice Squad deal with. So you've no immediate worry in that respect.'

Labiche sighed, heavily, like an actor displaying boredom. 'This is all foolishness, superintendent. You're wasting your time and mine. Foolishness and hypocrisy, when I think of your whore in the Pension Bernadotte, that Jew-boy in the bookshop and that slimy Arab pervert. Your own sheet isn't so clean. Don't forget that the Arab signed that paper, and I have two witnesses who would say he did so willingly. As for Father Paul, he holds you responsible for the murder of his brother. Don't forget that.'

'Oh I won't,' Lannes said. 'But the difference, Monsieur Labiche, is that I'm on this side of the desk, you're on the other, and your day is done. You're not going to get away to Spain. We're going to hold you on criminal charges, and then you will he handed over to whichever court is established to investigate and punish those guilty of collaboration with the enemy. In that respect you're guilty as sin. Meanwhile I think I know why you sent Marie-Adelaide to see me, and what you had to trade. Only someone else got in first. Fabien, wasn't it? He wanted the copy of the Liste Cortin, didn't he, with its record of the membership of the Cagoule. Only he didn't get it. He was shot instead. And I wonder why.'

'I don't know what you are talking about.'

'You don't?'

'We're getting nowhere, chief,' Moncerre said, getting to his feet. 'I understand this type better than you. He's conceited as the Devil, but there's one language he understands.'

He crossed the room, stood behind Labiche, took hold of his right arm and twisted it high behind his back till the advocate squealed in pain.

'That's just the beginning,' he said. 'Give me a half-hour with him in the cells and I guarantee he'll talk.'

'It's all right, Moncerre,' Lannes said. 'Let him alone. He'll talk here, especially now that you've shown him the cost of silence. Go and ask old Joseph to have the café send up beer and sandwiches. We've a long session before us.' When Moncerre with a shrug of the shoulders left the room, Lannes said, 'We call him the bull-terrier, you know, because when he gets his teeth into a case – or a suspect – he doesn't let go. Now you, Monsieur Labiche, prefer violence at one remove. So I don't think you shot Fabien yourself. I think that's why you brought a gunman along with you. Sigi de Grimaud, wasn't it.'

Labiche rubbed his arm.

'He hurt me,' he said. 'That's assault.'

'Don't be childish, Monsieur Labiche. Nothing happened. Nothing, as you would say, of any significance. I rather liked

Fabien, you know. Respected him anyway. And I was in his debt after you had the Milice arrest me. That was a mistake on your part, especially since that wretched chap d'Herblay lost his nerve. You don't choose your tools well – d'Herblay and that miserable Aurélien. I'd have thought better of you. It hadn't occurred to me you were such a bungler.'

'I don't know what you are talking about. This Fabien you speak of. I've no idea who you mean.'

Moncerre returned.

'Beer and sandwiches on their way. Is he talking yet?'

'He's thinking about it,' Lannes said.

'Want me to have another go at him?'

'Patience, my old bull-terrier. Remember who we're dealing with. Not only a member of the Bar which in his opinion entitles him to be numbered among the untouchables, but the Bordeaux director of the institute set up to handle the Jewish Question. So, an important person. Actually, Monsieur Labiche, it's indirectly your role in dealing with the Jews that has brought you here. You see, I've a witness to your meeting with Fabien in the Buffet de la Gare, and he recognised you because he had come before you to plead for his Jewish employer. You dismissed his appeal out of hand, of course, but he didn't forget you. How could he? So he was interested when he saw you with Fabien, and a few minutes later Fabien was shot as he stood pissing at the urinal. My witness was so disturbed by the sight of you and the memories this evoked that he was taken short himself and he was just about to emerge from the cabinet when he heard the shot, and then saw the back of your companion – the man in the trench coat – leaving the toilets where Fabien lay dead. Now, as I say . . . '

He broke off when the waiter from the café came in with a tray of sandwiches and six bottles of beer. He placed it on the desk, eyed up Labiche, turned to Lannes, smiled, nodded his head, and left them.

'Give the advocate a beer, Moncerre. I think he needs one.'

Lannes bit into a sandwich, and took a deep draught of beer. His headache had gone either because of the aspirin or because he was enjoying himself.

'As I say, I doubt if you killed Fabien yourself, because you prefer violence at one remove, and I don't think he got the List from you though it was the promise of the List that brought him to meet you. So it wasn't on account of the List, but for some other reason, something perhaps that he knew about you, that he was killed. And that's why you brought the man in the trench coat – it was Sigi, wasn't it – as a bodyguard in case Fabien wasn't alone – a bodyguard and hired gun. But you are – I've no doubt about it – an accessory to murder, and that's what I'm going to book you as, for the time being anyway. It's what we call a holding charge, but of course, as an advocate, you know all about that. I'd like to know what he had on you – of course I would – but that can wait. The accessory charge will stick.'

'This is absurd,' Labiche said. 'I suppose I knew he would have to go to the toilets? Knew there would be nobody else there, and dispatched my so-called companion in the trench coat to kill him? Yes, it's absurd, utterly absurd.'

'Absurd?' Lannes said. 'I don't think Judge Bracal will find it absurd. In any case we've been living in the absurd for four years now.'

*   *   *

Two hours later they were still at it. Lannes went over the ground time and again. Labiche admitted nothing. As to the meeting with Fabien in the Buffet de la Gare, which he realised he couldn't deny in view of the witness Lannes offered to produce, he shrugged his shoulders and said it had been a chance encounter. He had fallen into conversation with the man but had no idea who he was. What had they talked about? He really couldn't remember. Nothing of any great matter. Yes, he remembered that the man Lannes called Fabien had wondered how long it would be after the Germans had gone before they could get drinkable coffee again. He had no idea who the man in the trench coat was. If he had thought about it, which he had no reason to do, he would have assumed he was a friend or acquaintance of – what was his name? – Fabien. After all they had left together. No, he had no idea that there had been a shooting. Why should he have? Nobody had spoken to him about such a thing. Of course, when he learned of it later, he wasn't surprised, but only because such things were, sadly, all too common. He supposed he would have assumed that the Resistance was involved. They were criminals, murderers, capable of any barbarity. Everyone knew that. Why had he been at the station at that hour of the morning? Why shouldn't he have been there? He saw no reason or requirement to account for his actions. Nevertheless, if only to end this nonsense – he spat out the word, 'this absurdity' – he was willing to do so. He had intended to take a train to Bergerac, on the business of a client, but, as it turned out, the train, like so many, was cancelled. In short his presence there, like his meeting with the dead man, had been purely fortuitous. If Lannes really intended to hold him as an accessory to murder, he would have to produce some evidence. He couldn't understand why Judge Bracal had consented to sign that warrant merely on the strength, as it appeared, of the evidence of a single witness who, from Lannes' own account, had a grudge against him because he had quite properly in his capacity as director of the institute legally established to deal with the Jewish Question, been responsible for the arrest and – yes, he admitted – deportation of his employer. The man might be a Jew himself, certainly he seemed a Jew-lover, and his attempt to involve him in this crime was a typical piece of Jewish malice.

'That old tune,' Lannes said. 'It's out of date, Monsieur Labiche, and it does you no good to sing it. If there's one good thing that has come out of this terrible war, it's surely that anti-Semitism will never be respectable in France again. Your day's done, Monsieur Labiche.'

'I demand that you either release me immediately, or take me before Judge Bracal.'

'Both demands are refused. Arrange for him to be taken back to the cells, Moncerre.'

XXI

It was like old times, the three of them resorting for lunch to Fernand's bistro as they hadn't done for many months. There were no Germans there of course, and only a sprinkling of Bordelais had ventured out, pretending that normality had returned or in the hope that it was about to do so. Lannes was amused and even impressed to see that the silent elderly couple were there again. Young Jacques said they had become regulars.

'They never speak to each other, but they eat steadily through whatever we're able to put before them, and I have to warn you that's not much. Even the black market's not functioning efficiently at present.'

'So what can you give us?'

'A clear soup which is lacking in flavour, I'm sorry to say, followed by a rabbit stew and cheese. There's not even any salad, but at least the Boches haven't drunk the cellar dry.'

'Well, we'll have to make up on the wine, but actually a rabbit stew sounds fine. And we'll start with a bottle of champagne. We've got the advocate Labiche in the cells. So we've something to celebrate.'

'I'm glad to hear that,' Jacques said. 'He's been one of our best customers but I've never been able to stand the bastard. The champagne will be on the house.'

'Is your father about?'

'He said he might be in later if he can take time off from rounding up collaborators.'

He put his hand on Lannes' shoulder to draw him aside, out of the hearing of Moncerre and young René.

'I'm very glad you've come in. I've got young Karim here, up in the attic. He arrived last night, in a bad way. Someone has beaten him up. He wouldn't say who, but I'd say he's scared stiff. Would you have a word with him after you've eaten? And, by the way, if the old man does turn up, don't tell him Karim's here.'

'All right, but why?'

'It's just a feeling I have, that it would be better to say nothing. Now I'll see to the champagne.'

'Fine, I don't think we'll bother with the soup.'

'A wise decision, I'm sorry to have to say.'

'Fizz on the house,' Moncerre said. 'It's almost enough to make you believe in a post-war world. Are you sure we've got enough on the bastard, chief?'

'We've enough to hold him. Beyond that, I don't know, so far as the murder of Fabien is concerned. But don't worry. He's not going anywhere. There are lots of people who are going to be interested in seeing to Monsieur the Advocate.'

'I hope you're right. I'm with Jacques. Like he said, I can't stand the bastard, never could. But it's not like you to be so confident, chief. You must have got out of bed on the right side this morning.'

Jacques brought the wine, popped the cork and filled the glasses.

'Have one yourself, Jacques,' Lannes said.

'I don't mind if I do.'

'Here's to Peace,' Lannes said. 'I only wish I could believe in it. And we'll have a bottle of St-Emilion with the rabbit.'

'Of course.'

Lannes turned to René.

'Did you get anything from the clerk?'

'Nothing directly useful. He's still scared stiff of Labiche. Even when I told him we had him under arrest, he continued to say he knew nothing. I think he may have been telling the truth. He's a feeble fellow and I can't see Labiche entrusting him with anything important. Sorry.'

'I expect you were too soft with him,' Moncerre said. 'Give me ten minutes with him and he'd be singing.'

'Yes,' René said. 'He'd tell you exactly whatever you wanted to hear. But it would still be lies.'

Lannes repressed a smile. The boy had certainly grown up.

'There was just one thing,' René said. 'According to Jacques Bernard, the girl who was living with Labiche has walked out on him. That was the one you were looking for, wasn't it, chief?'

'Yes. I don't suppose he said where she had gone.'

'I asked him but he said he had no idea.'

'I don't suppose it's important. She came to see me, and she's certainly not the innocent child I was told she was. I would say she can look after herself.'

'This rabbit,' Moncerre said, 'has certainly been on Occupation rations. There'd be more flesh on a rat.'

*　　*　　*

220

Karim was lying face-down on the truckle bed in the attic, his legs stretched out straight. Lannes put his hand on his shoulder and the boy started. When he turned his head, Lannes saw that he had a black eye, his mouth was swollen and there were streaks of dried blood on his cheek.

'You just can't keep out of trouble, can you?' Lannes said. 'So what is it this time? Why did you land yourself on Jacques?'

Karim attempted a smile. It didn't get far.

'Nobody else,' he said, 'nobody else I could think of. The priest's dead. I didn't kill him, but he's dead. They put him up against a wall and shot him. I thought they were going to kill me too, but they just beat me up. Then one of them spat on me and then it was worse, and then they told me to get out of Bordeaux.'

He began to cry and his whole body shook. Lannes sat on the edge of the bed, waiting till the spasm passed. Eventually, 'You'd better tell, from the beginning,' he said, and placed his fingers lightly on the boy's cheek. 'Relax,' he said, 'and tell. You're safe here. No harm's going to come to you.'

'They raped me, all three of them, and one said, "This is what you like, isn't it?" '

'From the beginning.'

It took some time because Karim was incapable of speaking coherently. But gradually, something of a narrative emerged. He had been sitting in a café, couldn't say which, minding his own business, and happy. Yes, happy – 'because of my last conversation with you, superintendent, you remember that?' – then the priest came in, and sat down beside him. He would have gone away at once, but the priest prevented him. He began to speak again of his brother's murder. It was like he was obsessed. Really what he said made no sense at all, and twice Karim made to leave, but the priest took hold of him and said, 'No, you must listen.'

'Then these three men came in, not men really, young fellows, no older than me.' Two of them grabbed the priest, twisted his arm up behind his back and frog-marched him out into the street, round the corner into a little alley. The third one stuck a gun in Karim's back and made him follow. They set the priest up against the wall, and he cried out that he didn't want to die unshriven.

They laughed, and said it didn't matter because he was a collaborator and if there was a hell, that's where he was bound for. Then they shot him, just like that, and Karim was sure he was for it himself. He pissed himself in his terror, and that's when they began to knock him about, and one of them said, 'Let's have some fun with the pansy, let's give him what he likes.' Some people, alerted by the shots, came and stood at the entrance to the alley, and just watched, silently. 'The young men laughed, and, you know,' Karim said, 'they weren't thugs. They sounded like what they call well bred, students perhaps. And when they had finished, one said, "Fun's over." Another said, "Shouldn't we finish him off too," but they just laughed again, and they came and spat on him and left him there in the gutter.' He couldn't think of anyone to turn to but Jacques. 'He's always been my friend, even if . . . ' He began to cry again. 'What should I do?'

What could he say?

'I'll have a word with Jacques. For the moment you're safe here.'

He descended the stairs with a heavy heart. The priest, Father Paul, had been a scoundrel. He might have caused more trouble for Lannes, pursuing his allegation that he was responsible for the killing of his brother, the spook Félix. The charge was baseless. Nevertheless.

But his own murder, undoubtedly at the hands of the Resistance, was a crime which would certainly go unpunished. What was it Bracal had said? That, for the time being, the concept of legality was in suspension and the Resistance's revenge on collaborators would be a kind of wild justice? What sort of New France could be established on that sort of foundation? And the rape and humiliation of Karim? There was no justice there, merely a vile expression of power.

'Will you keep him where he is for a few days?' he said to Jacques. 'He's in a bad way. Not, this time, his own fault.'

'Yes of course,' Jacques said. 'I'm fond of him in a way. He's not such a bad chap, despite everything.'

'He's a bloody nuisance.'

'But you're fond of him yourself.'

'Am I? I suppose I am. What about your father?'

'Oh he's got no thought for anything just now, except his new girl, the Party and the Resistance. I don't understand it. It's not like him.'

'We must hope the enthusiasm passes.'

XXII

'The Charlemagne Legion of the Waffen SS,' Baron Jean de Flambard said, 'sounds grand, doesn't it? Almost medieval, like a heroic *chanson de geste*. Do you regret being here, kid?'

'Do you?'

Michel turned over to look at his corporal, and saw there was laughter in his eyes.

'Do you?' he said again.

'I know myself for a fool,' the baron said, 'but you shouldn't be here, kid.'

'Don't patronise me. I'm where I chose to be.'

The baron lit a cigarette and passed it to Michel, then another for himself.

'You don't know Paris, do you?' he said. 'I remember one evening in 1940, standing on the Ile des Juifs below the Pont-Neuf. It's where they burned the Knights Templar – there's a plaque on the wall commemorating it, and, as the flames rose around him, the Grand Master of the Temple Jacques de Molay called out a curse on the King, Philip the Fair, and on all those who had collaborated with him in the destruction of the Order. And I thought, even then, that curse still hangs heavy over France, more than six hundred years later. It was a beautiful May evening when I stood there and pictured the scene, the fires of persecution masquerading as justice, and now I think we're as surely doomed as the Templars were. And that's why I'm here.'

'I don't know what you're talking about,' Michel said.

'I don't know that I do either.'

Michel squinted along the sights of his rifle. He squeezed the trigger.

'That's one Ivan less,' he said. 'You talk too much, you know.'

*   *   *

François said, 'The General's an extraordinary fellow, you know. Did I tell you that when he was leading the march along the Champs-Élysées to the Arc de Triomphe, little Georges fell in step beside him. Without giving him so much as a glance, the General said, in his iciest tone – and tones don't come icier – "A few paces back, Monsieur Bidault." And poor Georges obeyed, even though as Chief of the National Council of the Resistance, he thought he had every right to be at de Gaulle's side, sharing the honour of the day. That shows what the General thinks of us in the Resistance; he thinks he's Joan of Arc and has saved France all on his own. He doesn't like me, as I've told you, Dominique. And he'll get rid of me as soon as he can. But he's not going to beat me, remember that. We're France too, those of us who served in Vichy and then organised the Resistance. You stick by me and I'll make you a great man. Our business is to effect a reconciliation between the France of Vichy and the France of the Resistance, the France of St Louis and the France of Voltaire. That's going to be my life's work, and I look to you to accompany me on what will be a long journey.'

He picked up his glass.

'Did you manage to telephone your mother? Yes? And what did she say?'

'She couldn't believe it was me, and then she burst into tears.'

*　　*　　*

Léon said, 'You'll like her, I'm sure you will. She's endured an extraordinary war. Well, I suppose we all have. But an English-woman, here in Paris throughout, it's remarkable. Of course I haven't ever asked her just what she has had to do to survive. But then,' he took hold of Anne's hand and squeezed it, 'my own last year since they broke the network and you were arrested has been shameful. Being Chardy's boy – that's not something I'm proud of. Yet I don't know what I'd have done without him. Anyway I'm sure you'll like Priscilla and in any case if it hadn't been for her and what she taught me about myself, I don't know that I would have dared to kiss you. Does that sound mad?'

'Only a little. And actually if you remember, I kissed you first.'
She leaned over and kissed him again.

'All the same,' she said, 'I'm not sure that I want to meet your Englishwoman.'

There was a knock on the door. For years now everyone had feared that sound, and for a moment they clung to each other in silence. The knock was repeated. Anne slowly disengaged herself, slipped from the bed, and opened the door. Two armed men in the uniform of the FFI stood there.

'A little love-nest,' one of them said.

He pushed Anne aside with the muzzle of his gun.

The other pointed his at Léon.

'Get dressed,' he said. 'We're taking you in for questioning.'

*   *   *

'It's hard to believe we're in Paris.'

The boy, Vincent, looked wide-eyed at the Boulevard St-Germain, and the girls who walked past them with a swagger that had survived years of malnutrition. He was a country boy and it was all strange to him.

'I never thought we'd escape from that cattle-truck,' he said, not for the first time.

'We were destined to be lucky,' Alain said. 'Anyway I never yielded to despair. I believe in France, you see.'

His arm was still in a sling, and he smiled with happiness as they sat outside the Flore watching the world go by as people savoured the reality of Liberation.

'I've always believed in France,' Alain said again, 'if not in the French people.'

'This friend of yours we're meeting, what's he called?'

'Jérôme, he's all right. Ah, here he is.'

Jérôme approached them, strolling, elegant in a bottle-green cashmere jersey, open-neck cream-coloured shirt and grey flannel trousers. He embraced Alain and said, 'I can't believe it.'

'This is Vincent, we've been through hard times together.'

'Delighted to meet you.' He held out his hand. 'It's extra-ordinary,' he said. 'I've just come from London, you know, and Paris seems less war-battered than London. It's like waking up from a bad dream. Do you have any word of Léon, Alain?'

'None at all. I don't even know if he's alive. Too many of us aren't.'

'We must find him,' Jérôme said, 'all for one and one for all, remember?' He took out a packet of Player's cigarettes and passed it round. 'The General smokes these himself,' he said. 'I've asked around about Léon, but nobody I've spoken to knows anything.'

XXIII

Under cover of darkness, during the night of 28 August, the convoy of German troops rolled out of Bordeaux. The city woke to find itself liberated. As the word spread the streets were filled with people experiencing the strangest and most exhilarating of feelings. Few could even then, however, fail to be mindful of the hundreds of resisters shot by the Occupying army and the Vichy police, and the thousands who had been deported for political or racial reasons. Nevertheless, as crowds surged through the streets laughing and singing the Marseillaise, almost nobody could restrain their expression of joy. Yet, even on this first day of freedom, there was bitterness too. A number of well-known collaborators were arrested and paraded in the Cours de l'Intendance, with placards affixed to their back and chest proclaiming their shame.

Lannes had woken to the unaccustomed sound of Marguerite singing, the happiness with which she had greeted that telephone call from Dominique scarcely disturbed by the continuing anxiety over Alain, of whom Dominique had been able to tell her nothing.

Clothilde said, 'It's astonishing to see Maman like she used to be.'

A tremor in her voice warned Lannes that she couldn't share her mother's undiluted joy. For months now she had known without doubt that her Michel had joined the wrong side, not only the wrong but the losing one; and he knew that she must now fear that she would never see him again. Such news as they had of the horrors of the war on the Eastern Front made it all but impossible for her to continue to hope. How long would it take her to free herself from his memory? And how terrible it was that she could not share in the unrestrained joy of Liberation! It was as if by loving Michel she had attached herself to the forces of darkness. Lannes took her in his arms and hugged her, but found himself bereft of any words of consolation.

And the man, Sigi, whose influence over the boy had led him so foolishly astray, had, Lannes feared, made his escape to Spain, along with Edmond de Grimaud whose nerve had seemingly, and unexpected by Lannes, failed.

He headed for the office, uncertain of what he might find there, but to his surprise all was normal. The Alsatian was even at his desk and greeted Lannes as if it was an ordinary day.

'I've already had a meeting,' he said, 'with the secretary of the newly-appointed Commissaire of the Republic, and our orders are to carry on as usual. It's essential, he says, that the organs of the Republic continue to function. For a little, he admits, the Resistance will rule the streets. There's nothing we can do about that, it's something we have to accept. But it won't be long before the Resistance is disbanded, its members either incorporated in the regular army, or returned to whatever was their proper station in civilian life. The commissaire's clear about that, but this is their hour, he says, and it would be foolish to attempt to rein them in. There will be some disorder, but it will soon pass. Do you understand, Jean?'

'I understand, but I don't like it.'

He lit a cigarette.

'You don't have to like it,' Schnyder said, 'just accept this is how it is, for the moment. We've come through dark times without compromising ourselves.'

'Yesterday,' Lannes said, 'three young men from a Resistance group murdered a priest. They put him up against a wall and shot him. He was probably a bad priest. Certainly I've no reason to think him a good man. But this was murder, mob rule and murder, perhaps a revenge killing, I don't know. But murder, I'm certain of that. And I've a witness. Do I do nothing? Do I tell the witness to forget about it?'

'That's just what you do. I'm sorry, Jean, but that's precisely what you do. We must do nothing that will compromise the PJ in the eyes of the new authorities. That's my prime concern. Now to another matter. I understand that you have the advocate Labiche under arrest.'

'Yes, as an accessory to murder. Are you happy with that or would you like me to release him?'

'There's no call for that,' the Alsatian smiled, and clipped the end off a cigar. 'Even two weeks ago it would have been different, but now I'm perfectly happy. You've done well. Labiche belongs to the past. His arrest will win us favours with the new regime. It's all a matter, Jean, of being alert to the way the wheel turns.'

The Alsatian was right of course. Lannes couldn't deny that. Nevertheless he felt soiled. Serving Vichy had been inescapable, also compromising, even humiliating. Were these days of Liberation any different? He picked up his stick and left the office. In the streets it was like a day of holiday. The crowd surged to and fro, cheering and singing. But the happiness wasn't undiluted. There was an undercurrent of anger too. People had suffered. They had experienced shame. Expiation demanded revenge. Anxiety quickened his pace towards Mériadeck.

The street was thronged as he approached the Pension Berna-dotte, and he had to push his way through a crowd, mostly of women, who were shouting and jeering. A platform had been erected, and Yvette was tied to a chair on top of it. The upper part of her dress had been torn away. Mangeot stood beside her, smiling. A couple of men stood over the girl. He recognised one as a local butcher. He was holding a pair of shears. 'Crop the bitch,' someone shouted. 'Crop the Boche-loving whore.' Lannes called out in protest, 'Stop this at once.' Yvette raised her head and met his eyes. Her face was without expression; she was like a dumb animal brought to the slaughter. 'Stop it at once,' he shouted again. 'Bastards, it's you who are a disgrace to France.'

Someone struck him on the back of the head. He fell to the ground and the crowd surging forward trampled on him. The last thing he heard was laughter and the repeated shout, 'Crop the bitch.' Then he passed out.

*   *   *

When he came to, he was lying on the floor of the bar below the

Pension. The proprietor, whom he knew to be a good man who had arranged for the funeral of the old tailor, Ephraim Kurz, said, 'You're a fool, superintendent. You're lucky they didn't do for you. The mood they were in. Beside themselves they were, with anger and self-righteousness. And you were trying to spoil their fun. Like a fool, as I say. You'll need to get your head seen to.'

Lannes ran his hand over his hair and it came away sticky with blood.

'What have they done with her?'

'Shaved her head, tore most of her clothes off and marched her away to be paraded in disgrace with other women, not all of them tarts, known or suspected to have had German lovers. It's disgusting if you ask me.'

'And you did nothing?'

'I did nothing. Just as we have almost all done nothing for the last four years. She's a nice girl, I know that, but I did nothing. In face of that mob, I did nothing. You ought to see a doctor, super-intendent.'

'Give me an Armagnac, please.'

'With a head wound? Not advisable, I'd say.'

'Give me one nevertheless.'

*   *   *

He felt bad, and his hands shook. He had dumped his head in cold water and washed the blood away, dried it with a towel, all the time the proprietor whose name he couldn't recall insisting he ought to see a doctor.

'I don't have time,' he said.

'Nevertheless you're in danger of becoming delirious.'

'I'll have to take the chance.'

*   *   *

'Fernand,' he thought, and walking unsteadily, even though he had been handed back his blackthorn, set off for the brasserie. He had little reason to hope Fernand would be there, but there was no one else he could think to turn to. The crowd surged around him. There was cheering and singing, and he hated them all.

'Jean,' someone called out.

He turned and saw his friend Jacques Maso.

'What's happened to you? You look terrible.'

'Nothing,' Lannes said, 'merely a casualty of Liberation.'

Jacques Maso took hold of his arm and guided him into the Rugby Bar.

'Sit down a moment and compose yourself.'

'I've been a fool,' Lannes said. 'A thoughtless fool. I was too late. It was horrible.'

Jacques Maso passed him a cigarette and called on the barman to give them two glasses of beer.

'It's only a bang on the head,' Lannes said. 'Nothing serious.'

'I don't know about that. You're not yourself.'

'I must see Fernand. You know him, don't you?'

'Of course I do. Your mind's wandering, for you know perfectly well we've all been friends for years. But what's happened?'

Lannes stretched out his hand for the glass, but found he couldn't lift it. He put his head in his hands and began to sob.

*   *   *

Fernand was in the brasserie, at the head of a table of a dozen young men, no doubt the members of his Resistance group. They were drinking champagne and singing. Fernand had his arm round the girl he called 'the peach'. He lifted his hand and beckoned to Lannes, an invitation to join his table. Lannes shook his head and sat down at the other side of the room. He crooked his finger towards Fernand who, in a little, disengaged himself from the girl, pausing only to kiss her on the mouth, and crossed over to join Lannes.

'Not sharing in the merriment, Jean?'

Fernand pulled out a chair, swung it round and sat on it, astride, resting his elbows on its high back.

'I told you you should have joined us,' Fernand said.

'So you did,' Lannes said. 'So you did, but I'm a police officer, a servant of the Republic. I have to play by the rules, most of the time anyway. The rules and the law. Some of your boys, not necessarily yours, but some like them, shot a priest yesterday, put him up against a wall and shot him. Just like that. Then they raped the boy he was with, and beat him up. You know the boy, young Karim whom you helped me get out of Bordeaux a couple of years ago. My boss says, "Fine, nothing to do with us." Nevertheless I'm not sure I'd have been happy if I'd signed up with you as you suggest.'

'It's the way things are, Jean. People have been afraid and humiliated for four years. It's natural that they want revenge.'

'Ah yes, revenge. A judge spoke of it the other day as wild justice. Not my sort of justice.'

'Believe me, Jean, it's necessary. Necessary. A cleansing of the stables. Why have you come here? You want something from me, don't you?'

'Yes, I want something from you. You're my oldest friend, Fernand.'

He hesitated, took out a cigarette and lit it, ashamed to find that his hands were still shaking.

'You're in a bad way,' Fernand said.

'Not really. Just a blow on the head, knocked me out for a moment, but that doesn't matter. There's a girl . . . '

'Good.'

'Yvette. She's a tart, nice girl.'

'Good again.'

Lannes drew on his cigarette, felt dizzy for a moment, swallowed twice, a taste of bile.

'They took her, shaved her head, tore her clothes. I tried to stop them. That's when someone clonked me. I don't know what they've done with her.'

He was amazed to see that Fernand was smiling broadly.

'And you've come to me for help? You want me to find her for you?'

'You've got the connections,' Lannes said.

'You fancy her, don't you?'

'She's a nice girl, whatever, caught up in the madness we've lived through.'

'But you fancy her. Have you fucked her?'

Lannes stubbed out his cigarette.

'No.'

'You should. You should have. Do you know the trouble with you, Jean? Self-denial. You've never allowed yourself to live. You take on responsibilities and you're not happy with them. Marguerite was never right for you, I've always known that. So this girl. You want to fuck her, but haven't allowed yourself to do so. Sad, really, old friend.'

'Perhaps. I don't know. Just at the moment I don't know anything. Can you do as I ask?'

'Expect so. Why not?'

The peach came over and settled herself on Fernand's knee.

'Mr Policeman,' she said. 'Mr Vichy Policeman. What does he want, darling?'

'He wants me to find his girl.'

'And will you?'

'Why not? Why not? It's Saturnalia time. Besides, a girl who can tempt Jean here off the straight and narrow must be worth a look.'

XXIV

'We lost contact with him. The wireless frequency was scrambled, and we heard nothing from him. He may be dead or in a German camp, we've no idea.'

The Gaullist captain, Colonel Passy's aide, a young thickset Breton, shuffled the papers on his desk.

'So I can't help you. All sorts of people disappear. It's the way things are.'

Jérôme said, 'Somebody must know something.'

Even as he spoke, he heard the feebleness, hopelessness indeed, of his words. He looked to Alain for assistance.

Alain said, 'Was the network betrayed?'

'Probably.'

The captain moved his papers about again. His tone was indifferent. It was obvious he wanted rid of them.

'Mind you,' he said, 'I advised the colonel against his recruitment. An obvious pansy, I said, they're not reliable.'

Jérôme felt himself flush.

'He was ready to risk his life,' he said.

'You're not suggesting that Léon betrayed his comrades, are you?' Alain said. 'If you are, I must tell you the idea's ridiculous. He's a patriot.'

'So you say. A Jew also, however. Not reliable, as I told the colonel. Not that I'm implying anything, you understand. You know yourself, Lieutenant Lannes, networks get broken. They're infiltrated. People disappear. That's how it's been. You've had experience of it yourself, I understand.'

'Yes,' Alain said, 'I have, but I know Léon well. I would trust him with my life . . . '

'No doubt you're right. But the fact is, I have no information and I can't help you.'

*　　*　　*

'He didn't give a damn, did he? Bastard,' Jérôme said as they left the office. Alain made no reply.

They stepped out into the sunshine of the Boulevard and went to join Vincent who was waiting for them at the Café de Quebec.

'What do we do next,' Jérôme said. 'Somebody must know something. But think of it. They send him to France, into danger, and they don't give a damn.'

'We keep looking,' Alain said. 'That's all we can do. People disappear, that's true, but sometimes they turn up again.'

'Léon was in love with you. You know that, don't you.'

Alain frowned.

'That's got nothing to do with anything.'

He remembered that November morning when they had parted in an English mist, and how Léon had trembled when they embraced, and then forced himself to smile. Two years ago. Whatever has happened since, whatever they had both experienced, had made them different people.

'You've been safe in London,' he said. 'You can't imagine how it's been here. We've all had to do things we're ashamed of. There are things I can't speak of, but I'll tell you this, it hasn't been like the Musketeers.'

Vincent was sitting in the corner of the bar, smoking.

'Any word of your friend?'

'None.'

'That's bad, isn't it?'

'Yes, it's bad,' Alain said.

'And that captain wasn't even interested,' Jérôme said. 'He couldn't wait to be rid of us.'

Thirty years later, he would write: 'It was when I looked at my friend's face in the dark corner of that café I have never been able to enter since that I realised how the experience of war had so hardened him as to kill what both Léon and I had loved in him. I realised that he had walked with Death, looked Death in the face, conspired with Death, and learned things about himself that he would never speak of. I felt hollow and wanted to break down and weep. Instead I ordered coffee.'

*　　*　　*

'We ought to get out,' Baron Jean de Flambard said.

'That's ridiculous.'

They had been pulled out of the line, briefly of course, and were sitting in a Bierkeller in a small town with a German name that had once been Polish and would doubtless be so again.

'That's ridiculous,' Michel smiled the smile of exhaustion as he repeated the words. 'You know we can't because there's nowhere to go.'

'Of course there isn't. Nevertheless you must admit, kid, that we've been cheated. Who would have guessed that the Boches could make such an unholy mess of their war? Or that little Adolf could be such an idiot.'

'Keep your voice down. There are things that are better not said.'

'Oh sure, let's pretend that we can still come through. Let's pretend that the Ivans will get tired and go home. Which of these girls do you fancy?'

'Neither much, they're a pair of scrubbers.'

'Beggars can't be choosers. And don't think you're cheating on your true love in Bordeaux. You know as well as I do that you'll never see her again. If she's any sense she'll be shacked up with someone else by now. I'll take the blonde, she looks a nice armful and the other's too young for a respectable man of my age.'

'You respectable? Come off it. But why not? The little one's really quite sweet, now I look at her more closely.'

'That's my boy. Take pleasure where it is to be found while you have the chance. There won't be many more opportunities on offer.'

*   *   *

Maurice was wary. He felt out of place in a Paris he scarcely knew, out of place and afraid. He didn't think of himself as a collaborator, and told himself he had no reason to be regarded as one, for in the years in Vichy he and Dominique had had no dealings, no direct dealings anyway, with the Germans. But service in Vichy was itself reason enough to be suspect. And his father had surprised him: that sudden panic – an expression on his face he had never seen before – his abrupt departure in the company of one of his grandfather's bastards, a man he had never met but whose appearance stirred in him a disquieting memory which however he couldn't place. Then the large envelope his father had given him with instructions to deliver it to Dominique's friend or master, François, who had moved, it appeared seamlessly, from Vichy to the Resistance and now to de Gaulle.

The Brasserie Lipp was packed, every table occupied, a babble of conversation, a haze of cigarette smoke, a smell of wine and sauerkraut. He hesitated, uncertain, recognising nobody. A waiter approached, and he asked for Monsieur Mitterand, was directed to the back of the long room, where François and Dominique sat on the banquette with plates of oysters in front of them.

Dominique rose to lean across the table to embrace him. François, smiled, an aloof and superior smile.

'So you're your father's emissary,' he said. 'I shouldn't have thought he needed one. He should have come to Paris himself, he's nothing to fear, I'm sure. Sit down. I hope you like oysters.'

Maurice handed him the envelope, glad to be rid of it.

'Do you know what's in this?' François said.

'Not exactly. It's a copy of some list my father said you will find useful. That's all I know.'

'Good, good. And so your father has made for Spain? Is that right? He had no need to do so, I'm sure of that.'

After the oysters, they ate *choucroute garni* and drank two bottles of Sylvaner, then millefeuilles with coffee and kirsch.

François analysed the political situation, the balance of parties. There were frequent interruptions as men approached to shake him by the hand, and exchange expressions of goodwill.

François said, 'Lipp used to be famous for having the best mille-feuilles and the worst coffee in Paris. The millefeuilles are as good as ever, aren't they, and the coffee is no worse now than it is everywhere else. Tell your father I'm grateful to him. This list is going to be invaluable, and you may assure him that I don't think his exile in Spain need be of long duration.'

*   *   *

Later Dominique and Maurice walked up the hill to the Luxembourg Gardens. They sat in the shade of the trees by the statue of *Le Marchand de Masques*.

'That's François,' Dominique said. 'I like him you know but I never know what he is really thinking. He wears a different mask depending on the company. You're worried about your father, aren't you? He may be safer in Spain for the moment. Any idea what that list is?'

'Won't François tell you?'

'Only if he thinks it useful that I should know. Not otherwise. So?'

'I suspect it's a list of members of the Cagoule.'

'Was your father one?'

'Probably. And François?'

'Perhaps,' Dominique said. 'Perhaps. How's Clothilde? You have seen her, haven't you?'

'Several times. I'm afraid she's sad. And I know what you are going to say, but the truth is she regards me only as a friend. I'm like that character in an opera who exists only to be on stage while the heroine pours out the anguish of her soul in a soaring aria.'

*   *   *

236

Léon stretched out on the bunk trying to think of nothing, but that was impossible. He was caught up in the Theatre of the Absurd, identified by two witnesses as a renegade Communist, turned Gestapo informant.

His companion in the cell in the basement of the house in the rue des Saussies couldn't keep still. He paced up and down the narrow cell, weeping.

'I was recruited in London by Colonel Passy of the Free French and flown into France to serve as a radio-operator,' he had said, again and again. 'Colonel Passy will confirm that. I'm not who you think I am.'

He had continued to say this even when they beat him up.

His companion, a middle-aged actor, said, 'How can you just lie there? They're going to shoot us, aren't they.'

Léon made no reply. There was nothing to say. He had no idea if his cellmate was innocent of everything, guilty of anything. He had read this scene often, thought of Julien Sorel on the night before he was guillotined. Perhaps Anne would have found someone to help, but there wasn't much time. It was stupid to hope, as stupid as it was absurd to be set up before a firing squad manned by men who were on the same side. Whoever he had been mistaken for was fortunate.

It was cold and dank in the cell and he didn't want to be found trembling. They were no more than ten minutes walk from the Arc de Triomphe where he had once arranged to meet Alain on the day of Liberation.

His cellmate stopped walking, subsided to the floor, hugged himself and began to howl. Léon wished he would stop.

*   *   *

Alain left Jérôme and Vincent in the café, and walked down to the river. He leaned on the balustrade of the Pont Neuf, above the Ile des Juifs where they had burned the Knights Templar. Jérôme had asked him how his parents were and he had been unable to say that he hadn't brought himself to telephone them. He should have done so. They must be anxious. They might fear he was dead.

But how could he speak to them? How could he pretend he was

the boy who had gone away? In Lyon he had been tortured, had talked and betrayed others. He didn't know the consequences. They might all have escaped. But he had talked, screaming in pain and terror, then whimpering where they were to be found, and it was no excuse to say, as the Gestapo officer, laying his arm around his shoulders had said, with sweetness in his voice, 'Everyone talks in the end.' That wasn't true. Some died rather than speak. But he had spoken, and ever since he knew he was fuelled only by hatred. Shame and hatred. When his wound healed and he was with the regiment of Hussars to which he had been assigned, he would kill more Germans.

He hadn't been able to speak of his war to Jérôme who had lived his own war safe in London and so knew nothing. He had been drawn to the boy Vincent because of his terror, but Vincent saw him as a hero. So he couldn't speak to him either. Perhaps Léon would understand if they ever met, if Léon was still alive. Yes, Léon might understand. Being Léon and being a Jew, he would surely understand; he would be the only person he could speak to. He looked over the parapet to where the Grand Master of the Templars had burned, cursing France, cursing the French.

XXV

'Of course you have to go,' she said. 'I understand that. Christmas is for families, not for your tart.'

'Don't call yourself that,' Lannes said.

He leaned over and stroked her hair which had grown in again. His lips brushed against her cheek.

'It's what I am,' she said. 'A *tondu* and a tart. It would have been all right if you'd taken me before, as you wanted, as I wanted. But now I don't know. Being under an obligation . . . '

When Fernand had been as good as his word, rescued her and summoned him to his brasserie 'for collection', as he said, Lannes had brought her to the Pension Smitt, and installed her in the room once occupied by Aurélien and Marie-Adelaide.

'I like the old woman,' Yvette said. 'She knows what I am, what

I've done and what has been done to me, and she doesn't give a damn.' It was true. When Lannes visited, as he did now every afternoon, Madame Smitt opened the door to him, nodded, sniffed, and shuffled off in her down-at-heel carpet slippers. Some evenings Yvette drank white wine with her in the kitchen; others she watched Aurélien laying out the cards in his endless games of patience. As she moved slowly towards recovery she had no questions for Lannes, at least since he had failed to find the cat that she had inherited from the old Jewish tailor and had no name but Cat.

Lannes said, 'I handed in my letter of resignation today.'

The last straw had been the decision of Bracal's successor to drop the charge against the advocate Labiche of being an accessory to Fabien's murder. 'How,' he had said, smiling, 'can we charge someone with being an accessory when we have no murderer to charge and no evidence that Monsieur Labiche had any connection with whoever that murderer may have been.' So the advocate had been released and had left Bordeaux, presumably for Spain. There was apparently no investigation under way concerning his role in the deportation of the city's Jews.

'And I'll be glad to be out,' Lannes said. 'I can't enter the office without feeling sick.'

Moncerre had greeted the news with a twist of the lips.

'I never thought that bastard would go down,' he said.

You could see that he thought Lannes a fool to be so disturbed.

'You've no call to resign, chief,' he said, 'but the truth is, you're a Romantic. Me, I'm a realist. So I soldier on.'

It was all Lannes could do to prevent young René from following his example.

'You're a good policeman with a career ahead of you,' he said. 'Mine's broken. There's no reason why this should concern you.'

It was the simplest explanation he could offer; a broken career, convenient too, and it would have seemed pretentious to have said that it was rather his belief in himself that was no longer tenable.

'How will your wife take the news of your resignation?' Yvette said.

'She's always hated my work, and now I hate it too.'

He leaned over to kiss her.

'Will you be all right?'

'Why not? I'll have a Merry Christmas drinking white wine with the old woman. And, like I said, Christmas is for your family, not your tart.'

'Don't speak of yourself like that,' he said again.

The trouble is, he thought, she feels the intolerable burden of gratitude. So it can't last.

*   *   *

His mother-in-law was already ensconced in her favourite chair.

'You'd think Monsieur Hitler would have had the sense to surrender and make peace,' she said.

'He'll fight till Germany's all in flames,' her son Albert said. 'To the last German. He's demented, you see, Maman.'

Lannes heard the words 'the last German' and saw tears in Clothilde's eyes. The last German, the last of the French volunteers against Bolshevism. It was madness indeed.

Albert had recovered his self-confidence. You wouldn't think to hear him speak now that he had worshipped the Marshal. His job in the town hall was safe, thanks to de Gaulle's order that functionaries should retain their posts and carry on with the necessary business of administration.

'He's a clever one,' Albert said. 'I've no doubt that he will see off the Communists. He'll discard them all when they've served their purpose.'

The war was being carried into Germany. Alain would not be home for Christmas. But at least he had sent a card posted from Strasbourg a fortnight ago.

Lannes went through to the kitchen. Marguerite looked up from the stove. He kissed her cheek and she didn't turn her head away.

'Your mother seems well,' he said. 'Albert too.'

'She's indestructible. They're both indestructible. And of course she's delighted we have Dominique home and safe, I've always thought it permissible for grandmothers to have favourites, unlike mothers. If only we had Alain here too.'

'It won't be long now. It can't be long now.'

'I don't know,' she said. "I'm like St Thomas, doubting till I see proof.'

'No,' he said. 'Alain will be all right, I'm sure of it. How long till we eat?'

'Half an hour perhaps.'

'Good.'

He took two bottles of Chateau St-Hilaire, premier cru Bordeaux, from the case that the Count had sent him for Christmas, with thanks, which he knew he didn't deserve, for restoring Marie-Adelaide to her family, drew the corks and set the wine on the sideboard in the dining-room.

Dominique and Maurice had returned from a visit to Henri in the rue des Remparts.

'How did you find your godfather?'

'In excellent spirits.'

'And Miriam?'

'On the road to recovery. Henri says they will get married in the spring.'

Madame Panard sniffed.

'Surely not,' she said. 'Miriam, that's a Jewish name. Surely Monsieur Chambolley won't marry a Jew.'

Dominique knelt beside her and took hold of her hands.

'Nobody cares for that sort of thing now, Grandma, nobody should anyway.'

'You've always been a sweet boy,' she said, 'but you don't know the world as I do. You can't trust the Jews. After all, they brought this terrible war on us, didn't they?'

Dominique smiled and kissed his grandmother's withered cheek.

Lannes said, 'It's about time to eat. Dominique, help your grandmother through to the dining-room. Your mother has cleverly laid her hands on a splendid boiling fowl, it's almost a miracle to find such a thing.'

'Well,' Maurice said, 'didn't Henri-Quatre say it was his ambition that every French household should have a fowl in the pot on Sundays. Perhaps de Gaulle thinks likewise.'

To Lannes' relief the meal passed off without incident, argument or embarrassment. There was even a mood of good feeling; it was as if everyone was holding their breath, aware that there was a moment of concord, fragile and dependent for its duration on restraint.

Later Marguerite said, 'I don't know if we've come through. I don't know if we've deserved to. But sometimes I think I understand more than you think I do.'

She kissed him good-night, and left him not ready to sleep. He gave himself an Armagnac and turned to an old friend, *Le Vicomte de Bragelonne*, and the disillusioned wisdom of the ageing d'Artagnan.

Envoi

Readers who have followed the lives of the characters through the four volumes of their story may wish to learn something of how they fared after the war.

As Lannes had feared, the burden of gratitude was too much for Yvette. She left Bordeaux and made for Paris where a couple of years later she found work as a model. He never met her again, but occasionally came upon her photograph in one of Marguerite's magazines.

Lannes withdrew his resignation. He and Marguerite continued to live together, with little that should have been said being said. In 1952 he retired from the police and went to live alone on the little farm in Les Landes which had formerly been his grandfather's. Occasionally, on birthdays and at Christmas, he returned to Bordeaux and the apartment where Marguerite continued to live. He died in 1972.

Dominique, to Marguerite's disappointment, never became a priest. He continued to serve in Mitterand's private office and was himself, briefly, a deputy in the last years of the Fourth Republic. He died of cancer in 1960. François Mitterand himself was President of France, 1981–95.

Alain remained in the army after the war. He served in Indo-China, where he won the Croix de Guerre, and Algeria. Angered by de Gaulle's betrayal of the cause of French Algeria, he enlisted in the OAS (Organisation de l'Armée Secrète) and participated in at least one of the attempts on de Gaulle's life. Arrested and sentenced to ten years' imprisonment, he was released in 1972, and became a successful right-wing journalist and an early member of Jean-Marie Le Pen's Front National.

Léon, as indicated, was shot in the basement of what had been Gestapo headquarters in the rue des Saussies, a victim of mistaken identity.

Michel is presumed to have been killed in the Battle for Berlin in which the Charlemagne Legion of the Waffen SS were among the last defenders of Hitler's bunker.

Five years later, when she had given up hope of his survival, Clothilde married Maurice. They had five children and Maurice agreed that their first son should be called Michel. Maurice wrote an account of his years in Vichy, entitled *A l'ombre du Maréchal*.

Jérôme became a successful novelist and was elected to the Académie Française. His novel, *Un ami de ma jeunesse*, a fictional memoir of Léon, won the Prix André Gide in 1969. It was published by a firm in which Léon's friend Anne worked as an editor.

Edmond de Grimaud was sentenced in 1947 to five years' 'national disgrace', but returned successfully first to journalism, then to politics.

Sigi de Grimaud remained in exile in Spain, teaching in a language school.

The advocate Labiche also remained there. In an interview given to a French journalist in 1957, he declared that there had been no death camps in Germany and insisted that the Holocaust was a Jewish invention, a typical example of Jewish lies.

Fernand continued to run his brasserie. He left the Communist Party when 'the peach' left him. She was soon replaced.

Henri and Miriam married and re-opened the bookshop together.

Moncerre at last left his wife, but remained in the police till he retired.

René Martin eventually became a commissaire in the PJ. He never married.

Marthe lived to be one hundred and two, still in that house which had seen so much wickedness. She survived Jean-Christophe who died of cirrhosis of the liver in 1951. Maurice inherited the house. Clothilde found no wickedness there.

Sir Edwin Pringle did indeed marry, if only for show, but lost his seat in Parliament in the Labour landslide of 1945. He returned to the Commons in 1950 and was given a peerage by Harold Macmillan in 1959. His boyfriend, the American dancer Max, survived the air-crash, and after the war kept an antique shop in

Chelsea. One afternoon in the early Sixties I bought a First Empire cup from him.

In 1947 Karim was spotted – picked up – on a beach by a film director called Jules Faguet, and, though the relationship didn't last, enjoyed some success as an actor in 'film noir' movies. He sent Lannes a Christmas card every year.

Freddie Spinks became a publican in the East End when he left the Royal Navy in 1952. He married three times and had six children, but every spring for forty years spent a few days with Jérôme in what he still called 'Gay Paree'.

*   *   *

Snatches of brief lives, crossing each other's paths, all deeply and inescapably stained by memories of the dark years, 1940–44.